Chris glared at Matt. 'She gets on that bike with you over my dead body or yours. And we both know it will be yours.'

Oh God this was so typical of Chris – coming on all macho and sexy just when I don't want him to be. Because it was too late now, I'd made up my mind. I was going with Matt. Just wish I didn't have to break Chris's heart to do it.

But Chris had his arm wound round my waist tight as a python's death grip. Looked like I would have to break his arm as well as his heart to get free.

And why didn't Matt do anything? He was just staring at me with a glazed expression. OK, I suppose I did look a bit odd tonight. This yellow and black helmet clashed badly with my scarlet prom dress and high heels but I hadn't grown another head for God's sake and at least it stopped my hair frizzing in the rain so I'd be fine when I took it off. Wish Matt would stop gawping at me and get off his bike and help.

Praise for *My Desperate Love Diary*:

'Heartfelt but at the same time fantastically funny, this is a must read' MIZZ

'A feel-good summer read' SUN

'Very funny ... the reader is d~~~~~ ~~~~~~~ into Kelly Ann's world' WRITER'S NEWS

www.kidsatrando~

D0582724

MY ROCKY ROMANCE DIARY

by kelly Ann

LIZ RETTIG

CORGI BOOKS

MY ROCKY ROMANCE DIARY
A CORGI BOOK 978 0 552 56208 9

Published in Great Britain by Corgi Books,
an imprint of Random House Children's Books
A Random House Group Company

This edition published 2010

1 3 5 7 9 10 8 6 4 2

The Random House Group Limited supports the Forest Stewardship Council
(FSC), the leading international forest certification organization. All our titles
that are printed on Greenpeace-approved FSC-certified paper carry the
FSC logo. Our paper procurement policy can be found at
www.rbooks.co.uk/environment.

Mixed Sources
Product group from well-managed
forests and other controlled sources
www.fsc.org   Cert no. TT-COC-2139
© 1996 Forest Stewardship Council

Set in 11/16pt Palatino by
Falcon Oast Graphic Art Ltd.

Corgi Books are published by Random House Children's Books,
61–63 Uxbridge Road, London W5 5SA

www.**kids**at**randomhouse**.co.uk
www.**rbooks**.co.uk

Addresses for companies within The Random House Group Limited can be
found at: www.randomhouse.co.uk/offices.htm

THE RANDOM HOUSE GROUP Limited Reg. No. 954009

A CIP catalogue record for this book is available from the British Library.

Printed and bound in Great Britain by
CPI Bookmarque, Croydon, CR0 4TD

For My Daughter Carol

With special thanks to Lauren Buckland,
Kelly Hurst, Ruth Knowles and Seriously
Sassy author Maggi Gibson.

Thanks also to the long-suffering men
in my life – my husband Paul, son Chris
and ever charming agent Guy Rose.

And finally a huge thank you to all
you Kelly Ann fans around the world.

MONDAY JANUARY 7TH

First day of term and Mum woke me up at eight but I'd two free periods first thing so I mumbled, 'Leavemealoneandgoaway'. Then I snuggled back under my duvet. Bliss.

By the time she'd left for work I'd dropped back off to sleep but unfortunately didn't wake up again until eleven so was late for maths and got a punishment exercise from Mr Simmons.

I mean, a punishment exercise at my age! Surely seventeen is too old for childish sanctions like that. It's ridiculous. Decided to tell him so.

'You can't give me two hundred lines like I'm a first year, sir. I'm seventeen, way too mature for this now.'

'You're right, Kelly Ann,' he said, taking the exercise from me. He scribbled something on it and handed it back to me with a self-satisfied smirk. 'Now you're older, you can do *four hundred*.'

Great.

Still, except for Mr Simmons, sixth form isn't too bad. The best things about it are the free periods and our own common room where we can chat, make tea or coffee and hide alcohol. School is much more civilized now and, yeah, almost bearable. But, oh God, how I've missed my boyfriend Chris since he left for university last year.

I can't wait to go to uni too where there will be student bars and so much free time that some days I'll have no classes at all. Or that is what I've heard anyway from people who are doing arts courses like me. Medical students, like Chris and his flatmate Jamie, have to work like galley slaves on amphetamine. Don't know why anyone would want to do that, but I suppose if you're dead set on being a doctor like Chris is, you just have to put up with it.

At lunch time I hurried to the common room. My friend Liz was already there and waved me over.

She offered me a Malteser from a large box. 'Want one?'

I nodded and took a couple. Well, no one can eat just *one* Malteser.

'Not on a new year diet then?' I asked. 'You usually start one round about now – not that you need to.'

'Yeah, I am actually. A chopstick diet.'

'A chopstick diet?' I asked, puzzled.

Liz has been on some weird diets before, like the watercress-soup-and-boiled-egg-only diet which failed because she doesn't like either food. Or the white-coloured-food-only diet which lasted a bit longer but ended with her scoffing my wine gums. This one sounded the most stupid yet.

'Yeah,' Liz said. 'I can eat anything I want but only if I use chopsticks. Takes so long I hardly get to eat anything. Watch.'

She took a pair of chopsticks from her school bag and tried to snare a Malteser with them. Half the contents of the packet were rolling on the floor by the time she managed to get one to her mouth. Liz finished it and smiled contentedly. 'See. No wonder Chinese people are all slim.'

'Yeah, Liz. I think this diet might actually work.'

But then she tossed the chopsticks aside and popped a handful of Maltesers into her mouth. 'Just until I get the hang of them,' she said.

Hmm.

Don't know why Liz bothers dieting anyway. I suppose she *is* slightly plump but she's blonde and busty so has no problem attracting guys. In any case her boyfriend Julian adores her curves and doesn't want her to lose an ounce. Not that there's any danger of that as Liz always abandons diets shortly after starting them. Often by lunch time.

'Have you seen the new boy, Matt Davies, yet?' Liz asked. 'Everyone's talking about him.'

'Not yet. What's he like?'

'Very interesting. It's rumoured he's been expelled from practically every school in Glasgow before coming here. And some people say his dad is serving life in prison for gangland murders.'

'Oh my God, really?'

'Yeah but other people say his dad is an accountant who lost his job so Matt had to leave his private fee-paying school to come here.'

'Hmm, so what do you think?' I asked.

'I think he's going to be popular – with girls anyway.' She moved closer to me and whispered. 'Look, here he is now.'

The new boy strolled into the room. He was tall – easily over six feet – and slim, with dark hair and eyes. While our school wasn't really strict about uniform, most people at least kind of vaguely complied with the navy blue and grey dress code. Not him. Wearing black jeans and T-shirt he'd ignored it completely. He'd a strange black tattoo on his arm – a dagger with a serpent curled around it – and one dull silver earring shaped like an eagle on his right ear. He looked different all right and well, kind of . . . dangerous. Like a panther in a pet shop.

He scanned the room lazily as he made his way to a chair by the window but didn't attempt to talk to anyone, just sat there, seemingly quite comfortable with his own company. It was weird. Most new people would be anxious to make contact and feel awkward sitting by themselves. Not this guy.

'So what do you think, Kelly Ann?' Liz asked.

'Looks . . . interesting,' I said.

I noticed that a large group of females were casually migrating closer to him, some openly checking him out, others giving him surreptitious glances. Matt didn't seem to be aware of the stir he was causing. Or if he was, he didn't show it. Maybe he was used to this reaction. In fact, he just gazed out the window in the direction of the football pitch, probably watching the five-a-side I knew some fifth years had organized.

A couple of girls moved to the window nearest him and pretended to be interested in the game as well. That's a laugh. Knew those two had as much interest in football as I had in learning to crochet tea cosies. Their ploy didn't work anyway as Matt completely ignored them. I shook my head and smiled.

Suddenly he turned round and caught me looking at him. He stared right back; dark eyes focussed on me. Then he raised his eyebrows and smiled as though the two of us were somehow sharing a private joke. I flushed and looked away.

Yes, Liz was right. Matt was going to be popular with girls. But not with me. I had a gorgeous boyfriend; my, well ... soul mate really, I suppose. We've known each other since we were kids and were best friends for ages before we realized we were in love and started going out together. Nothing will ever come between Chris and me. I could never be attracted to anyone else. Never.

TUESDAY JANUARY 8TH

Matt didn't come into the common room until nearly the end of our lunch hour, this time accompanied by Felicity, a leggy blonde whose boobs are so big it's rumoured she's had implants. Well, I started the rumour she'd got implants actually, but honestly it's not fair for any one person to have that many assets. I mean, what about short, skinny brunettes like me who still can't get into a B-cup bra? Thank God for Chris who thinks I'm gorgeous anyway.

Matt and Felicity sat next to each other in the corner by the pool table. Felicity looked smug, basking in the envious glances of her friends. But to everyone's surprise, after chatting with her for a few minutes, Matt deliberately wandered off by himself to a seat by the window again.

Don't think anything like this had ever happened to Felicity before. Her mouth gaped half-open in surprise and stayed that way like a moray eel's. Felt a bit sorry for her really. Can't be easy getting rejected for the first time ever. But why *had* Matt knocked her back? OK everybody knows Felicity is incredibly boring and totally up herself but it's never put off any other guy. This new boy was definitely different.

He was supposed to be in my drama class after lunch but he didn't show. In fact he didn't go to any classes in the afternoon. It's rumoured he's been expelled already for dealing drugs to first years although other people say he just had a dental appointment. I hope it's the dental appointment. Matt Davies is the most interesting thing to happen at our school since, well, Mr Simmons' affair with my English teacher Ms Conner. I actually caught them snogging in the maths cupboard last year which was interesting but also kind of gross. She's been seconded to work for the exam board this term, thank God, but I always knock before going into any school store cupboard now. Just in case.

WEDNESDAY JANUARY 9TH

Saw the new boy roar out of the school car park riding a huge black and silver Harley-Davidson motorbike. Or donor-bike as Jamie and Chris call them since so many young people have fatal accidents on them they are a major source of healthy transplant organs. I know this should put me off, but watching Matt speeding away on his powerful, beautiful machine was definitely, well . . . sexy.

Oh yes, he was going to be popular all right but maybe not with everyone. Certainly not with Mr Smith, our deputy head, who he cut right across at the lights. Or Mr Simmons who was forced to brake and pull in when Matt overtook him from the inside. I wondered how long he'd last at our school before he was expelled.

Found myself hoping it would be quite a while. Not that I fancied him or anything. It's just that he was unusual. Exciting.

FRIDAY JANUARY 11TH

Chris picked me up from school. Saw people eyeing me enviously. Yeah, it was so cool to have a gorgeous boyfriend who also had a car. And his own flat. Well, not his *own* flat – he shares the rent with three other pals who are also students – but still, at least he doesn't live with his parents. And Chris has told me his flatmates are all going out tonight so we can be alone together, just the two of us.

We're going to cook spaghetti bolognese and eat it with scented candles. Well, scented candles on the table anyway. So romantic. Then we'll probably just hug up on the sofa and watch a chick flick, or maybe, OK, a thriller if Chris really can't hack it. Then afterwards we'll, well do whatever we like really . . . mmmm. Oh yes it was going to be so good. I hadn't seen Chris all week because he'd been busy studying or working. And even though he texts me every morning and calls every night it's not the same. I've missed him so much.

We stopped off at my house so I could change and collect my stuff then we went to the supermarket. Seemed really grown-up, shopping together for groceries like mince and garlic. Weird. But nice.

By the time we got to Chris's place it was nearly six. I could hear the telly in the living room so I popped my head in on the way to the kitchen to see who was at home. Ian had already gone out but Jamie and Gary were still there watching football. They assured us they were leaving soon.

'Hot date tonight,' Gary boasted. 'Blonde.'

'Mustn't waste good pub drinking time,' said Jamie.

Good. Reassured that they were definitely going, Chris and I dumped our shopping in the kitchen then went back to the living room where we chatted for a bit and watched the football with Jamie and Gary. When we were sure Scotland had lost (4-0 down) we decided to make dinner.

As the garlicky aroma wafted through the flat, Jamie and Gary seemed less keen to shift and sloped into the kitchen. 'My date just texted,' Gary informed us. 'Says she's gonna be late. Needs to wash her hair again or something. Blonde, you know.'

'May as well have a few more beers here first,' Jamie said. 'Cheaper. And, em, best to eat something too maybe. Shouldn't drink on an empty stomach. There wouldn't be any spare bolognese going would there?'

'No way, I'm not your mum. Get your own dinner.'

'C'mon, Kelly Ann,' Gary begged. 'All this week I've been living on Pot Noodles and beans. Have mercy.'

'Honestly, you two are pathetic,' I said. 'You should never have left home if you can't look after yourself.'

They looked sheepish but continued to beg, so in the end, to stop them moaning, I put some more pasta in and we shared our meal. Didn't bother with the pink rose-scented candles though, as it wasn't exactly the romantic occasion I'd been hoping for.

Jamie and Gary told us they were really grateful, but of course, as soon as they finished eating they left without helping to clear up. 'Sorry, Kelly Ann, no time to wash up. Late already,' they chorused.

After putting their dirty dishes on their beds, Chris and I had just settled down to watch the chick flick in the living room when Ian and his girlfriend came back.

'Oh, I love this film!' Valerie said, squeezing in beside us. 'Haven't seen it in ages though. And it's just started.'

Brilliant.

After five minutes Ian and Chris decided to play the Xbox in Ian's room while Valerie and I watched the movie.

At least it was a good movie. Might have been better if Valerie hadn't kept saying stuff like, 'Oh this is the bit where she catches her boyfriend cheating on her and pours pasta down his trousers.' And, 'Wait, this is so funny, ohmigod, just as she's dancing with the hottest guy in the club and her ex is staring at her and he's, like, sooo jealous, totally gutted, guess what? Her knickers fall down. No really. You'll laugh.'

Not any more.

When it finished we went off to Ian's room but they were in the middle of a game playing against some people in the US and didn't pay any attention to us. Well, if you can't beat 'em join 'em. I grabbed a spare control and got stuck in. We played well but were outclassed by our opponents, who humiliatingly enough turned out not to be nineteen-year-old students from the Massachusetts Institute of Technology like they'd said but twelve-year-old boys from the Bronx who taunted us: 'You guys really suck. We beat your asses.'

'We should have known from their squeaky voices,' moaned Ian. 'I just thought we had a bad connection. Bloody little squealers.'

When Valerie was ready to leave, Ian offered to walk her home, even though she lives less than two minutes away, and put a protective arm round her shoulder. Not that Valerie really needed protecting. At just over six feet and built like a Valkyrie I couldn't see anyone hassling her. But Ian, who is nearly six-five and broad as a tank, treats her like a delicate china doll. I think it's nice and though they've only being going out since Christmas I can't see them ever breaking up. They get on really well and anyway neither of them has a hope of finding anyone else the right height.

When the door closed behind them I reached for Chris and he pulled me into his arms. It was midnight already and apart from a quick kiss when he picked me up we hadn't had a chance to snog never mind anything else. But the outside door opened again almost immediately. It was Gary, grumping that he'd spent a fortune on his date but he hadn't even got a goodnight kiss.

Two minutes later Jamie came back with a bunch of other medical students. 'Sodding club bouncers wouldn't let us in because some of us had trainers on,' he grumbled. 'Just wait till we're all doctors and one of them turns up at Accident and Emergency having a heart attack, or with a potentially fatal wound. He'd better not be wearing trainers.'

Chris grinned. 'You'd turn him away? A bit unethical.'

'Fair's fair. Serves him right,' Jamie said. 'Is there any beer left in the fridge? Let's have some sodding music as well. Friday night after all.'

Oh God, this would go on for hours.

I put up with it for a while but soon, grossed out by disgusting medical jokes about cadavers and body parts plus the stink of beer, I wandered off to brush my teeth and get ready for bed.

Sleepy now, I pushed open the bathroom door and switched on the light. A large skeleton sitting on the loo grinned at me. Before I could stop myself, I screamed.

Chris was with me in an instant. He pushed me from the door and stood protectively in front ready to deal with whatever threatened me. His adrenaline-fuelled rush relaxed when he spotted the skeleton.

Jamie was next on the scene, followed by the others. 'It's OK, Kelly Ann,' Jamie said, striding into the bathroom. He lifted the skeleton's wrist and made a show of taking its pulse. 'Can't say for sure until we've done further tests but I think the intruder is dead.'

Very funny. Bloody medical students.

SUNDAY JANUARY 12TH

Chris drove me home. We stopped outside my house but both of us were reluctant to part right away so we hugged and chatted for a bit longer.

Chris brought up the skeleton incident again. 'Jamie's sorry he scared you, Kelly Ann.'

'I wasn't really scared. Knew it was fake. Obviously. Just, um, took me by surprise for a second. I'm more annoyed with Gary eating our cheesecake and never replacing the toilet paper when it's used up. And tell him the fake plastic turd in the toilet bowl was not funny, just totally childish.'

Chris smiled ruefully. 'Gary won't change, but never mind, one day we'll have our own place, just the two of us.'

I smiled. 'Sounds good. Maybe once you're a doctor earning loads of money and I'm a famous actress or something.'

Chris groaned. 'Another five years? No way. I was thinking this summer. The lease is up then and you'll have finished school and be starting uni.'

'Six months! You're joking.'

'No,' Chris said. 'I'm serious. Why not?'

'Well . . . I don't know.'

He pulled me towards him and kissed me. 'Sure you don't know?'

Mmm. Chris and me together all the time. Sleeping together, waking up together, hugging, kissing and . . . well doing anything we wanted. All day if we felt like it.

Hmm, not all day. I suppose we'd need to eat something occasionally.

So we could maybe cook together too. And wash up afterwards. Clean the flat. Do the laundry. Iron. But when would I shave my legs, put a facepack on? And who would clean the loo? Hmm. Not quite as romantic as I thought.

'I . . . well, I'll think about it,' I said.

'What's wrong? Don't you want us to be together? I thought you'd be pleased. Excited.'

His hurt expression got to me. 'Course I do. One day. But not right now. I mean, well, it would be like being married or something. Old and sensible. We're too young to give up having fun yet.'

'You think living together wouldn't be fun?'

'Yeah but . . . look, Chris, it's late. And I've got school tomorrow.' I yawned to make the point.

'Sorry. You're right. We've got plenty of time to talk about this.' He kissed me and I got out the car. As usual he waited until I opened my front door and turned to wave at him before driving off.

Mum and Dad were still up.

'What kind of time do you call this?' Dad said crossly. 'And where have you been all weekend?'

'Just gone ten, Dad. I've been staying over at Chris's. You and Mum are fine about it, remember?'

'Yes well that was more your mother's idea. I'm not so sure I *am* fine about it. Young Chris is a nice enough lad, and I realize you've known each other since you were kids but still . . . he's having his cake and eating it, if you ask me.'

I looked at Mum for support. 'What's all this about?'

She stubbed out her cigarette, took another swig of her Bacardi and Coke then rolled her eyes at Dad. 'Well, Kelly Ann, it seems your father here has decided he's no longer happy living in the twenty-first century so you'll just have to away up and put your chastity belt on. And you're not to take it off, mind, until he's saved up enough for your dowry.'

Dad scowled at her. 'All I'm saying is—'

'Night, Dad. Night, Mum,' I said quickly and made my way upstairs to bed leaving them to argue it out without me. I wasn't worried. Mum would win. She always did.

I brushed my teeth and frowned at my dark curly hair reflected in mirror. I'd spent ages straightening it this morning but the rain had frizzed it again. Just as well Chris likes my hair curly even if I don't. At least my skin looked OK – only two spots – maybe the pill was clearing them up. Hadn't done anything about increasing my boobs though as I'd hoped. Don't think I'll ever fill a B cup properly now unless I go for implants. Chris says they're fine and right for my slim shape but he would say that. I still long for curves like Liz, whose double-D boobs have most guys drooling over her.

In my bedroom I unpacked the rucksack I'd taken to Chris's then undressed and threw my thong and push-up black Wonderbra into the laundry basket. I pulled on warm thick flannel pyjama bottoms, fluffy socks and an old greying T-shirt – which was at least three sizes too big for me – and sighed contentedly. It was nice to be comfy and cosy when I didn't have to worry what I looked like.

I snuggled under the duvet and lay for a while listening to the familiar sound of my parents arguing and slinging insults at each other. Dad said Mum had her head in the sand and was asking for trouble. Mum said Dad was as much fun as the ruddy Taliban these days and to shut his face. Dad told Mum to go jump off a cliff, the impact might knock some sense into her. Mum invited Dad to away and boil his head.

I know it wasn't really serious and they care about each other deep down but I wonder if they've always been like this. Maybe when they first started going out they were nice to each other. Like me and Chris.

Seems difficult to imagine now. In fact, I don't know anyone whose parents talk really nicely to each other. Maybe because they live together. Hmm.

MONDAY JANUARY 14TH

My friend Stephanie is back from an extended winter skiing holiday. Must be nice to be like Stephanie and have parents who are loaded even if they are divorced. In fact, her parents being divorced is probably an advantage as she goes on separate holidays with both of them.

Of course Stephanie has missed the first week of term of her fashion-and-design course at college but she's never let small matters like term times and schedules interfere with the much more important business of having fun. Having said that, she's doing really well at college as there's nothing she doesn't know about fashion and she has a real talent for design. There's nothing she doesn't know about guys either and she has had hundreds of boyfriends before gobsmacking everyone by getting engaged last year to Dave – who also has rich parents.

Since she is the most experienced friend I have I decided to ask her advice about moving in with Chris after the summer.

Stephanie was horrified. 'Share a pokey little flat with your boyfriend? Are you mad? Let him see you without concealer when you've got spots and PMT? Or when your legs need waxing? Next thing you know you'll be laughing at fart jokes together and sharing razors.'

'Well *you're* getting married this year,' I said, annoyed.

'But Dave and I won't be living together all the time. We'll maintain separate apartments as well as a joint one. Go on different holidays most times. We won't ever be sharing a bathroom. Gross.'

'You think it will spoil the romance? The mystery?'

'Duh!'

Hmm.

Asked Liz, but warned her I wanted a straightforward, sensible, normal opinion. No psychobabble rubbish.

Liz has wanted to be a psychologist practically since she could talk and can be a pain when she analyses everything to death, even stuff like your choice of lipstick colour. Scarlet, for example, means you're signalling to guys that you have a healthy vagina and you're practically gagging for sex but if, grossed out by that interpretation, you change it to pink then you are desperately seeking a father figure as you can't cope with growing up, and your arrested development will probably attract paedophiles. And it's useless to point out you chose your lipstick colour to go with your new top because your choice of top means . . .

Liz said Stephanie had intimacy issues and not to listen to her. She thought that Chris and I had both reached a stage of psychosocial development where it was necessary for us to move on to a greater degree of commitment. She asked if Chris and I got a flat could she come over and stay sometimes when she gets bored with being at home? Or when Julian comes back from New York to visit her?

We'd need two bedrooms, of course. A one-bedroom flat might impact negatively on a couple's relationship. Liz would bring her own duvet and hot-water bottle. And we wouldn't mind if she kept a few things there, would we; some posters, photos etc to personalize her, erm, the spare room? Impersonal rooms could be psychologically damaging.

Hmm. Get the impression that Liz is thinking more about herself and her boyfriend than me. Still, I do feel bad for her. Julian, who's also Stephanie's brother, has been working in New York for ages now so Liz hardly gets to see him at all. Although he's just a couple of years older than Liz, he's a total genius with computers, so they are paying him a fortune over there. He's told Liz he's just going to stick it out for another year or so then he'll have enough to retire and do nothing for the rest of his life. Which has always been his dearest ambition.

He's nice but totally nuts, of course, so he suits Liz perfectly. Hope he comes back soon so she can analyse him as much as she likes and give the rest of us a break.

WEDNESDAY JANUARY 16TH

Matt was in our drama class today. Last time he'd said practically nothing and didn't take part in any of the exercises Mrs Kennedy set. Today though, when we were talking about stage lighting, he surprised everyone by contributing some helpful and knowledgeable suggestions. Afterwards we discussed *West Side Story* – a musical Mrs Kennedy plans to modernize and adapt to a Glasgow setting for us to perform at the end of school along with the music department. He didn't seem too interested in this at first but when the teacher asked me to demonstrate some dance movements from it, and the group applauded me when I was done, he joined in enthusiastically.

At the end of the lesson he came up alongside me as I was leaving class. 'You're good,' he said. 'Where did you learn to dance like that?'

I flushed, pleased by his unexpected praise, but tried to shrug nonchalantly. 'Oh, I just copy stuff. You know pop videos or musicals, that kind of thing.'

He raised a sceptical eyebrow. 'You look as though you've trained.'

'A long time ago my mum sent me to ballet lessons. I used to be a bit of a tomboy so this was her way of trying to stop me hanging around my dad's garage learning about cars and swearing from the mechanics or playing football in the mud with the boys.'

He smiled. 'And did it?'

'Not really, and I hated the stupid tutus I was made to wear. I like dancing though but now I prefer modern stuff. What about you? How come you know so much about stage lighting? You ever done that before?'

'A bit. But it's really music I'm into. I play the guitar.'

'Are you any good?'

'Yeah.'

Hmm. A lot of the boys say Matt is totally up himself. I thought they were probably just jealous but maybe they're right. On the other hand maybe Matt *is* really good and is rightly confident about it.

Matt said, 'I think you've just gone past your class. You've got maths next, haven't you?'

'Oh yeah, right. Thanks,' I said, blushing at my stupidity.

'See you around later.'

'Yeah. See ya.'

What was it with this guy that he could distract me so much I walk past my class? And how come he knew already what my schedule was? He'd hardly had time to learn his own timetable. Was it possible he was interested in me? Found me attractive even? Must admit the idea of someone like Matt fancying me was exciting.

What am I thinking? This is all wrong. I have a gorgeous boyfriend I'm mad about. I am not interested in anyone else. Not in *that* way. Definitely not.

THURSDAY JANUARY 17TH

Gerry brought his guitar into school today. He'd been taking lessons since last summer and is getting quite good. I don't think he's that interested in music. Like a lot of guys, he's taken up the guitar as he thinks it will help him pull girls. Not that he needs much help. Gerry is probably the nicest looking guy in sixth year so even though he's a bit of a tosser and a serial cheat lots of girls fancy him.

He started strumming a few tunes in the common room at lunch time but was getting stuck on some difficult chords. Matt strolled up to him. 'Nice guitar. Can I have a look?'

Gerry frowned but passed it to him anyway as it would have looked stupid not to.

Matt adjusted the tuning slightly first then started to play. Oh my God. When he said he was good he wasn't exaggerating. The music just seemed to flow out of him like the instrument didn't matter. And he could play anything; pop, rock, classical, jazz, indie. He played short pieces in each style. Casually and easily, like he was doodling. Everyone was quiet, spellbound, staring at him. Not wanting him to stop. Finally he paused, looked across the room and stared straight at me. 'This is for Kelly Ann.'

I blushed scarlet as attention suddenly shifted to me. Everyone was looking at me curiously as though I'd been keeping some secret from them but it wasn't true. I was as surprised as they were by Matt singling me out. I tried to give a nonchalant, I've-no-idea-either kind of shrug however my hot, tomato-red face probably meant nonchalant shrugs were pretty unconvincing. But when he started to play Abba's 'Dancing Queen' I forgot about being embarrassed and just swayed along to the music totally enthralled.

When he finished the whole room applauded. Except for Gerry who, as the end-of-lunch bell rang, grabbed his guitar back and muttered, 'Naff song.'

Had a feeling that Gerry wouldn't be bringing his guitar to school any more.

Matt didn't try to talk to me afterwards or pay me any particular attention later but it didn't stop people gossiping about whether there was anything going on with us. Even Liz has asked me if I've been keeping something from her. I've told everyone Matt just thinks I'm a good dancer because of seeing me in drama and have tried to act cool about the whole thing.

But there is absolutely no doubt about it. A guy who plays that well and dedicates the number to you is flattering. Very. And attractive. Even if there is no chance of me ever doing anything about it.

FRIDAY JANUARY 18TH

Hadn't seen Chris all week as he's been busy with coursework so I was really looking forward to tonight.

Chris picked me up at my house straight from uni and

we went to his flat so he could dump his books and get changed before we went out to the cinema.

The first person I saw was Gary. 'Have you replaced the cheesecake you stole yet, Gary?' I asked.

'Borrowed not stole. Theft is a serious accusation you know.'

I sighed. 'You can't *borrow* a cake. Now, have you bought me another one, you thieving tosser.'

'Sorry, I forgot. I'll, um, get you one tomorrow. Anyway I'm glad you're here because I wanted your opinion. I've got a hot date tonight. How do I look?'

I scowled. 'You look like you need a black eye.'

'Oh c'mon, Kelly Ann. Seriously. I really want your opinion.'

I looked him over. Nice, loosely fitted denims, black shirt with sleeves rolled up to the elbows and new, but not too new, trainers. Hair gelled a little and, yes, after-shave that actually smelled nice and not like pine disinfectant for a change – a Christmas present from Liz and me.

'Hmm, I've seen you look worse. Who's the girl? Still the blonde?'

'Yeah, Samantha. Sexy name, right?'

'So, she's special?'

'Well,' Gary hesitated, 'special date anyway.'

'Special date?'

'Third.'

'So?' I asked, puzzled.

'So I might get to sleep with her. Bloody hope so anyway. If you don't get a shag on the third date there's no telling when you'll strike lucky. Could take months.'

'You're disgusting, Gary.'

'Thanks.'

'Where is everyone?' I asked, deciding a change of subject might be a good idea.

'Jamie's out getting pissed with some other medics then they're planning to go clubbing if they can still stand up.' Gary shrugged on his jacket. 'Ian's meeting Valerie. Going for a curry or something, I think.'

'Oh,' I said.

'Yeah, so you and Chris will definitely have the place to yourselves tonight. No shagging in my room though. I want it pristine when I bring Samantha back.'

'You're—'

'Disgusting, I know.'

'Anyway Chris and I are going to the cinema, like we said.'

'Sure, right. So, wish me luck?'

'Hope she slaps you.'

But, like Gary said, we had the place to ourselves tonight. So we could be together – hug, snog and maybe, mmm yeah, make love without worrying that anyone would overhear us. And the film hadn't had great reviews. Anyway, maybe we could go to a later showing.

Chris didn't need any persuading. He picked me up and carried me to his bedroom. I put out the light which I know disappoints Chris a little but he understands that I still feel shy about making love with the lights full on. However since our bedroom door was ajar some soft, muted light reached us from the hall. So romantic. And flattering. Oh God it felt so good to be alone with Chris at last.

Then I heard a key being inserted and turned along the hall. The front door opened. A gruff, deep voice said, 'See, I told you no one was here. Only the hall lights on.'

Ian.

A contented giggle. Valerie.

Shit.

Chris wanted to get up and tell them we were here but I stopped him. 'We can't come out of a dark bedroom at eight o'clock,' I whispered, blushing. 'They'll know what we've been doing.'

'So,' Chris said. 'It's not a crime.'

But I couldn't face it so in the end we just lay quietly. Not moving or speaking and even trying to breathe as silently as possible.

Soon wished I'd taken Chris's advice though. They started in the hall, for God sake. Noisily snogging and laughing before finally throwing open Ian's bedroom door which is diagonally opposite ours and what sounded like jumping onto his bed and bouncing about on it. We had to lie there for what seemed like hours listening to Valerie giggling and calling Ian her 'gorgeous big heffalump' while Ian moaned stuff like, 'Valerie, my hot wee carrot top.'

Oh God it was embarrassing.

Chris and I were trapped until they finally fell asleep and we could creep out.

The film was rubbish.

Maybe Chris is right. Perhaps we do need our own place.

MONDAY JANUARY 21 ST

Spent the whole weekend with Chris. Bliss. Except for having to get up to brush my teeth early each morning.

Chris says there's no need and that I smell and look gorgeous first thing but I think he's lying so as not to hurt my feelings. And he's pointed out that he doesn't bother so why should I? But I know Chris doesn't suffer from morning breath, probably because he sleeps with his mouth closed, a trait I don't think I share. We tried making love without kissing so I wouldn't have to get up but Chris didn't like it. Said it was like having sex with a prostitute. Or what he imagined having sex with a prostitute was like anyway.

Still it was fantastic spending the whole time with Chris when he didn't have to work or study. And it put all stupid thoughts of fancying anyone else totally out my head. I didn't think about Matt even once all weekend.

OK, maybe once, when Chris was in the shower singing tunelessly to himself. Normally this just makes me smile indulgently but this time it kind of annoyed me somehow. I bet Matt has a nice voice. Someone that musically talented could never sing out of tune.

WEDNESDAY JANUARY 23RD

Matt brought his electric guitar into school and played a tune he'd composed himself. Wow, he really is so talented. And he's told everyone he's just joined a band called Rock Rampage. They're new but all the guys in it are in their twenties and have played in other bands before. Have decided to avoid him as much as possible. Shouldn't be difficult as he is now constantly surrounded by hordes of groupies from first year up.

SATURDAY JANUARY 26TH

Nearly everyone went off to the pub after school yesterday. Not the one nearest to the school as teachers go there and some of us, like me, are still legally underage but the one on the other side of the park which doesn't look at fake IDs too closely. Matt went too but so what? There was a huge group of us. However it was only Liz and me that he offered to buy a drink for. I was going to refuse but Liz cut in with, 'Great, thanks, and could you get us some crisps too?'

Fortunately I wouldn't be tempted to stay long as Chris was picking me up at seven.

Chris texted. SORRY CAN'T MAKE TONIGHT. ASKED TO COVER FOR SICK STAFF AT WORK. C U TOMORROW. LUV U xx

Hmm.

Got drunk, danced on table and was barred by the pub manager. I said, 'You can't bar me. I'm underage.'

Manager had no answer to that one.

But other than that didn't do anything too embarrassing like pole dancing upside down (a party last year – don't ask) or coming out of the loo with my skirt tucked into my knickers (Liz).

And I didn't tell Matt I fancied him and ask for a snog, thank God, although I suspect my restraint was helped by the fact that he left after just one drink.

Wish I'd left after just one drink too. Was sick all morning and still feeling awful by the time Chris picked me up at six.

Tried to tell him that I just had an upset stomach from something I ate earlier but I needn't have bothered. 'Something you drank more like,' Chris said. He handed me his phone. 'Have a look at the texts you sent me last night.'

LUV U SOOOOOOOOO. LUV EVERY PEOPLE INTHE WOOOORLD SOOOOOOOO MUCK. KA

THE PUBIC MINGER HAS BARED ME. FOR BING DRUNK. IN A PUBLIC! WANT KILL THE MINGER.

'My predictive text's been playing up?' I said.

Even without the stupid texts my condition must have been pretty obvious. As soon as we arrived at Chris's, Jamie took one look at me and said, 'Ah, a serious case of alcohol poisoning I see. For which there is only one known cure.' He disappeared off to the kitchen and returned with a glass of what looked like fresh orange which he handed to me with a flourish. 'Your medicine. Vodka and orange. Best followed by a fry-up or chicken-tikka curry.'

Chris took the glass from me and scowled at Jamie. 'You idiot.'

But it was too late. Just the thought of Jamie's 'cure' had me running for the bathroom to throw up again.

Of course we couldn't go out then.

Most medics are pretty callous with ill people unless you've got cancer, or something equally serious, but Chris has always been kind and caring when anyone is sick. Even if it's self-inflicted. So he held my hair back from my face when I was on my knees hurling into the toilet and put a cold cloth on my forehead afterwards.

Later, when I'd recovered a bit, he made me tea and toast then we went to bed and he just hugged me until I fell asleep. It wasn't exactly the most fun night I'd ever had but it did remind me of how much I loved Chris and how lucky I was to have him.

SUNDAY JANUARY 27TH

Oh God, the sheer joy of feeling well again was almost worth getting ill for. Almost. Jamie apologized for his 'hair of the dog' hangover cure but said it worked for some people.

Hmm.

It was a lovely crisp frosty day so Chris drove us to Loch Lomond. We parked the car then walked hand in hand by the calm blue water and gazed at the snow-capped surrounding mountains. So romantic. Later we went for lunch at one of the cafes by the shore. Starving now, I wolfed down my chicken and chips but kept some bread to feed to the ducks and a pair of swans afterwards.

A perfect day. And Matt never entered my head at all. Until the evening.

Back in Glasgow Gary suggested we all go to this pub in the city centre where a new rock group was playing. The Rock Rampage. He'd heard they were good. We didn't go. Everyone was too broke. But still, after that, I couldn't get Matt out of my mind. Not entirely.

MONDAY JANUARY 28TH

This stupid thing with Matt was getting seriously annoying. Decided to talk to Liz. Wish I hadn't bothered.

'It's his guitar, Kelly Ann,' Liz said.

'His guitar? That's it?'

'Of course.'

'I'm attracted to Matt just because of his musical talent? Don't think so. I mean, sad Nigel McDuff is good on the violin but I don't fancy him. And his pal Kevin isn't bad on piano but—'

'Violins and pianos aren't phallic symbols. Guitars are.'

'Don't talk rubbish,' I said, exasperated now. 'Guitars aren't anything like penises.'

'No? Think about where they're placed. Right at the groin. And how they're played. All that sexy hip grinding. Oh yes. Unconsciously you're thinking all the time: *Matt's got a massive one and knows how to use it.'*

'This is bollocks, Liz. But OK, let's say you're right. How come *you're* not affected then?'

'Once you've studied how the unconscious mind works as I have then these things don't affect you the same. My super ego can rise above it.'

Hmm.

Decided I'd get more sense out of Stephanie so went round to her place after school.

'Of course you still love Chris, Kelly Ann. You just fancy this Matt. A lot, it has to be said.'

'So what should I do?'

Stephanie shrugged. 'You could try shagging him.'

'What! I couldn't do that!'

'Why not? At least it would get it out of the way. After a few times you'd probably be bored with him.'

'Cheat on Chris? How could I possibly explain *that* to him?'

'You don't explain anything, you idiot. Just keep your mouth shut. Honestly, I despair of you, I really do. You don't need to share every tiny little detail of your life with your boyfriend you know.'

Hmm. So either I spend my entire life trying to understand the complete works of Freud or live with the guilt of cheating on Chris for the rest of eternity. Brilliant.

No, there has to be a better way of dealing with this.

But then again maybe I wouldn't have to do anything. Most likely Matt didn't fancy me anyway and he was just being friendly. Probably he had a girlfriend already – a guy like him was almost bound to.

I should have felt relieved by this but I didn't. More depressed really. Oh God, why did this have to happen now? Just when I'd finally got my life sorted out. Of all the schools in Glasgow he could have gone to why, oh why, did he have to come to mine?

FRIDAY FEBRUARY 1 ST

Matt hasn't been at school all week. He came in briefly today and was suspended for two weeks for truanting. Well, actually one week for truanting and one week for making a rude gesture to Mr Smith when told about it.

I'm glad. I had made up my mind to ignore Matt as much as possible but now this won't be necessary. And out of sight is out of mind. Hopefully anyway. Also I'm beginning to think I've imagined or at least exaggerated how attractive I find him. He's just a guy after all. OK, he can play the guitar a bit and is new, so obviously he is bound to be more interesting than other boys I've known for years. But that's all.

Anyway I've got more to worry about than my stupid crush on Matt. Mum is determined to have an Ann Summers party at our house on the weekend before Valentine's and neither Dad nor I can talk her out of it.

And she is going to invite everyone she knows including Liz's, Stephanie's and Chris's mums.

Of course their mums will be too classy, mature and well, *decent* to attend such a thing but just the thought of her asking is mortifying. Why can't my mum act her age for God's sake and be respectable?

TUESDAY FEBRUARY 5TH

Don't believe it. Everyone is coming. Well, everyone except Great Aunt Winnie and that's only because she has to go into hospital to get her hip replacement checked. I mean, are there no middle-aged women anywhere who are prepared to grow old in a dignified, graceful manner?

Mum has asked me to stay in on Saturday to help out but there is absolutely no way I am prepared to have any involvement with this stupid event.

FRIDAY FEBRUARY 8TH

Mum said I should think myself lucky to have a modern mum like her. A mum who lets her teenage daughter spend weekends at her boyfriend's flat. If it was up to my father on the other hand . . .

Total blackmail, but what choice did I have? Just hope

these parties aren't as depraved and sordid as I've been led to believe.

SATURDAY FEBRUARY 9TH

Given the choice between poking my own eyes out with hot knitting needles and attending such a . . . thing again there would be no contest. Hot knitting needles would definitely be the less painful option.

It wasn't so much the tacky, and sometimes downright disgusting, underwear, or the 'toys' – don't ask – but the attendees. How any of these women can criticize teens is beyond me. They were shameless. Utterly shameless.

Can you imagine a room full of forty- and fifty-year-old drunk women all wearing frilly knickers or see-through baby-doll nighties and dancing to *Mama Mia* music? Oh God, I wish I could wipe the awful memory from my head but even now it's over, no matter how hard I try, I keep getting horrible flashbacks.

Mum wore a French-maid outfit which was hideously embarrassing especially as you could see a bit of her bum cheeks when she bent over, but Chris's mum was the worst. I can never tell him about it or he'd be psychologically scarred for life. She was wearing a red balcony bra with tiny nylon pants and black stockings, yet strolled over to talk to me as calmly as though she'd proper clothes on.

Oh it was nice to see me again. She didn't see much of me now Chris had moved out. Didn't see much of Chris either but medicine was such an intense course wasn't it? And how was I doing? How was school? Was I looking forward to going to university next year?

I mean all this normal talk from a woman who was practically naked. Come to think of it a woman who would have looked more decent if she *had* been naked. I was speechless – too shocked to say a single word – so at first I was glad when Mum came over and started talking to her. That was until I realized she was trying to sell her one of the gross toys. And Chris's mum bought it.

My jaw practically hit the carpet. Just couldn't believe that Chris's mum could behave like this. I mean she's a senior nurse for God's sake. Nursing is a respectable, responsible profession. How could she stoop to this?

But she was completely unfazed. 'Have you bought anything yet, Kelly Ann?'

I flushed. 'Um, no.

'Better hurry up or all the best things will be gone.'

Best things! Bloody hell. 'I'm not really interested in any of this, erm, stuff,' I said stiffly.

'Of course you're not,' Chris's mum smiled at me indulgently. 'You and Chris. So young and in love.' She paused. Sighed nostalgically. 'I remember when I was your age. Wonderful time. Those were the days all right. But, you know, when you've been married as long as I have, well, it's important to add a little variety to your relationship. Stop things getting stale.' She looked at Mum. 'Isn't that right, Moira?'

Mum took a drag of her cigarette, blew the smoke out of her nose and nodded. 'Too right. After a few years it can get boring. You need to spice things up a bit in the bedroom. Now your dad and I— '

Right that was it. I refused to listen to my mum and my boyfriend's mum discuss their sex lives. Without another word I fled upstairs to my room only to find Aunt Kate there trying to wriggle into a leather basque and asking for my help with the hooks. Would this torture never end?

When I eventually went back down I noticed Mum and Chris's mum looking over at me and giggling like, well, like schoolgirls really. Hmm, probably all that sex talk was a wind up. Was more relieved than annoyed to be honest. The thought of either of them being serious about it was way more disturbing.

Finally they left – after putting their clothes on, thank God – but not before Mum made me buy something because 'every party girl has to buy at least one item'. In the end I opted for the cheapest and least offensive thing on display which was a plastic ice-cube tray. Not that I'd ever find a use for penis-shaped ice.

At least it was over and I'd never have to endure a night like this again.

SUNDAY FEBRUARY 1OTH

Mum made over £200 last night on commission and is determined to do more Ann Summers evenings.

Told Mum I would join Dignitas who would no doubt assist me in committing suicide, as the quality of my life would be unbearable if she went ahead with her decision.

But Mum just cackled and gleefully counted her earnings again.

MONDAY FEBRUARY 11TH

'maybe you should just move out,' Liz said. 'Go live with Chris.'

'Leave home altogether? That's a bit drastic,' I said.

'Not as drastic as suicide.'

'Suppose. But where would I find the money to pay for a flat? I only get twenty pounds pocket money a week.'

'Well,' Liz said, 'now that your mum will be earning lots more . . . ?'

'Yuk. That would be like . . . like . . . living off my mum's immoral earnings!'

'It's a dilemma,' Liz agreed. 'But since she's going to do it anyway? You wouldn't want her to spend it all on booze and fags would you?'

Hmm. Liz had a point. Looked at that way, maybe it

wouldn't be wrong to accept Mum's money. In fact it might even be my moral duty. But did I really want to move in with Chris? Live, eat, sleep and clean the toilet bowl together? Maybe end up telling fart jokes in bed. Where's the romance in that? And I'm only seventeen. Much too young to settle down with a boyfriend. Even one as gorgeous as Chris.

TUESDAY FEBRUARY 12TH

Dad says Mum can't use our house to sell stuff any more; that's what shops are for. He was really determined about it and for once Mum didn't argue. Said she'd become an official rep and would be organizing parties at other people's houses anyway. She showed us the mobile she got from the company then gobsmacked me by texting people on it. Mum texting! I never thought she'd ever be capable of learning to use modern technology. She can barely work the remote on the TV. She must really be serious about this job.

But I've refused to help out. 'Family's one thing but I'm not doing this in strangers' houses, Mum.'

She didn't say anything at the time but a few minutes later I got a text: AWAY AND BOIL YOUR HEAD.

My first ever text from Mum and it's an insult. Typical.

WEDNESDAY FEBRUARY 13TH

Gary, Ian and loads of other people who left for uni last year visited the school today. The invitation came from the guidance staff, who organize this ex-pupil thing every year. I was surprised so many people accepted. When I leave I don't think I'll ever bother to come back.

The teachers greeted them like long-lost friends, even pupils they'd hated for the entire five or six years of school. Well, except for my maths teacher Mr Simmons who told the ones he didn't like to sod off and don't annoy him – he didn't need to put up with them any more.

And the former pupils were just as bad, going all sentimental about how they really missed school. Even people who'd hated it and got into trouble for truanting. God, there was no way I'd ever be that sad or hypo-critical. I couldn't wait to leave and I'd never come back when I finally got my freedom.

A lot of the teachers asked about Chris and how he was doing but he'd been unable to come because no medical student can afford to take even half a day off. In fact most medics have to study every night after lectures as well except at weekends so I practically never see Chris during the week. Still, I'd see him tomorrow night as it's Valentine's.

It's nice to have a boyfriend on Valentine's and know that I'll definitely get a card – especially after years of never getting any except the ones Mum or Aunt Kate used to forge for me out of pity – but it's a bit unexciting too. No *Will he? Won't he?* excitement or wondering if you might get a surprise card from a mystery admirer.

I know that in the morning I'll get a nice tasteful card from Chris in the post which will say *Guess who?* Then he'll pick me up in the evening and hand me a bunch of long-stemmed red roses. He's suggested going out for a romantic meal but I pretended I didn't want to as it's too expensive now Chris has to pay for a flat, so I expect we'll just stay in and watch the DVD I've bought him as a Valentine's present. Then he'll take me home as he's got a lecture at nine tomorrow.

It will be nice I know but . . . kind of predictable.

Chris called me tonight. He was going on about tomorrow; how he couldn't wait so see me, how much he loved me, what a lucky guy he was that I was his Valentine etc, etc then he stopped. 'You don't sound too enthusiastic, Kelly Ann. What's wrong?'

'Nothing. God, no, nothing's wrong. It's great, yeah, really looking forward to seeing you too.'

'But?'

'But nothing. Yeah, can't wait to see you. It's just that well . . . '

'Well what?'

'Well, I love you and everything, and it's great having

a steady boyfriend, but Valentine's isn't quite the same any more. I mean, it's romantic of course but, well, not as exciting as it used to be. Sort of predictable really.'

'You think I'm predictable?' Chris said.

'Well, yeah. But, you know, that's a good thing I suppose.'

'Hmm.'

THURSDAY FEBRUARY 14TH

Was gobsmacked when Chris walked into my maths class just before lunch.

Mr Simmons was delighted as Chris had been his star pupil. 'Oh, Chris, great to see you again. This is an unexpected visit. A pleasure. How are you doing?' Mr Simmons said.

But Chris had his eyes fixed on me. 'Sorry, Mr Simmons. Don't have time to chat right now.' He strode up the aisle to the back of the class where I sat, pulled me into his arms and kissed me full on the mouth. The whole class, except for Mr Simmons, applauded.

'Happy Valentine's, Kelly Ann. Can't wait for tonight,' Chris said. Then he left with a wave to Mr Simmons.

Two minutes after he'd gone there was a Tannoy announcement from a giggling school secretary to say that a bouquet of flowers had just been delivered to the school office, 'For Kelly Ann, the most gorgeous, sexiest girl in the school'.

Have never been so embarrassed in my entire life. I'm going to kill Chris for this.

FRIDAY FEBRUARY 15TH

But he'd booked a really nice hotel room for us for the night. And the next morning we both decided to skip classes. I even felt so happy and comfortable with Chris that for the first time I didn't bother with brushing my teeth before we made love in the morning.

Afterwards we just lay in each others arms blissfully happy until Chris said, 'Christ, you smell awful, Kelly Ann. What a stench!'

'*Arrgh.* Oh my God! You should have said something before! Oh God,' I squealed, as I tried to twist free of him.

But Chris held on to me and started to laugh. 'You should have seen your face. Wish I'd taken a photo!'

Hilarious.

SUNDAY FEBRUARY 17TH

We didn't go out anywhere at the weekend as neither of us had any money. Well, that's not quite true. I've got some left over from Christmas and some saved up but I'm keeping that to buy Chris a really good present for his eighteenth next month.

It's weird to think he'll be an adult then and legally allowed to drink beer, smoke, get into debt and go to prison. Can't wait till I'm eighteen too and free to do what I want. Not that I'd want to do all those things, of course – prison definitely doesn't sound much fun, for example – but it's the principle.

MONDAY FEBRUARY 18TH

Matt is back. But after spending a whole weekend with my gorgeous, loving, romantic and occasionally-very-unpredictable boyfriend I wasn't bothered at all. Matt is just a quite-nice-looking guy who plays guitar. And rides a bike.

WEDNESDAY FEBRUARY 20TH

'Want a ride home?' Matt said.

We were leaving early as both of us had a free period last thing on a Wednesday. I looked over longingly at his huge black and silver bike parked in the head teacher's space. Deliberately, of course. It might not be long until he was suspended again.

'I don't have a helmet.'

'I've got a spare.'

'I'm not allowed to ride a motorbike. Too dangerous,' I said, aware just as the words formed in my mouth how pathetic I must sound.

'You always do what your parents tell you? Why not break out? Live dangerously for a while.'

I flushed. Actually it was Chris who'd warned me about motorbikes. When he worked as a hospital porter last summer he'd had to wheel the bodies of three teenagers, all killed in motorbike accidents, to the mortuary. Afterwards he'd made me promise never to ride on one. It hadn't bothered me at the time. But now? Not everyone who rides a bike gets killed after all. And there are lots of motor-car accidents too, yet Chris drives.

Matt must have seen the indecision on my face because he grinned and said, 'C'mon, you know you want to.'

I smiled back nervously and followed him into the car park. He handed me a too-large helmet and helped me tighten the straps to fit under my chin. It was yellow and black, and probably made me look like a giant bumblebee, but so what? It's not as though I cared whether Matt found me attractive. In fact it would be better if he didn't.

Matt got on first and I climbed on behind him. He looked back at me. 'Hold on.'

I wound my arms lightly around his leather-jacketed

waist but kept my body away. However, I tightened my grip when we started to move.

But he drove slowly and carefully to my door. I live near the school so we were there in minutes.

'Thanks, Matt. That was, um, great,' I lied, tugging at the helmet straps as I prepared to get off.

'Liar. Now how would you like to go for a real ride?'

I hesitated.

'Trust me,' he said. 'I'll have you back inside an hour. In one piece. Don't be scared.'

'I'm not scared it's just—'

'OK then, let's go!'

We roared off. Matt weaved through the traffic jumping several red lights until we turned into a slip road, accelerated onto the motorway, cut straight into the fast lane and then flew along fast as a bullet, overtaking everything in our way.

I'd left my stomach somewhere back on the slip road and at first I was too terrified even to scream but just gripped Matt. However when I noticed the speedometer hit ninety miles per hour I managed to shriek into the wind, 'Slow down!'

He turned and shouted, 'It's OK, there's no speed cameras here!'

'Keep your eyes on the road!' I screamed.

He grinned at me but looked ahead again and brought his speed down to eighty.

After a few minutes, when I realized there was a chance that my bloodied, broken corpse might not be strewn over the motorway, and that I may actually survive this trip, I calmed down enough to notice that the fingers of my ungloved hands would probably drop off with frostbite as the cold wind whipped them to frozen stumps. I put my hands in Matt's deep front pockets and hoped fervently that he didn't think I was groping him.

That was better. After another few minutes I actually started to enjoy the speed. Matt was a confident, skilful, expert biker who knew exactly what he was doing. Of course I'd be safe. Ten minutes later I was whooping with joy when we raced another biker and left him for dust behind us. Yeah!

When Matt finally deposited me outside my house again I was on a total high.

I got off the bike and turned to him gabbling excitedly. 'Oh my God that was brilliant. Just brilliant. Like doing the extreme velocity twister ride of death at last summer's fair, but better. Oh my God.'

'Cool, glad you enjoyed it. So, maybe we'll do this again sometime?'

'Yeah definitely.' Impulsively I put my arms around his neck and we clunked helmets. 'Thanks. I, um, expect you'd like your spare helmet back?'

Well it wasn't kissing him was it? Not when we both

had helmets on. But when Chris called later that night and asked how my day had been I didn't tell him about Matt or the motorbike ride. Because I didn't need to tell my boyfriend every tiny little detail of my life, did I? And I'd nothing to feel guilty about. Nothing.

THURSDAY FEBRUARY 21 ST

But I did feel guilty. I wasn't Stephanie, and keeping information – no matter how totally innocent – from Chris felt wrong. I'd tell him about my bike ride with Matt. I know he wouldn't approve because of his views on donor-bikes but . . . he wasn't my dad after all. And there was no reason to tell him about the helmet clunk. A clunk isn't a kiss after all.

MONDAY FEBRUARY 25TH

Didn't mention anything about Matt to Chris at the weekend. Well, the opportunity didn't really come up. Although we *had* talked about a movie we'd watched, about a rock star who died in a motorbike accident. But he'd been much older than Matt, and the film was made in the eighties, so it wasn't really relevant. Also it seemed kind of negative. I'll tell Chris next weekend.

Meantime I'm determined to avoid Matt as much as possible. And I won't be going on any more rides with him. Chris is right, it's dangerous, but maybe not for the reasons he thinks. Fact is, someone at school must have seen Matt give me a lift home and now there's an ugly rumour going round that we're dating.

I've denied it of course. Matt hasn't bothered. Just told people who mentioned it to him to 'Get a life, saddos.' He's right. Malicious gossips like that should be treated with contempt. But what if they tell Chris?

WEDNESDAY FEBRUARY 27TH

Have avoided Matt so far this week. I don't go the common room any more and even skipped two drama classes. This is getting stupid. I'm going to tell Chris myself and then I can act normal. But not over the phone. I'll tell him on Friday when I go over for the weekend.

Chris called tonight. Said he was really sorry but he couldn't see me this weekend as he was working at the hospital Friday and then he'd need to study all of Saturday and Sunday for a biochemistry exam. It was a bitch but really important.

Not sure whether I was relieved or disappointed by this news, which didn't seem right somehow.

THURSDAY FEBRUARY 28TH

Matt cornered me this morning at break. 'Hey,' he said, 'you been avoiding me?'

'God no,' I lied. 'Why would I?'

Matt shrugged. 'Dunno.' He smiled. 'Maybe I'm getting paranoid. Anyway, thing is, I'm glad I ran into you. I wanted to tell you about a gig we're doing in Ashton Lane tomorrow. Me and the band. Want to come?'

OK, now was the time to draw a line. Tell him about Chris. Make things plain to him and the rest of the school. 'I'm sorry, Matt,' I said, 'but I think you should know I've got a boyfriend.'

'So?' he said.

'So, I'm not single. You'll have to ask someone else.'

'Hey, wait a minute, I don't think I quite get it.' He smiled and raised his eyebrows sceptically. 'You think I'm asking you out? On a date or something?'

'Well, um, no. Not really. I mean, I'm not sure, but well—'

'Look, I just thought you'd enjoy the music. Like to hear the band. So, yeah, no worries, bring your boyfriend too. That would be cool. He into rock?'

I blushed furiously. Oh God. He must think I'm totally up myself imagining he fancies me. 'Chris? Yeah, but he's, um, busy this weekend. Working. Look, I didn't really think you ... Well, it's this stupid school. Full of gossips and—'

'Tell me about it,' Matt laughed. 'I've just got to look at a girl, next thing I know everyone thinks we've shagged in the toilets.'

'Oh God, yeah that must be awful for you. Some people are just so nasty, small-minded and totally—'

'Of course sometimes they're right.' Matt grinned to show me he was only kidding. *I think.* 'So anyway you want to come?

'Oh, erm, I don't know if—'

'And you like music don't you? Someone who dances like you must love music.'

'Yeah of course I do, but—'

'Great. I won't be at school tomorrow – need to practice and set up – but I'll pick you up at your place seven o'clock.'

Then he was gone.

Was going to tell him at lunch time that I'd changed my mind, couldn't make it, but he must have cut classes and gone home as I didn't see him in school for the rest of the day. How had this happened? Matt was picking me up tomorrow and taking me to a gig. But it wasn't a date. Of course not. I didn't tell anyone about it though. Not even my best friends Liz and Stephanie. And not Chris. Definitely not Chris.

FRIDAY MARCH 1 ST

By eight o'clock matt still hadn't showed. I should have felt relieved but I didn't. Instead I felt disappointed and a bit humiliated. Because even though it wasn't a date it still seemed somehow like I'd been stood up.

Wished now I'd arranged to go see *Psycho Stalkers* with Liz, even though I'm not keen on stalking movies, or agreed to help Gerry baby sit Morgan, his baby girl who was the result of a one-night stand with Linda last year. Even teaching Gerry to change a dirty nappy while simultaneously trying to keep his hands off my bum (absolutely nothing puts Gerry off sex) seemed preferable to spending a Friday night at home watching repeats of last year's repeats or programmes about home decorating. Obviously producers think only very sad people stay in on a Friday night.

Even my parents are out – quiz night at the pub – and they are about as sad as you can get.

Decided to go and get a DVD from the video-rental shop to pass the time and climbed upstairs to get my purse. Frowned at my reflection in the wardrobe mirror. New black velvet jeans, heels, strappy top and full make-up. All dressed up and nowhere to go. Kicked out of my shoes, peeled off jeans and top then changed into old denims, a bobbly grey jumper and comfy Converses. My scarlet lipstick and heavily mascared eyes now looked stupid with my casual outfit so I wiped off my make-up before going back downstairs where I grabbed a hoodie from the coat stand and opened the front door.

Matt was standing on the step, finger poised to press the bell. He grinned at me. 'Christ, you psychic? Or did you just hear the van screech to a halt outside? Paul really needs to get the brakes fixed on that. Never mind, thank God you're ready. We were supposed to be on stage half an hour ago.'

He turned and jogged towards the van parked outside my house. It had ROCK RAMPAGE painted in large, electric-blue, jagged letters along the top. Underneath were pictures of demons playing guitars with orange and yellow flames licking around them. Any hope I'd had of nosy neighbours not noticing Matt's arrival vanished.

I followed him quickly to the van, opened the passenger door, climbed up and poked my head inside. 'Matt, I've got to go back in first and—'

'Sorry no time for that now.' He revved the engine and

took the handbrake off. 'Quick, get in and shut the door.'

The van started to move. Bloody hell, I was going to be dragged. I scrambled in quickly and closed the door. Matt accelerated away.

'Where's the rest of the band?' I said.

'Left them at the gig setting up the equipment. Should be done by the time we get there.' He turned his face to look at me. 'Christ you're amazing, Kelly Ann!'

'I am?'

'Yeah, definitely. You know, most girls would have got dressed up for something like this. Make-up, heels – clubbing stuff. But not you.'

'Well I—'

'I mean, look at you. Old torn denims and worn jumper. Like you just don't give a shit.'

'But you didn't give me t—'

'I really admire that.'

'You do?'

'Yeah, I mean, it's like you're saying to the world, *Hey this is me, this is who I am – take it or leave it, I couldn't care less.* So confident. And real. You're incredible.'

Hmm.

Must admit I was flattered by Matt's comments but I didn't feel so great when we got to the club and started pushing our way through the crowded room hoaching with really nice-looking girls in clubbing gear. Felt a bit like Cinderella turning up at the ball still dressed in rags.

When we'd pressed to the front Matt introduced me to the other three band members as 'Kelly Ann, the dancer I was telling you about,' ordered me a vodka and Coke then hurried onto the stage.

They were all dressed in black like Matt but none were as tall or nice looking. They started to play. The drummer, bass guitarist and the guy on keyboard were all good but nothing compared to Matt who played lead guitar. And I was right about Matt's voice too. He could sing!

After the first number everyone broke into wild applause and some girls screamed 'Matt! Matt!' So even though they were a new band he must already have some fans. Couldn't help enjoying the envious stares I was getting from these girls who obviously thought I was his girlfriend. Not just envious but incredulous too as they eyed my outfit. Wondered if next time they'd come dressed in old denims and bobbly jumper instead of pulling clothes.

I was seated at a table right in front of the band with another two females; a tall blonde American girl who was the drummer's girlfriend and an old woman who turned out to be the base guitarist's gran. Although she'd brought her knitting with her she was dressed more trendily than me.

After about an hour the band stopped for a break.

'You were fabulous, Matt,' I said. Then added politely, 'And, well, the band too. All of you. Brilliant.'

'Thanks,' Matt said, sitting down and wrapping an arm casually around my shoulders.

It would have seemed like really bad manners to have objected or shrugged his arm off. After all, it was just a friendly sort of gesture. The kind of thing a guy might even do with another guy for instance. But when he took a swig of beer, pulled me towards him and kissed me on the forehead I wondered if I should say something. No. A kiss like that is the kind you could give to your sister or elderly aunt. Nothing wrong with it. It wasn't a pass. Definitely not.

However, when his arm slipped from my shoulder and his hand touched the side of my bum I was just about to complain when I saw Gary. He was with a girl, probably Samantha who he is still seeing despite the disappointing third date. Oh My God!

Fortunately he hadn't seen me yet but they were headed towards the bar to the left of us. Frantic now, I dropped down and hid underneath our table.

'What are you doing, Kelly Ann?' Matt said, leaning down and squinting at me.

'Shh, don't talk so loudly. I'm, erm, looking for something.'

'What?'

'Oh, em, something really important.'

'A bomb?'

'Keep your voice down! No of course not. I'm, erm, looking for money. Yeah, I dropped a pound coin down here.'

Matt seemed satisfied with that and chatted with the rest of the band. Peering through people's legs I recognized Gary's trainers by the bar. But he was turned sideways so I couldn't come out without the danger of being seen. I'd have to wait until he was served and turned round.

After a good two or three minutes he still hadn't been served. Matt peered at me under the table. 'Kelly Ann, why don't you just forget it?' he said, sounding more amused than impatient. 'It's only a quid after all. Look, tell you what' – he handed me a pound coin – 'now come up and join the company.'

Saw Gary turn round and start back along the room holding two drinks. This was my chance. I reached for my hoodie and crawled out from under the table but kept my body low then I made to dart for the side door. Matt caught me.

'What are you doing?'

'Sorry, Matt. Gotta go. Diarrhoea!'

He let go of me immediately without asking any further questions. Diarrhoea does that to people. I've used it on forged sick notes at school ever since I learned to spell it. Teachers never question further. I bolted for the door. And never looked back.

* * *

Wish I'd remembered to take my bag with my purse and mobile in it but I didn't. Had to walk all the way home, but luckily at least I'd my comfy Converses on. The only lucky thing about tonight. Not that I deserved to have a good night – sneaking out with Matt and not telling anyone about it, well it wasn't right. Even though it was totally innocent, of course, and not really cheating or anything, it was just all wrong. Never again.

SATURDAY MARCH 2ND

Matt turned up at my door at one o'clock. Handed me my bag.

'How are you feeling now?' he asked. 'Got over your, um, upset?'

I didn't let him in. Just reached for my shoulder bag and murmured, 'Thanks.'

'Your boyfriend texted you a few times.'

Oh God.

'Hope you don't mind but I thought it best to text back. Pretended I was you. Said you were going to bed early.'

I flushed. 'I *do* mind actually.'

He shrugged. 'Sorry.'

'I didn't need you to lie for me.'

'Yeah you did. You didn't tell your boyfriend you were with me, did you?'

'No reason why I shouldn't. We didn't do anything.'

'But you didn't.'

My silence confirmed what he knew already.

'I get it. Your boyfriend's the jealous type. Bit of a control freak, right? Why complicate things.'

'He's not a control freak.'

'But he does get jealous?'

'Sometimes.'

'So now he won't suspect anything.' Matt smiled. 'Not that there was anything for him to get worked up about.'

'There wasn't.'

'Like I said.'

'Yeah, well, um, thanks, Matt.'

'No worries.'

But I did worry. It seemed wrong somehow that Matt lied for me and so we now both had a secret we were keeping from my boyfriend. After Matt left I called Chris. He sounded so happy to hear from me and apologized again for not being able to see me this weekend. Felt so guilty. But I hadn't really done anything wrong, had I?

MONDAY MARCH 4TH

Avoided matt today. Even persuaded Liz to go to MacDonald's at lunch time so I wouldn't see him in the common room. Wasn't difficult to persuade Liz as she'd only brought boring cheese sandwiches for lunch. I was surprised when she took out her chopsticks to eat the Double Quarter Pounder.

'You can't eat a burger with those, Liz.'

'Yeah I can. It's easy. Look.'

Liz speared the burger with one of the chopsticks and, holding it like a kebab, bit off a large piece.

Hmm, Liz has stuck with this chopstick diet much longer than any other, but I think she may have gained a few pounds.

'Have you heard the latest rumour about Matt?' Liz asked.

I flushed. 'No and I don't believe it anyway.'

'How do you know you don't believe it if you haven't heard it?' Liz peered at me suspiciously. 'Why have you gone red?'

'I haven't gone red. Anyway all the rumours at our school are rubbish.' I tried to give an unconcerned, dismissive laugh but somehow it came out sounding wrong, more like a witch's cackle really. 'I mean, people have even said I've been seeing Matt. Total lies.'

'They're not saying that now. Rumour is,' Liz said,

putting her head close to mine and nearly poking my eye out with her chopstick in the process, 'he's dating the French teacher Mademoiselle Laroche. He was spotted snogging her in the language lab at break last Thursday.'

'Don't believe it.'

'Three people saw them. Then they were seen coming out of Findlay's pub on Friday night about eleven o'clock. They were holding hands and kissing. Both of them got into the same taxi and it drove away, with them snogging the faces off each other in the back.'

'No way. Matt was doing a gig in Ashton Lane on Friday night.'

'So he's said but no one believes him. Everyone's saying it's a cover-up to protect her.'

'Well they're wrong. I know for a fact. I was there!'

Oh God.

Liz's eyes narrowed. 'Tell me all.'

TUESDAY MARCH 5TH

I suppose when your best friend is the nosiest person in Scotland it's going to be difficult to keep stuff a secret from her. Anyway I'm glad Liz knows now so I've someone to talk to about it. And she says she won't share my secret with anyone. Anything I tell her about Matt will be absolutely confidential. Psychologists are ethically bound to keep their clients' secrets to the grave and beyond. Usually.

WEDNESDAY MARCH 6TH

Stephanie called round. 'This is fabulous, Kelly Ann. I'm so proud of you. Who'd have thought after all those years when you couldn't get a single date with a decent-looking guy and now you've got two drooling after you. Liz says Matt is pretty hot.'

'I don't have two guys drooling after me. Only Chris. And he doesn't drool.'

'When will I get to see Matt?' Stephanie asked, ignoring me.

'Never.'

THURSDAY MARCH 7TH

Chris's eighteenth birthday. His parents have persuaded him to take the afternoon off to attend a family get-together at home. Only Chris would need to be persuaded to take time off on his birthday! Afterwards he and I are supposed to be going out to dinner for a quiet celebration just the two of us as he said he didn't want any fuss.

Of course there was no way his pals were going to let him get away with that so a surprise party has been organized at the union by Gary, Ian and Jamie, although Chris's parents have agreed to foot most of the bill. To be honest I am really doubtful about the whole thing as every surprise party I've been to has ended up a disaster.

Called Gary straight after school to check on final arrangements.

'Relax, Kelly Ann. Everything is sorted.'

'Hmm. You better not have hired a stripper.'

'Of course not.'

'Or organized any stupid games like arm-farting competitions.'

'Like I'd be that juvenile. What do you take me for? Frankly, I'm offended.'

'I still think you should have left the arrangements to me. Liz and Stephanie would have helped.'

'Yeah right. Left to you lot we'd all be drinking Bacardi Breezers or Chardonnay while listening to the soundtrack of *Dirty Dancing* or something just as naff.

'There's nothing wrong with *Dirty*—'

'Look, Kelly Ann, the party's all fixed. Chris will love it. Honestly. Trust me.'

Hmm.

Although I don't approve of surprise parties I have got

Chris a surprise present which I know he'll love. He's asked for a DVD but there is no way I was getting him something as cheap and ordinary as that for his eighteenth. Instead, I've bought him a skeleton. OK, I know it's not the most romantic gift ever, but he's been saying for ages how he'd like one like Jamie's because it's useful for learning anatomy and anyway makes a cool ornament but they were too expensive.

Wore a short red dress which was Chris's favourite and high heels. Opted for scarlet lipstick and tried not to think about Liz's daft talk of advertising healthy vaginas. Then I put on just a little mascara as Chris doesn't like a lot of make-up. Says I'm beautiful just as I am. Cheesy but nice. I picked up my skeleton and got Dad to drop me off at Chris's.

It was a bit awkward dragging Jimmy, as I called him, up four flights of stairs. Dad said I should have kept him in the box but that wouldn't have been as exciting as presenting Chris with a fully formed skeleton. For a laugh I gave him a wee jimmy tartan cap with orange hair attached, and a cheap fake sporran.

When I got to Chris's door I propped Jimmy up against the wall where Chris wouldn't see him right away and rang the bell.

Chris opened the door, pulled me into his arms and kissed me. 'God, you're beautiful, Kelly Ann.'

I smiled. 'Happy Birthday!'

'It is now,' he said. He put an arm round my shoulder. 'Come on in. I've got a surprise for you.'

'Wait, me first. I brought someone with me I'd like you to meet.'

Chris frowned. 'You brought someone?'

'Yeah, I think you'll like him.' I stepped back out and grabbed the skeleton. 'Meet Jimmy!'

'Oh!'

'I know you asked for a DVD but there was no way I was getting you just that so I thought, *What would Chris really like?* and well, you know, I . . . What's wrong? You don't seem very happy. I thought you'd be excited.'

'Oh yeah I am. Of course, yeah. It's just that, you know, skeletons are so expensive. You shouldn't have.'

'You're worth it. I wanted to do it.'

'Right. Great. So, um, could you just wait here a minute. I've, um, just got something I want to do first.'

'Don't be daft. You can't keep us both at the door like this.' I looked at the skeleton as I dragged him in and tutted. 'He's not usually rude like this, Jimmy.'

And then I saw it, leaning seemingly nonchalantly against the wall at the far corner of the hall. A large skeleton (taller than Jimmy or Jamie's) wearing a policeman's helmet and carrying a baton.

'A surprise present from my parents,' Chris explained unnecessarily. 'I've called him Percy.'

'Oh.'

'But I'll still need yours too.'

'Don't try to humour me, Chris. It's useless. My own fault. Surprise presents are a stupid idea.'

'No, you see Jimmy isn't really a Jimmy. Look at the pelvis. She's a girl. It's just as important for medics to know about female anatomy.'

I grinned. 'Jenny then. A girlfriend for Percy.'

Chris kissed me. 'Now for my surprise for you.' He opened the living-room door. '*Voila!*'

The table had been laid for two with flowers and candles. Sooo romantic. And the delicious aroma of Marks & Spencer's lasagne was wafting from the kitchen. Oh God, if only.

'I thought we were going to the union then off for pizza?'

'Yeah, but I just realized yesterday everyone was going out tonight so we'd have the place to ourselves. I can't think of a better way to spend my birthday.'

'Oh but, em, I'm not hungry right now,' I said, salivating.

'OK we don't need to eat now. I'm sure we could find ways to pass the time.' He pulled me towards him again and kissed me but I was looking at the clock. We'd need to get going soon.

I broke away from him. 'Look it's a Thursday night. Thursday is the new Saturday, right? Cheap drinks everywhere. And you can buy them legally for the very first time. We don't want to be stuck in here.'

Chris looked hurt but agreed reluctantly. Hated making him upset on his birthday but he'd soon get over it. Unlike the nearly one hundred and fifty guests who'd be really cheesed off if we didn't show.

More than one hundred and fifty by the looks of it and of course, since it was organized by guys, mainly girls. I didn't recognize most of them, who I guessed must be students from uni, but spotted Liz and Stephanie and waved them over. However, Jamie and a gang of other medic guys got to us first, hoisted Chris up on their shoulders and carried him off to the bar. I watched resignedly as they poured a pint down his throat while counting to eighteen by which time he was supposed to have downed the lot.

A roar went up as Chris downed it at sixteen and Jamie took up the challenge to outdo him.

Responsible teenage trainee doctors' drinking.

Thought briefly about going up and trying to stop them. But what was the point? I'd have had more chance persuading a tiger to eat muesli instead of meat than preventing this lot getting Chris completely plastered on his eighteenth. Decided I might as well give up.

'So,' I said, turning to Liz and Stephanie. 'What do you think of the party? Has Gary got everything organized OK?'

'Have you noticed how many girls are here?' Stephanie moaned. 'Just as well I brought my own guy.' She nodded over at her fiancé, Dave, who was standing at the corner of the bar facing away from us. He had his arm round a blonde girl's shoulders. She was hanging on to him, her head resting on his chest.

'Oh, er, right. But, em, aren't you annoyed about the girl?'

Stephanie laughed. 'The blonde in the skinny jeans and polo top? Jamie's skeleton. But yeah come to think of it he's spending too much time with her. You can't trust thin blondes – even dead ones. I'll go get him.'

Chris eventually made his way back to me grinning happily and planted a wet, beery kiss on my mouth. Forced myself to smile back – it was his birthday after all – and resigned myself to the fact that this was never going to be the romantic evening I'd have preferred.

Chris was whisked away again by other pals offering to buy him drinks so Liz, Stephanie and I headed for the buffet, while Dave and Gary were sent off to get us vodka and Cokes.

When they returned Gary started telling us about what he and Jamie had organized for later on that night. A gay male kissagram for Chris, a pole-dancing competition (which Stephanie was sure to win) and some game involving guys drinking beer from condoms.

'Sounds fantastic,' I said sarcastically.

'Yeah, took a lot of organizing but it's been worth it for my best pal,' Gary said, ignoring my tone. 'And guess what?'

'I don't know. Oh yeah, you forgot the arm-farting competition.'

'I told you we'd grown out of that. Give me some credit,' tutted Gary. 'No, I was just going to say I've organized a live band for later. They're fairly new and still trying to make their name so we got them quite cheap, but they're good. Saw them at a gig a couple of weeks ago and they were shit hot.' He looked over my head towards the door. 'In fact here they are now. Bang on time.'

I followed Gary's gaze and saw him immediately, even though he was behind the others, his tall frame silhouetted in the doorway, guitar slung carelessly across his back. Intent on making his way to the stage at the far corner of the room, he didn't notice me right away but then he scanned the crowd lazily and his eyes locked with mine. He stared at me for a moment, surprised, then gave me a slow smile.

I flushed, turned my head away. This was my boyfriend's eighteenth-birthday party. I shouldn't, I mustn't feel this attracted to another guy. Especially not tonight.

But I did. Attracted, excited, and horribly guilty.

Oh God. Of all the bands Gary could have hired, why oh why did he have to choose Matt's?

FRIDAY MARCH 8TH

Of course, Chris got absolutely plastered last night and made a complete idiot of himself. Not that I can talk about people doing stupid things when they're drunk, I suppose, but honestly it's just not like Chris to make a total show of himself.

It started with him doing a passable Michael Jackson moonwalk across the bar to huge applause until he fell backwards off the end. To even louder applause.

Ian and Gary helped him up then Jamie shoved a whisky shot in his hand. 'This should dull the pain. Repeat dose as necessary.'

I tried to take the drink off Chris but he'd already downed it.

Mistaking my hand on his arm for an affectionate pat he lunged at me drunkenly and gave me a whisky-drenched kiss. 'Christ, I love you so much, Kelly Ann!' he yelled. Then he started singing, if you can call it that, 'You Are So Beautiful'.

How he managed to get not a single note, even accidentally, in tune was beyond me but Chris was blissfully unaware of how awful he sounded.

Mercifully Gary intervened. 'Shit, even if you could sing, that song would make me puke. C'mon let's go, it's time for the cake.'

Jamie wheeled a trolley with a huge cake and candles

on it to the centre of the room and called for silence. The cake was in the shape of a girl's torso. A very curvy girl's torso. Don't ask where they'd put the candles.

Despite Chris's drunken state, he managed to blow out the candles first go. There was applause and calls for a speech. For a laugh Jamie gave him some helium balloons to inhale before talking. As if he needed a ridiculously high girly helium voice to sound totally stupid given how pissed he was.

Chris told everyone he loved me so much. And his mates – Gary, Ian and Jamie – who were the best mates in the world, he really loved them all so bloody much too. From the heart. He really did. He wanted them to know that. And the barmen, who were his best friends in the whole effing world. He loved them as well. And he wanted them to know.

Then he collapsed face first into the cake.

No taxi would take us with Chris in that state so Ian, Jamie and Gary had to carry him back to the flat with me trotting beside them trying to pretend I wasn't with them. It didn't help that his pals weren't completely sober either and dropped him several times while laughing hysterically like it was hilarious or something. Especially as they slid down two flights of stairs on the way up to the flat.

I suppose it could have been worse. At least Chris had refused to snog the gay kissagram – although he did tuck a tenner in the band of his tight leather shorts – and he'd resisted calls to do a full-monty strip, but even so I was mortified for him.

Chris, however, is totally unembarrassed and except for a slight headache he is completely recovered. Around twelve o'clock he made a huge fry-up for me, Gary and Ian which he wolfed down while his flatmates reminded him, between forkfuls of sausage, black pudding and scrambled eggs, of his drunken exploits. Instead of curling up into a ball of shame, Chris just laughed good-naturedly, 'Yeah, what a great night.'

Not for me, I couldn't help thinking, but then instantly felt guilty. It wasn't as though Chris had done anything really bad, like grope another girl or anything. And it's not like he's always getting wrecked and behaving like an idiot. But, oh God, he'd just been so embarrassing last night.

After the meal, Chris offered to drive me to school before going off to uni.

'It's okay, I've got the day off,' I said. 'Well, not officially, but Mum said I could stay off because of your party so long as I forged my own absence note. She couldn't be arsed.'

Chris grinned. 'Diarrhoea again then? Want me to spell it for you?'

'I know how to spell it. I'm not stupid you know.'

Chris frowned. 'Sorry. Hey, what's wrong. You feeling OK? A bit hungover maybe?'

'Me? Of course not. But, erm, why don't you skip this afternoon? I mean, you must still be feeling at least a bit off after last night. Jamie said he'd give you a copy of the lecture notes.'

'Have you seen Jamie's handwriting? I'd have more chance translating Sanskrit. I'll go in. I'm fine. Want a lift home first?'

'No it's OK I'll make my own way back.'

Chris tried to persuade me to let him drive me, or wait in the flat until he got back, but I refused. The truth was I was finding Chris's cheery good humour kind of annoying. I'd have had to spend most of the day with my head in the toilet if I'd drunk as much as he did, yet Chris seemed totally fine. It wasn't fair. And he clearly wasn't suffering any agonies of regret over making an arse of himself in public either. If anything, I was more humiliated than he was.

As soon as I got home I called Liz to moan about Chris at the party. 'Oh God, Liz, he was awful. I mean, doesn't he realize yet he just *cannot* sing? Or dance come to that. The moonwalk on the bar!'

'Well, it's not as though he was the only drunk guy at the party to do something stupid.' Liz giggled. 'Remember the idiot who bought Jamie's wigged skeleton a drink?'

I smiled. 'Yeah, suppose.'

'Anyway I thought you wanted Chris to be less

sensible and responsible all the time. Lighten up a bit.'

'Not that much!'

Later, still upset, I called Stephanie.

'Chill, Kelly Ann,' she said. 'Nearly everyone was pissed.'

'Not as pissed as Chris.'

'You think? What about the guy who threw up on his girlfriend's mum's shoes when she came to give them both a lift home and then – get this – told her he'd always fancied her.'

'Oh God, really?'

'Really.'

Talking to Liz and Stephanie did help a bit. I suppose they are right. Maybe I am making too much of it. But neither of the drunk guys they mentioned was my boyfriend and I still cringe at the thought of last night, particularly as Matt was there. Don't know why Matt's presence makes it so much worse but it does somehow. And it's hard resisting the temptation of a cool and sexy rock band musician when your boyfriend is acting like a total idiot. But I did. Well, except for agreeing to one slow dance when I held Matt a bit closer than maybe I should have. And enjoyed it way more than I should have. But that doesn't really count. Doesn't count at all. It was nothing.

SATURDAY MARCH 9TH

Shit – I just remembered it's Mum's birthday on Monday and I haven't got her anything. Also I'm broke after spending a fortune on Chris's skeleton. Worse than broke, as I've borrowed money from absolutely everyone and will have to pay it back. Feel a bit guilty about Mum but, well, it's not as though Chris will ever be eighteen again. Suppose Mum will never be forty-two again either but it's not the same. She's been able to drink, smoke and vote for ages. And done lots of it . . . well except for the voting thing as she says, 'All politicians are greedy, useless, lying buggers, the whole sodding lot of them.'

Still she *is* my mum and I'll have to get her something, but what can I buy for £1.26? I will have to ask Chris, even though I know he's broke too as his student loan is nearly used up. But he should be able to spare me a tenner.

Called Chris but he didn't pick up, then I remembered he was at football practice all afternoon.

Dad was busy at the garage too. I'd have to wait then dash out and get something before the shops closed. Or try and find something tomorrow.

Have just been reading a feature about frugal living in a magazine, and it's got some fantastic ideas for inexpensive but thoughtful presents. It says, *Why not make your own personalized cards and gifts? Your loved ones will* really appreciate the time and thought you've put into producing something original and unique for them to treasure.

Sounds great and just what I need. Thoughtful and, more importantly, cheap. Yeah. I'll do it.

SUNDAY MARCH 10TH

Made Mum a fantastic birthday card which I decorated by sticking bits of red-yellow-and green-coloured tissue paper and pasta shapes onto the front in a kind of 3D collage thing. Also composed a poem for her on the inside.

Then I made her a necklace from coloured beans and string – *Ethnic Chic*, the magazine said. Wasn't quite sure Mum was the ethnic-chic type, so just in case I made bath salts as well with Epsom salts and lemon-coloured food dye. Found an old bottle of bath salts my sister Angela had left behind half-used. The bottle was a nice shape and had a gold ribbon on it so I chucked out the rest of the contents and filled it with my home-made stuff. Sorted. Mum will love it.

Wrapped the presents in last year's Christmas paper but at least it didn't say *Merry Christmas* or anything like that on it. And anyway recycling gift paper is better for the environment. Thoughtful, environmentally friendly, creative gifts and card. Mum would love them.

Mum did not love them.

She looked at my card. 'What the **** is this?'

'It's your birthday card. I made it myself. Took me ages.'

'Looks as though you've vomited over the front.' She tossed it away.

'Aren't you going to look inside? I composed a poem for you.'

'For God's sake. What do I want with sodding poetry?'

Charming. But she picked it up and read it anyway. Out loud in a totally sarcastic voice:

'Happy Birthday, Mum

Happy Birthday, Mum. I'm so glad you were born
Because if you'd not I'd be so very forlorn
Worse than forlorn really, my mother so dear
Because without you, I'd not even be here.'

Then she said, 'Here's a poem for you:

'If only your dad's condom hadn't split
You wouldn't be here to write this shit.'

Then she nearly wet herself laughing. Charming. When

she finally managed to stop I handed her the presents. She looked at the snowmen on the wrapping paper.

'Call me Sherlock but this looks likes last year's Christmas paper.'

'Recycling paper helps save the rainforests. You wouldn't want to make baby orang-utans homeless would you?'

She muttered something which sounded a lot like wanting to make *me* homeless but otherwise didn't go on about it and unwrapped my necklace present.

Mum stared at it in disbelief. 'What am I supposed to do with this, eat it or wear it?'

'Took me ages to make that,' I said. 'Surely it's the thought that counts!'

'Aye, and the thought was bloody cheap. The next one better be a proper gift or you've had it.'

She opened the bath salts. 'Hmm, at least you actually *bought* something for me even if it didn't cost much. Time you acted your age and got me something decent.'

'If you'd give me enough pocket money I might.'

'Pocket money? It's time you got a job. I was paying my mother digs at your age.'

My sister Angela who lives in Manchester with her new husband Graham and baby Danny didn't even bother to come and visit. Just sent Mum a bunch of boring flowers, a naff pink and lilac card which said *To a very special Mum*

– *hope you enjoy your very special day* and a bottle of expensive perfume. I mean, how creative and imaginative is that? But Mum was delighted by her totally conventional, unoriginal gifts. It's so unfair.

However at least they put Mum in a better mood. As did Dad's offer, when he came home from work, to take her to a really posh Italian restaurant. She went upstairs to have a bath and get ready for her night out taking my bath salts present with her.

I smiled contentedly. At least she'd liked something I'd got her.

But fifteen minutes later Dad and I heard a scream coming from upstairs. After a stunned pause we both leaped up and made for the door to the hall but before we could get to it Mum burst into the room.

At first I thought she'd contracted some awful disease and I was going to call for an ambulance. Her whole body, except for her red, furious face, was stained yellow, so that she looked like someone whose liver had packed in and was suffering from terminal jaundice. But then she screamed. 'Bloody bath salts! I'll swing for you, so I will!'

I blame the magazine and their stupid recipe, but Mum didn't and Dad had to drag her off me. Several times in fact, as he seemed to find Mum's appearance hilarious and kept losing his grip on her when he was bent over laughing.

Decided to make myself scarce and ran over to

Stephanie's. She wasn't very sympathetic when I complained about Mum's negative attitude to my gifts and her violence following the bath-salts incident.

'Face it, Kelly Ann. They were crap presents. You need more money so you can buy decent stuff.'

'Yeah you're right. I'm absolutely fed up being broke all the time. But my parents aren't rich like yours. They won't give me any more allowance.'

Stephanie shrugged. 'Get a job then.'

'Hmm. It's not easy finding a job especially since I'm still under eighteen. I won't be able to work in bars or even supermarket checkouts. Anyway I've no experience in anything.'

'Why not try dog walking?'

'Dog walking? That isn't a job is it?'

'Of course it is. Loads of people have dogs they're too busy to take for a walk. Or can't be bothered to walk. Pay's not bad either. At least ten pounds an hour.'

'You're kidding me? Ten quid?'

'At least. Mum knows two dog owners who're looking for someone right now. You interested?'

Was I interested? Bloody hell this was fantastic! Ten quid just to take a dog for a walk! What could be easier?

TUESDAY MARCH 12TH

Matt was back at school today. He didn't turn up yesterday; come to think of it he's off most Mondays and Fridays now, probably because he's busy with gigs at the weekends. After the suspension no one seems to bother, or even notice, that he doesn't attend regularly now. I suppose the teachers know he doesn't care about school work or exams and just leave him alone.

I avoided him for most of the day but he always sits next to me in drama now and it would have looked odd if I'd moved away. Or refused to talk to him. Matt was, of course, totally relaxed as usual.

'So, cool party,' he said. 'Your boyfriend enjoy it?'

I flushed. 'A bit too much. He doesn't usually act like an idiot. He was drunk.'

Matt shrugged. 'Eighteenth birthday – be weird if he *wasn't* drunk. I was totally off my face on mine last year.'

'Last year?'

'Yeah, I had to repeat a year at school.' He smiled. 'I'm not as smart as your boyfriend, obviously.'

'Chris isn't a nerd, just really keen on being a doctor,' I said defensively.

'Hey, it's cool. I didn't say he was a nerd. Seems like a nice guy. Popular.'

'He is.'

We were silent for a while after that, both working on

an exercise on the use of music in film which Mrs Kennedy had handed out.

For once Matt looked completely absorbed in school work, but I was finding it hard to concentrate. Despite my vow to ignore Matt as much as possible I found myself glancing sideways a lot watching him as he wrote and trying to work out why he affected me so much.

Totally engrossed like this, he reminded me of Chris, whose single-minded concentration on the task in hand couldn't be distracted even if poltergeists were trashing the room around him and aliens had just declared war on us. Also like Chris, Matt was tall and dark. But there the resemblance ended. Matt was normally laid-back and casual whereas Chris was focussed and determined. Matt was unpredictable, dangerous even. Chris was depend-able, safe. Chris loved me. And I loved him. So why was I fascinated by someone so completely different?

Hmm, maybe it was because Matt seemed so mysterious. Probably if I got to know him better I'd find out he was just an ordinary guy after all and my stupid crush would disappear. Yeah, determined to find out as much as I possibly can about Matt.

'So how come you repeated a year?' I asked Matt as we walked along the corridor on the way to maths. 'Don't tell me you're thick because I know you're not.'

He shrugged. 'When I hit sixteen I decided school

wasn't for me so I left. Hitched round Europe – made some money busking, fruit picking, whatever. My dad wasn't happy. Persuaded me to come home, finish school.' Matt smiled. 'Bribed me with a motorbike.'

'What did your mum think?'

'Who knows? She took off years back. Ran away with some plumber Dad hired to put in a fitted kitchen.'

'Oh God, that's awful, Matt.'

'Yeah. Guy didn't even finish the kitchen. But hey, no worries. Dad found another workman. Did a good job.' He smiled crookedly but it didn't reach his eyes.

Impulsively I reached out and patted his arm. 'Sorry, Matt. Must be horrible for you to have your mum to run off and never come back.'

He shrugged. 'I guess she had her reasons. Dad isn't the most exciting guy in the world. Maybe she got bored.'

Hmm, so his dad probably isn't a gangland murderer then. People like that would be more likely to have dismembered the plumber before hiring another one. Probably weren't likely to be boring either. So much for rumours.

'What are you thinking about?' Matt asked, interrupting my thoughts.

'Murderers,' I blurted.

Matt laughed. 'Christ you're random sometimes, Kelly Ann.'

I blushed. 'Yeah, I suppose that must have sounded mental. Sorry, it was a stupid—'

'You've gone past your class again.'

Damn. Still, at least I found out he has an ordinary boring dad.

WEDNESDAY MARCH 13TH

Liz and Stephanie aren't convinced that getting to know Matt well instead of ignoring him is a good idea.

We were watching a horror movie at Liz's – which was pretty crap but had some really nice-looking actors – when Liz started quizzing me about what I'd found out about Matt.

'Hmm,' Liz said. 'Hitching round Europe. Busking in Paris, Madrid, Amsterdam at just sixteen. Very boring and normal. Totally uninteresting. What do you think, Stephanie?'

Stephanie shrugged. 'I still think she should just shag him. Get the whole thing out of her system.'

Brilliant.

Didn't want to get into an argument and decided to change the subject. 'So, Stephanie, you were saying you'd set me up with a dog-walking job. Did you bring the address?'

Stephanie shook her head. 'Left it at home. I'll text it

tonight.' She turned her attention to the screen. 'I think the grave digger is sexier than the vampire. Got bigger biceps. What do you think?'

'Hmm,' Liz said. 'Not sure. I feel vampires are a bit stalkerish really. But the grave digger is too stupid for me. What do you think, Kelly Ann?'

'I like the vampire. He's kind of scary and mysterious.' Didn't add that he looked a lot like Matt. Except for the fangs.

Liz stared at me, her eyes narrowed suspiciously. 'You know, he looks a bit like Matt, doesn't he?'

I shrugged. 'Looks nothing like him.'

THURSDAY MARCH 14TH

Liz isn't sure about the dog-walking thing. She says I'm not a dog person, whatever that means. And she's also pointed out that I have no experience of dealing with dogs at all.

'C'mon, Kelly Ann, you've never even had a pet in your life. Well, except for three goldfish who all died within a week of purchase.'

'And a gerbil.'

'Which escaped the same day you got it when you tried to take it to school in your lunch box. Ate your peanut butter sandwiches too.'

But I refused to be put off. I mean, I was only six when I lost the gerbil and anyway I won't have to look after the dog for ever. Just an hour. What could possibly go wrong in an hour?

Straight after school I made my way to the address that Stephanie had given me. It was a pity I didn't have time to go home first as I hadn't brought my umbrella and it had been raining on and off all afternoon but it was dry now so maybe I'd get away with it.

As I hurried along I was thinking how great it was to earn real money I don't have to ask my parents for. At last! I've worked out that I could probably handle as many as four dogs at a time. If I take them out just on school days I could earn £200 a week for five hours' work and have the weekends free to shop and spend it. It's going to be brilliant.

I should have asked Stephanie what kind of dog it was. I eyeballed a Great Dane warily, my face about level with its. Bloody hell it was huge. Size of a pony. Wasn't sure whether I was expected to walk it or stick a saddle on its back and ride the thing.

The owner, a grey-haired woman in a tweed suit and sensible shoes stared at me doubtfully. 'Well, your friend said you're a dog lover who's worked in kennels before and even helped out at Crufts. Is that right?'

'Oh, um, yeah, absolutely.'

'Right then I'm sure you'll be fine with Titan. He's a good boy really. Just make sure not to let him off the leash though. He's a bit of a wanderer I'm afraid. Last time he got loose he ended up in Edinburgh, the little rascal.' She tugged its ears affectionately. 'Didn't you, Titan?'

She paused, still smiling at it as though waiting for an answer. I mean what did she expect the dog to say? *'Oh God yeah I remember that. Got totally lost. Nightmare.'*

She handed me the leash and a plastic bag.

'What's the bag for?' I asked.

She looked at me as though I was stupid. 'Well, Titan's toilet of course. You just scoop it into the bag and deposit it in the dog-waste bin.'

Yuk, no way. 'Oh yeah, right, of course.'

I shoved the bag in my blazer pocket. Took a deep breath. 'I'll be off then. Back in an hour.'

The woman waved goodbye. 'Have fun. And remember. Don't let Titan off his leash.'

I trotted along anxiously beside my canine companion wondering what I'd do if it suddenly attacked me. Get eaten I suppose. However, by the time we got to the park gates and Titan had shown no interest in biting my head off I relaxed. Instead, I tied the leash around my wrist to make sure I wouldn't lose him and prayed that he wouldn't need the toilet before the walk ended.

God didn't listen. We'd done one lap around the park when Titan squatted on the grass beside the footpath and produced a huge steaming turd the size of large cowpat but ten times as smelly. Then he turned and waited expectantly for me to deal with it.

I hesitated, fingered the plastic bag inside my pocket, tried to visualize myself scooping the pile into it. Failed. I looked about me furtively. No one watching. Good. I yanked Titan's leash. 'C'mon.'

He resisted at first, obviously unused to this antisocial behaviour, but eventually moved off with me. Did feel a bit guilty, but honestly £10 just wasn't enough payment for such a gross job.

Was taking a short cut to the pond along a dirt track surrounded by high bushes when I spotted three neds drinking lager and smoking. Of course they started making sarcastic remarks about Titan. 'What you been feeding yer dug? Miracle Gro?' And, 'Is yer pet no a bit big for ye? Or did ye shrink in the wash?'

Hilarious.

I ignored them. But Titan didn't. He turned and gave them a low menacing growl, baring his teeth and straining against the leash.

The neds shut up and backed away. Then they ran off, but not before I'd given them a rude and energetic gesture. They were furious but what could they do? Oh yes there were definite advantages to having a huge canine companion.

Had just about completed another lap of the park and

was thinking about going back and collecting my earnings when I spotted a cute squirrel just in front of us. Unfortunately so did Titan who suddenly bounded off to chase it. Tried reining him back by tugging hard on the leash but I might as well have attempted to stop a tank falling down a cliff and I was forced to run full out behind him.

The terrified squirrel ran for its life but Titan picked up speed too. I held on to the leash, grimly determined not to lose him as we galloped faster and faster. Then I slipped on the huge pile of dog crap that I hadn't binned earlier and was dragged along the muddy wet grass.

It's the kind of thing my English teacher Ms Conner would call 'poetic justice' and I call really, really annoying.

When the squirrel ran into a tree Titan gave up the chase, thank God, and I took him home. His owner was delighted to see him.

She patted his head. 'Did you enjoy your walkies, Titan? Who's my good boy then.' She beamed at me, not even registering my stinking dishevelled state. 'I think he likes you.'

The feeling was so not mutual. 'Thanks.'

'So did he, er, do his business then?'

He certainly did.

The woman paid me – it might even cover most of the cost of dry-cleaning my blazer and skirt – and asked if I'd be back tomorrow. Have never been more sure of an answer in my life.

FRIDAY MARCH 15TH

Unusually Matt was at school today. Working on my new plan of getting to know him really well so I'd lose interest, I got talking to him at break and suggested he come along with a group of us to the pub around six o'clock.

'Thought you were barred,' Matt said with a smile.

'Oh, you heard about that? Well, um, it's been a while so I'm kinda hoping I won't be recognized. Anyway Liz says the last manager has moved on.'

'OK, yeah, sure. I can come for a while. Haven't got a gig tonight.'

'Great. My boyfriend's coming later so maybe you can meet him when he's not totally plastered this time.'

'Cool.'

Liz, Stephanie and I all turned up just after six. There were already a bunch of people from school there including Gerry and Felicity – who were now dating and snogging in a dim corner – but no Matt.

By half past six he still hadn't showed and, yeah, I couldn't deny it, I was disappointed. Flat. Hopefully this was only because my plan to get bored with him by familiarity had suffered a setback.

Chris turned up at seven, exactly when he said he would. He spotted me right away and smiled like I was the most beautiful girl in the whole world. Which to him I suppose I am. Oh God, he always makes me feel so good.

I smiled back and he hurried over, enveloped me in a bear hug, lifting me off my seat. He said hi to Liz and Stephanie then went off to the bar to get us all drinks.

Took a long time – loads of people from school wanted to talk to him on the way as they hadn't seen him in a while. I'd forgotten how popular Chris was, and smiled over at him indulgently.

Liz wasn't smiling though. 'What's keeping him? Honestly, guys have a nerve talking about *us* gossiping.'

'You've still got half your drink left, Liz, what's the hurry?' I said.

'But I haven't got my salt and vinegar crisps and I'm starving.' She got up. 'I'm just going to go and see what the hold up is.'

Stephanie rolled her eyes. 'Hope she doesn't eat them with her chopsticks this time. Did you notice if she brought them with her?'

I shook my head. 'Didn't notice. Surely she wouldn't bring them to the pub.'

Stephanie laughed. 'Wouldn't surprise me. Tried to eat

soup with them once until I mentioned the Chinese *did* use spoons. Probably invented them.'

Stephanie went off to the toilet to redo her make-up so I was sitting alone when I saw Matt stroll in. I wasn't the only one to notice him either. Nearly every girl in the place eyed him as he made his way to the bar, seemingly oblivious to all the attention.

I thought he was going to walk right past me and wondered if I should say something but he glanced down and stopped by my seat. 'Hey, Kelly Ann, not dancing on the table tonight? Pity, I'd like to have seen that.'

I flushed. 'I don't usually make an idiot of myself.'

'That's not what I heard.' He smiled and added quickly, 'Only joking. Can I get you a drink?'

'It's OK, my boyfriend is getting mine.'

'Cool.' He shrugged and went off to the bar.

Chris and Liz returned. 'Who's the guy you were talking to?' Chris asked. 'Don't think I know him.'

'He was one of the guys playing at your birthday do. Don't you remember?'

Chris smiled ruefully. 'Don't remember much about that night.'

'And he goes to our school now. I'm sure I must have mentioned him to you,' I lied.

'Maybe,' Chris said vaguely.

When Matt got back I introduced him to Chris. He pulled up a chair and sat next to me. So there I was sandwiched between two really fit guys, and I had to admit it felt good.

Chris was polite and friendly to Matt and other than draping a protective arm round my waist, which he'd do anyway, didn't seem at all jealous or suspicious. Not that he'd any reason to be of course.

The busty barmaid who collected our empty glasses made sure Matt got an eyeful of her cleavage as she leaned unnecessarily low over the table. In fact she practically dangled her boobs half a centimetre from his nose. Not exactly subtle.

And she was back and forward every five minutes afterwards. We had the tidiest, cleanest table in the pub while empties cluttered nearly everyone else's. Obviously Matt was the only thing *she* was interested in picking up. Soon she'd struck up a conversation with him about music and promised to talk to the manager about signing Matt's band up for a gig. Of course this gave her an excuse to ask for his phone number.

Matt gave it to her, but only because he was interested in the gig, of course. Or so I thought until he asked for her number too then suggested they meet up some time next week.

This was just so wrong. Not that I was jealous. It's just that she was so not his type. I mean, she's way too old for him for a start. Twenty-one she told him but she's most likely lying. I'd say she was twenty-two at least. And she's probably an airhead too. Certainly acts like one although she claims she's a biochemistry student. Hmm. Another lie. Definitely. Whoever heard of a biochemistry student with dyed blonde hair and big boobs for God's sake? Or one that would flirt with customers when they should be working.

Decided to leave the pub early. Chris was surprised but didn't argue and just asked me to wait until he finished his pint.

I went to the toilets with Liz to fix my make-up. She tried to persuade me to stay.

'It's only half past eight and it's a Friday night. What's the matter with you? You're not jealous because Matt's flirting with the barmaid are you?'

'Of course not. Why would I be? He's not my boyfriend.'

'Hmm, why are you leaving so early then?'

'I've just decided I've had enough vodka tonight and prefer to drink responsibly.'

Liz raised her eyebrows. 'That'll be a first.'

'Yeah well, OK,' I laughed. 'Maybe I just prefer to drink in pubs where barmaids don't flash their boobs and shove their tongues down customers' throats right in front of me.'

'Hmm so you *are* jealous. Knew it!'

There was no arguing with Liz when she'd made up her mind like this so I didn't bother. But she was totally wrong. I wasn't jealous of the barmaid coming on to Matt. Definitely not. Why would I be?

SATURDAY MARCH 16TH

Honestly though I'm glad I went because last night has totally put me off Matt. I mean, a guy shallow enough to fancy a total bimbo like that blonde barmaid doesn't interest me at all.

No, I'm lucky to have Chris. Intelligent, interesting and gorgeous. What more could I want?

Well, maybe it would be nice if he closed that thick-as-a-tombstone textbook and paid me some attention on a Saturday afternoon.

I glanced at the page he was reading. *Condyloma acuminata.* Disgusting close-up pictures of people with genital warts. I sighed. 'Do you have to read that now? We don't get to see each other that much any more since you left school, and those photographs aren't exactly romantic.'

Chris dropped the book, pulled me onto his lap. 'You're right. Interesting maybe but not very attractive. Unlike you for instance.'

'Flatterer. Good to know you think I'm sexier than a genital wart.'

'Way sexier.'

Chris kissed me and I tried to respond but to be honest the warty pictures were still on my mind. Don't know how he can just switch off like that.

I pulled away and tried to engage him in a bit of gossip but should have known better.

'What did you think about that barmaid last night? Total slut, wasn't she?'

Chris shrugged. 'Didn't notice.'

'You must be the only person. She practically flashed her boobs for the whole pub to see.'

'Claire's got a good figure.'

'You know her?'

'Not really. I've seen her around the campus. She's a biochemistry student in her final year. Supposed to be brilliant. Gary had a thing about her for a while.'

'Oh.'

'What's wrong?'

'Nothing. It's, erm, just that it's not like Gary to be attracted to brainy girls.'

Chris smiled. 'Don't think it was her brains that attracted him. You know how he is about blondes. And Claire's a natural. Mother's Danish according to Gary.'

'Oh.'

'What's the matter? You're not jealous are you?'

'Don't be stupid. Of course I'm not jealous. Why would I be? Matt's just a friend.'

'I didn't mean of Matt,' Chris said, genuinely

surprised. 'I meant jealous of Claire. Being blonde and, um, curvy.'

'Oh right. Yeah well sort of. Bloody blondes.'

'You shouldn't be. You're perfect just as you are,' Chris said, meaning it.

I smiled, nuzzled closer to him and rested my head in the crook of his neck. Oh God I was so lucky to have a boyfriend like Chris. I'd hate to lose him. Especially if it was my own stupid fault.

We stayed like that for a few minutes not speaking just comfortable being close. I pulled my head up and looked at his profile. He seemed deep in thought concentrating on something. I hope he wasn't thinking about what I'd said about Matt. Maybe getting suspicious of my interest in him. I wondered if any of the rumours had got back to him.

'What are you thinking about?' I asked, hoping I didn't sound too anxious.

'Nothing.'

'You can't think about nothing.'

'Honestly, you don't want to know.'

'Yeah I do.'

'Really you don't.'

'Really I do,' I insisted.

'OK . . . well, um, if you're sure.'

I nodded.

'Genital warts.'

He was right; I really didn't want to know. It's just as Stephanie always says. You should never ask a guy what he's thinking. Especially not medical students.

SUNDAY MARCH 17TH

Wasn't going to do any more dog walking but Stephanie says the second one's a Chihuahua not much bigger than my hand and totally harmless. So cute, I'd love it.

Hmm, I wasn't totally convinced but when she also told me the owner will pay time and a half, that is £15, because she wants me to walk it on weekends, I gave in. I mean, how much trouble could a thing that size be?

Chris drove me home after lunch. I changed, walked round to the address Stephanie had texted me and pressed the buzzer.

A tall, elegant woman wearing an expensive-looking wool dress and high heels greeted me brusquely, 'Ah, you'll be the dog walker then. Please come into the living room so you can meet Lavinia and we can discuss your duties.'

Bloody hell – felt like a Victorian servant or something.

'My name's Kelly Ann,' I said pointedly.

'Quite, yes.' She turned her back on me and click-clacked her way along a long gleaming hallway.

I followed resentfully but, determined not to be

intimidated, I tried to strike up a conversation. 'So, with a name like Lavinia, I guess it's a girl dog then?'

She turned round and looked at me suspiciously. 'She's a bitch, yes. Are you sure you're a trained dog handler?'

'Um, yeah, course I am.'

'Hmm, we'll see,' she sighed resignedly. 'Still I suppose you'll have to do for now.'

'Bitch,' I muttered under my breath. And I didn't mean the dog.

We went into a large living room, with thick rugs and heavy dark furniture.

'Well there she is,' the owner said.

I scanned the room but couldn't see a thing at first until I heard a squeaky pathetic yap and my eyes followed the source of the noise to the enormous sofa.

Oh my God. I know Stephanie said it was small but this was just ridiculous. It couldn't be a proper dog surely. Looked more like a bald newborn rat, except for the ears which were bigger than its head and stuck out like a fox's.

'She's a short-haired teacup Chihuahua,' she said. 'A person of your experience will be familiar with the breed, of course.'

'Oh yeah, um. Right. Of course I am. Yeah.' I stared at the miniscule creature doubtfully. She couldn't seriously expect me to take the thing out could she? It looked as though it could be knocked over by a gentle breeze.

Oh but she did, although first she dressed it in a tiny woollen striped coat to keep it warm and attached it to a leash and harness which looked like it had been made out of dental floss. I would be a laughing stock.

On the other hand at least I was unlikely to be dragged through the mud. This excuse for a dog couldn't drag a piece of fluff across a polished floor if its life depended on it.

'Now take good care of Lavinia because, as you know, teacup Chihuahua are a very delicate breed. Easily damaged and frightened.'

'Right, yeah, no worries.'

Although it wasn't raining or cold I put up my hood and hoped no one I knew would recognize me then set off for the park which was just diagonally opposite her house.

I got some odd looks but no one said anything. The only trouble I had was with an Alsatian who took a fancy to Lavinia. I mean, really, you'd have thought that even a dog is smart enough to know that this was an impossible relationship. Apparently not, so I had to lift Lavinia up and tuck her inside my pocket while the Alsatian owner dragged his frustrated pet away.

Put Lavinia down again and took a quieter route back along a dirt track at the rear of the proper path so I wouldn't bump into many people or canines. It wasn't muddy and everything was fine until I spotted the three neds who'd annoyed me last time I dog walked.

Oh my God. Put my head down and pulled my hood further over my face. Desperately hoped they wouldn't recognize me.

Of course they smirked at Lavinia and made stupid comments about her size and stripy wool coat. 'Haw, you! Taking yer caterpillar for a walk then?'

I kept my head lowered and said nothing, just hurried past them. Thought I'd made it until I heard one of them say, 'Is that no the lassie that that gave us the finger the other day?'

'Bloody hell, aye. I think it wiz. Cheeky slag – let's get her.'

I ran for it. They chased me up the hill, along the back of the glass house and down the footpath to the park exit. Fortunately I'm a fast runner, so even though I didn't lose them they didn't manage to catch me. Unfortunately Lavinia's tiny legs couldn't keep up with me so she bounced along behind spending most of the time flying in midair but occasionally her minuscule paws would hit the ground and she'd be dragged.

Just as well she wasn't attached to the leash by a choker chain or she would have been throttled but I guessed she'd probably have skid marks on her paws. Still, this was an emergency and canine lives weren't as important as human ones, in this case mine, so it couldn't be helped — though I don't suppose Lavinia's snobby owner would agree.

I sprinted out the park gates and across the road to the house not stopping to look back. I pressed the door buzzer keeping my finger on it then looked over my shoulder. The neds were crossing the road at a leisurely pace but keeping their eyes on me the whole time.

Oh God when would the woman answer?

Finally the door opened. Lavinia dashed in immediately but I wasn't so lucky as the owner was blocking my way.

She frowned and looked at her watch. 'You're early – almost fifteen minutes. I'm afraid I'll have to reduce your fee accordingly. Please wait here while I get it.'

I glanced back. The boys had crossed over and were leaning on the next-door neighbour's fence. Waiting.

'Sorry,' I panted, barging in past her. 'I need the toilet. Now.'

She wasn't pleased, but what could she do? Decided I'd have to stay in the toilet until they got fed up and left. Hopefully.

After five minutes she knocked on the door. 'Aren't you finished yet?

Would they be gone yet? 'Don't know.'

'I beg your pardon.'

'I mean, not yet. Nearly,' I groaned loudly. 'Constipation.' Heard the click of her heels hurrying off.

Gave it another five minutes and crept out, closing the door quietly behind me. I scurried along the hall and, standing on tiptoe, peered out the stained-glass window over the front door. Shit, they were still there. Although they did look bored and impatient.

Jumped when I heard her voice behind me.

'Ah, you're going. Don't you want your fee?'

'Yes thanks and, um, could I have a glass of water too please?' I moved past her to the living room. 'Mind if I wait in here? It's kind of cold in the hall.'

She sighed. 'Very well, I'll be back in a moment.'

She was back almost immediately with a glass of water and handed it to me impatiently. 'If you don't mind hurrying up I have to go out soon.'

'Oh yeah, right. I won't be long.' I took a tiny sip and sighed happily. 'This is excellent. What kind of water is it?'

'Excuse me?'

'I mean is it Perrier or—'

'It's tap.'

I took another tiny sip. 'Well it tastes lovely. In fact, do you mind if I sit down to savour it properly.'

'Actually—'

Before she could object I plonked myself down on her sofa. And felt something soft and squiggly under my bum. I leaped up and Lavinia dashed off yelping in pain and shock.

I took one look at the woman's horrified, furious face and decided I'd take my chances with the neds.

Fortunately they'd got fed up and gone off to annoy someone else. I trudged home.

When I got there, realized that I hadn't collected my money but I didn't fancy going back to ask.

This job had been a disaster. Maybe Liz was right and I'm not really a dog person after all.

MONDAY MARCH 18TH

Matt strolled into the common room near the end of lunch time accompanied by a gaggle of girls like he was a rock star already with a groupie following.

'God, how does he do it?' asked Billy. 'They swarm around him like bees on a jam jar.'

'Or flies on a turd,' Gerry said sourly.

'Don't care. I'm gonna learn guitar,' Billy answered. 'That's got to be it.'

I tried to ignore Matt but somehow I was always aware of him. Probably, as Liz said, because I kept tracking him out of the side of my eyes and straining to hear what he was saying instead of paying attention to my best friend's theories on group dynamics and sexual attraction.

After a while Matt broke away from his group of

admirers and went to his favourite seat by the window. They didn't follow him. Everyone now knew this meant he didn't want company as he'd always pointedly ignored anyone who tried to talk to him there.

I'd just glanced in his direction when he turned from gazing out the window and caught me staring at him (momentarily of course).

God, he probably thought I was nosy, or worse, a sad stupid groupie too.

But he smiled and, to my surprise, waved me over.

I settled down in the seat next to him, conscious of being watched by almost everyone.

'So how was your weekend?' Matt asked.

'Oh, um, great.' *Apart from narrowly escaping being beaten to a pulp by a bunch of annoyed neds and almost squashing a defenceless pup to death.* 'How about you? Did you meet up with Claire?'

'Yeah.'

'Oh right. She's very attractive isn't she?'

He shrugged. 'She's OK.'

'A bit old for you though.'

'Not really.'

'Oh, so you're, um, going out with her now then?'

'No. Just the one night. Wanted to make sure of the gig.'

'Oh.'

He smiled. 'What does "Oh" mean? You disapprove?'

'Of course not. No. It's not my business. I'm just surprised that's all. Most guys wouldn't knock her back.'

'I'm not most guys,' he said, frowning.

'God, sorry, I didn't mean to be nosy.'

I got up to leave but he put his long, surprisingly strong fingers around my wrist.

'Don't go.' He smiled. 'All girls are nosy.'

I sat down again. 'Not me,' I lied.

He shrugged. 'Claire just isn't my type that's all.'

'What's your type?'

'Well, I prefer brunettes.'

'You do?'

'Yeah.' He stared at me intently, his dark, almost-black eyes boring into mine. 'And I like girls to be, well, a bit more difficult to persuade. Less . . . available.'

I stared back, hypnotized. 'Me too.'

He grinned. 'You like girls like that as well? Yeah, so we've got something in common then.'

I flushed. 'Oh God, no I didn't mean . . . I'm not gay or anything. I meant well, em, yeah Claire was a bit obvious. Flashing her boo— I mean showing off a bit that night.'

Mercifully the bell went. I got up quickly. 'Right, bye then, gotta go.'

He stood up. 'Yeah, me too. Mind if I come with you? We've both got drama next.'

God so we did. He must think I'm some idiot taking this long to learn my timetable. Ignoring people's nosy stares and Liz's concerned frown I nodded and we headed off.

Drama was really interesting. We've been working for a while now, along with the music department, on the Glasgow version of *West Side Story* scripted by Mrs Kennedy. A boy and girl from two gangs fall in love but of course their relationship faces horrible problems because the gangs are sworn enemies. We're going to team up with fifth years and produce a school play for June.

I tried out for the main part today and think I did okay. Hope I get it as there's a lot of dance in the role. Everyone expects Gerry to get the male lead but I'm not so sure. Mrs Kennedy specifically asked Matt to have a go today, and though he wasn't as good as Gerry at the talking bit, when she asked them both to sing one of the songs from the play Matt, of course, was way better.

I think doing a musical is a great idea but this version isn't going to be as romantic as the original though. Here's the first love scene:

Barry: Ah know yir big Malkie's sister but ah pure fancy ye so ah dae.
Kylie: Yir no that bad yersel.
Barry: Aw right then gonna geez us wan?
Kylie: Aye, am pure gagging fur ye, so ah um. But big Malkie's gonna gut ye if he finds oot.

Hmm. Mrs Kennedy said she wanted it to be authentic Glasgow. Bit too authentic for me. Still, the music and dance should make it fun. Really hope Mrs Kennedy picks me for Kylie.

TUESDAY MARCH 19TH

Brilliant news in drama. Mrs Kennedy said I've the main part. And – get this – Matt has landed the other.

Gerry was gutted because he is a good actor, but it's a musical and Matt's singing voice is way better than Gerry's.

At first Matt refused. Not his thing. But Mrs Kennedy and I persuaded him to accept the part. Well maybe just me actually as he said, 'Anything to please the dancing queen.'

Oh God it's going to be so good. Matt and I can work together on this and no one will think anything is going on between us. I can get to know Matt as a cast member and friend. Which is exactly what he will be. I can have it all. Chris, my reliable, faithful boyfriend who I adore and Matt – exciting, fascinating, enthralling, totally platonic pal.

Perfect.

What could possibly go wrong?

Saw Matt heading downstairs for the exit at the beginning of last period and caught up with him.

'Matt, wait!'

He turned round. Smiled. 'You heading home too? Want a ride?'

'No. I wasn't intending to leave just yet. I was just thinking. About the play.'

'What about it? I said I would do it, didn't I?'

'Yeah I know. But, well, we've both got a free period now and Mrs Kennedy says the drama room is free. Why don't we go and discuss our approach to our roles in the play and maybe do some rehearsing. We've both got such big parts. It's going to mean a lot of practice.'

'Do more time at school than I need to? No offence but screw that, I'm out of here.' But then he smiled. 'You want to talk about it though, meet me in the pub. Same one as last time, seven o'clock. See ya.'

And then he was gone.

Hmm. Still the pub is, well, a public place, just like the name says. And we're just going to discuss our roles in the play. So it's no way a date and there's nothing wrong with it.

Had to beg mum for money. Just asked for a tenner to go to the pictures but she'd only give me five. 'Enough to

buy one drink and a packet of polo mints to disguise it,'
as she put it.

I really have to get a job.

Put on some make-up. Not to impress Matt, of course,
just to make sure I don't get knocked back for being
underage. Even with a really good fake ID sometimes
barmen get suspicious if you look too young.

I got there at ten past seven. Although it wasn't a
date, I didn't want to seem too keen by arriving exactly
on time – you don't want even platonic friends to think
you don't have a busy, interesting life after all – but Matt
didn't show up until seven-thirty. Got some pitying
stares from customers who thought I'd been stood up
even though I waved the play script around and
loudly told the barman I was waiting for a fellow artist to
arrive.

'Only get piss artists in here, love,' he'd said.

Nice.

When Matt eventually turned up he didn't bother to
apologize. 'You here already, Kelly Ann? Want another
drink?'

Hmm.

When he came back from the bar I started to talk about
the play, but he interrupted me. 'Later. Let's just chill for
a while. Get to know each other better.'

'Well I don't—'

'Look, if we're going to work on something like this it

helps to understand where your co-star is coming from. Right? Create a little chemistry.'

'Yeah . . . I suppose.'

'Definitely. So tell me about yourself.'

'Oh, well, nothing much to tell really,' I hedged, desperately trying to think up something interesting to say.

'OK then we'll talk about me.'

'Oh, um, right.'

He smiled. 'That was a joke, Kelly Ann.'

'Yeah, well, let's start with you anyway.'

'OK, what do you want to know?'

'Well, um, how come you left your old school?'

He shrugged. 'They kicked me out.'

'What for?'

'Got caught smoking.'

'Oh, I didn't know you smoked. Still, it seems a bit over the top. Loads of people get caught smoking at our school but they're not expelled.'

'Smoking hash.'

'Oh.'

Matt smiled. 'Don't tell me you're shocked. I can't believe you're that naïve.'

'Of course not. It's just, well; I don't really think drugs are a good idea.'

He looked at the vodka and Coke in my hand and raised an eyebrow. 'You don't?'

'Well, not illegal drugs, anyway.' I blushed. God, I must sound like a prim great-aunt.

'Better put your drink down now – you can finish it when you turn eighteen. Coke might go a bit flat by then though.'

He was right. I was a total hypocrite.

We never did get on to discussing the play as after two drinks I'd no money left. I suppose Matt would have paid if I'd told him – he always seems to have plenty of cash, and isn't mean, but I didn't want that. Letting him pay would have made it seem like a date. Which it definitely wasn't.

He seemed really surprised when I cut our meeting short and tried to persuade me to stay but I told him I'd stuff to do.

When we left the pub he lit up a cigarette. I was pleased as I hate smoking so this would definitely put me off him.

He saw me looking at him. 'Yeah, I smoke cigarettes too, occasionally.'

'Good,' I blurted without thinking, then flushed scarlet. That must have sounded mental.

He laughed. 'God you're random, Kelly Ann. Don't think I'll ever work you out. What's good about it? I thought you'd disapprove.'

'Oh I do. Yeah. I, um, meant it's good you only do it sometimes. Smoking's bad for you. Gives you cancer.'

He shrugged, took another drag of his cigarette. 'Only when you're old. I plan to die before then.'

I smiled uncertainly not really sure whether he was joking or not. He said nothing more, just continued to casually smoke his cigarette. I watched him, fascinated.

I've always hated smoking. It stinks, gives you wrinkles, and rots your teeth and lungs. Then why, oh why, when Matt smoked, did he look so bloody attractive? Sexy. Maybe Liz was right and getting to know Matt better so I'd go off him wasn't going to work.

Well, I've got to go now,' I said.

'Sure I can't persuade you to stay a bit longer? We've still got the play to discuss.'

'No I'd better go. Busy.'

'OK. Maybe some other time?'

'Maybe.'

I walked off feeling his gaze following me. Hmm. Matt seemed as interested in me as I was in him and I couldn't help feeling flattered. Who wouldn't be? But there was no harm in another guy finding me attractive and enjoying my company was there? After all, nothing has happened between Matt and me. And nothing was going to happen. Ever.

THURSDAY MARCH 21 ST

Was moaning to Stephanie about being broke again so she suggested I do some modelling.

'Not fashion modelling *obviously*. You're skinny but not nearly tall enough. I mean modelling for artists' classes. You get fifty pounds a session. Not bad for a couple of hours' work.'

'Fifty quid. That's brilliant. But well, um, I don't know. Do you think I'm, well, nice looking enough?'

'God, yes. In fact, looks don't matter. You can be fat and ugly or old and wrinkly and still pose for artists. Makes you more interesting, in fact. All you have to do is sit still for a couple of hours. Even you could do that.'

'Thanks, Stephanie,' I said sarcastically.

She ignored my tone. 'The art lecturer at my college is looking for models for his evening class. I'll let him know you're interested then?'

'Yeah definitely.'

'You're supposed to be eighteen but just flash him your fake ID. It's cash in hand and they won't check that carefully.'

I nodded.

'Oh and he's looking for a male model too. So if you can think of anyone who might be interested bring him along as well.'

FRIDAY MARCH 22ND

Didn't bother to ask Chris as I knew it wasn't his thing but Gerry had been complaining about being broke lately. Also someone as vain as he was wouldn't mind lots of people looking at him. And he's already eighteen.

Just as I thought, he was really keen. 'Fifty quid just for sitting there? Cool. Thanks for asking me, Kelly Ann. I could really do with the money. Dating a hot girl like Felicity is bloody expensive.'

I scowled. 'And looking after your baby. Morgan comes first. Right?'

'Oh yeah, of course. Don't look at me like that, Kelly Ann. I bought her a new teething ring last week.'

Hmm. I know Gerry does love Morgan but he's not the most responsible of guys. Or generous – except to girls who look like Felicity.

WEDNESDAY MARCH 27TH

Was a bit nervous when I arrived at the college with Gerry but really what could possibly go wrong? All I had to do was sit there and do nothing then leave with fifty quid.

The receptionist signed us in then directed us to a large brightly lit studio which had two circles of chairs and easels around couches draped with white cloth. The art lecturer, a small thin guy with a beard wearing skinny black jeans and a pink T-shirt, waved us over.

You'd think that an artistic person would know that guys should never wear skinny jeans, but obviously not. He seemed really nice though. Thanking us for coming and not asking about previous experience or anything as the students filed in and took their places.

They were mainly adults in their thirties and forties but there was one boy I recognized as a fifth year at our school and two old women with thick glasses, elasticated trousers and polyester cardigans.

The lecturer told us just to adopt any pose we liked for the first twenty minutes of sitting but afterwards he might direct us to adopt a different stance.

When everyone was in, the lecturer talked to the class. 'We are fortunate today to have two life models with us, male and female. Hopefully everyone will get a chance to sketch both during the course of the lesson.'

He turned to Gerry and me. 'Right then, just pop all your clothes off and put them on the chairs here and we'll get started.'

Oh my God. No way. I froze in sheer disbelief. Scanned the faces of the class. They looked so normal. Respectable. (Well, except for the fifth-year boy who was leering at me.) This was Glasgow. Surely asking people to strip off in a public place then staring at them for hours was illegal?

'Oh my God, Gerry, let's get out of here,' I hissed turning to him. 'I'm so sorry. I'd no idea that—'

But Gerry wasn't listening. Too busy getting undressed. I stared at him horrified as he climbed out of his jeans. 'Stop it. What are you doing?'

Too late. Gerry was soon starkers and, for a laugh, I suppose, striking Rodin's The Thinker pose.

He grinned up at me. 'C'mon, Kelly Ann, get your kit off and we could do The Kiss.'

I turned and fled.

THURSDAY MARCH 28TH

Stephanie wasn't at all apologetic.

'Of course it was nude modelling. It's an *art* class, for God's sake, not a fashion shoot for British Home Stores Catalogue. If you're going to be this picky about jobs I'm not sure I can help you any more.'

'Picky? Well, yeah, excuse me but I *do* prefer to work with my clothes on, thanks all the same.'

'And how was I supposed to know that? You never said so. I'm not a mind-reader you know.'

Matt hadn't learned his lines for the short scene Mrs Kennedy wanted us to try out today which kind of annoyed me but at least he turned up. Most often he's not at school on Fridays. But any frustration I felt disappeared when he sang the first song. He knew the lyrics perfectly and his golden, sexy voice had everyone spellbound. All the girls anyway.

Afterwards I did ask him though if he was really interested in performing in the play. If not he'd maybe best give the part to Gerry.

'No, it's a great story. Interesting. Don't worry, I'll get my head round it before the night. There's plenty of time.'

'Yeah it's a fabulous story. Really sad too though. How gangs can ruin peoples' lives. I hate them.'

'Gangs?'

'Yeah. Don't you?'

He shrugged. 'Used to be in one.' He pointed to his tattoo. 'That's where I got this. But you're right, they're a stupid idea. I got bored with it.' He saw me staring at his tattoo. 'You don't like it?' he asked.

'I don't usually like tattoos, or I thought I didn't anyway, but . . . yeah, on you it looks good.'

But then everything about Matt seemed absorbing. Attractive. Even things I thought I didn't like. I wished Chris hadn't left after the fifth year. If he were here every day with me I was sure I wouldn't be so interested in Matt. Tempted by him.

Thank God I was seeing Chris tonight so I could remind myself of the gorgeous loving boyfriend I already had. Stop me longing for anyone else.

We didn't go out as both of us were broke but I didn't care. Instead we had beans on toast with a bottle of cheap wine mixed with lemonade (well mine was anyway as Chris has given up trying to persuade me it's an awful way to drink it).

Everyone else was staying in too for the same reason as us except for Gary who I think must be getting into serious debt trying to impress this blonde, Samantha.

Afterwards we went into Chris's room for some privacy. Chris sat on the bed by the wall and I curled up in front of him to watch a film on his PC. It wasn't a particularly good movie – I'm not that keen on sci-fi – but after a whole week apart I was just happy to be wrapped in Chris's arms again where I belonged.

He had nice arms, toned and muscular, better than Matt's really. I traced the tips of my fingers round his biceps. Wondered what a black tattoo would look like on *him*.

'Have you ever thought about getting a tattoo?' I asked.

'A tattoo?' Chris smiled. 'That's an odd question. What brought this on?'

'Nothing. I don't know. Just wondered I suppose. Anyway, have you?'

'No. Why?'

'Well, it's just I think some tattoos can look good. Sexy. Lots of really interesting, creative people have tattoos.'

'And criminals.'

'What?'

'Over ninety per cent of criminals have tattoos.'

'God, you're so conservative sometimes. Having a tattoo doesn't make you a criminal.'

'I didn't say it did,' Chris said calmly. 'Just that lots of criminals have them. Well, the ones who get caught anyway.' He put on an aggrieved high voice. 'Yes, officer, that's the man who mugged me. The one with MUM tattooed on his knuckles.'

'But seriously though wouldn't you like to get one? A proper artistic design. Nothing naff.'

'No.'

'Why not?'

Chris shrugged. 'Just not interested. Of course I suppose I could have I LOVE KELLY ANN etched into my forehead so everyone will know how I feel but I reckon, why bother?' He twisted me round to face him. 'Anyone can tell how I feel about you just by the expression on my face every time I look at you.' He cupped my face in his hands and smiled. 'No need to spell it out.'

Didn't see much of the movie after that.

SATURDAY MARCH 30TH

Chris drove us back to my house this afternoon as my sister Angela and her husband Graham are visiting with my adorable nephew Danny.

I love my sister really but God she's boring. I used to call her MNP, short for Miss No Personality, which was a bit cruel I suppose so I stopped it, but honestly she's about as much fun as a damp duvet at a sleepover. And her nerdy husband Graham is even worse. How the two of them produced my gorgeous giggly Danny I'll never know.

They were all already there when we got in. Danny gave me a wide goofy grin and pointed at me. ''Kay!' He toddled towards me as fast as his small legs would go. I knelt and spread my arms out. He hurled himself at me and I hugged him.

Could have hung on to him for ever but he got restless and wriggled free. He looked up at Chris and stretched out his arms. 'Kiss, Kiss.'

Everyone laughed except for Angela. 'It's Chris, Danny. Say Chris.'

'Kiss! Kiss!' Danny squealed proudly.

Angela frowned. 'No, Danny, it's—'

'Oh for God's sake shut your face,' Mum interrupted. 'He's only one year old. You weren't saying a bloody word at that age. Still just dribbling into your bib. Didn't start talking till you were nearly three.'

'I'm sure that's not true,' Angela protested.

'Bloody is,' said Mum. 'And I sometimes wish you hadn't bothered your arse learning to talk. Liked you better when you said nothing.'

Mum cackled at her own joke, ignoring Angela's scowls.

Chris, as usual, stayed diplomatically neutral in our family squabbles and was busy throwing Danny gently up into the air and catching him again, each time rewarded by delighted squeals and chuckles.

I watched them both, smiling, until inevitably Angela asked Chris to stop so as not to overexcite Danny. Chris immediately put him down.

Mum shook her head at Angela and went off to the kitchen muttering. 'Christ. God forbid the child should have any fun.'

Angela frowned. 'C'mon, Danny. Let's play.'

She opened a large box labelled DANNY'S TOYS. I looked inside. Just as I'd thought. All boring educational stuff – mainly plastic, primary-coloured shapes and beakers with letters of the alphabet painted on them.

'What is he supposed to do with these?' I asked.

'They're to teach him his colours and shapes,' Angela said. 'Watch.' She took a red plastic triangle from the box and waved it in front of the baby. 'What shape is this, Danny?'

Danny said, 'Ba da ba.'

Angela beamed at him. 'That's right. It's a *triangle*. Clever boy. Now can you tell Mummy what colour it is? What colour is the *triangle*?

Danny said, 'Ba ma da.'

'Yes it's *red* isn't it? *A red triangle*. Good boy.'

She put the shape back in the box, selected a blue cube and waved it about. 'Now, Danny, can you tell Mummy what colour this is?

Danny grabbed it, put it in his mouth, covered it in drool then dropped it on her lap and toddled off to the kitchen to see his gran.

'That's right. It's *blue*,' she called after him.

We had lunch: burgers followed by chocolate éclairs. Delicious. But poor Danny was only allowed plain boiled rice with steamed fish and puréed, unsweetened apple for dessert.

Afterwards Mum managed to shoo Angela and Graham out. 'Danny will be fine. Away out and enjoy yourselves now.' She shut the door on them and muttered, 'Not that the pair of you know how.'

As soon as they were gone Mum got the jelly and ice cream she'd been keeping for a delighted Danny.

Mum's all right sometimes.

Later Chris and I took Danny to the park. We took his pushchair with us though we shouldn't have bothered as

Danny insisted on walking or being carried. Noticed that every other tot was doing the same thing. It's mad. Pushchairs are just another thing to look after. Just as well Chris was here as Danny was too heavy for me now but Chris could swing him up and carry him on his shoulders no bother. Well, except when Danny would put his hands over Chris's eyes for a laugh so he'd to walk blind.

We reached a small kids' play area so Chris put Danny down and he toddled off to the sandpit.

I smiled fondly at my nephew. 'I wish he wasn't going back tomorrow. Wish he still lived with us like before.'

Chris gave me a sympathetic look. 'I know you miss him but most married couples don't want to live with parents or in-laws. And they're not that far away. You can still keep in touch.'

'Hmm. Suppose.'

'Anyway, one day we'll have our own kids.'

'We will? So you're a fortune-teller now? How many will we have?' I asked.

'How many do you want?'

'Eight, I think. Four boys and four girls. I can make them naff clothes from curtains and teach them to sing 'Doh a deer' like in *The Sound of Music*.'

'No way.'

'Eight too many?'

'Teach them *Sound of Music* songs? It's the only film

I've seen which had me cheering on the Nazis. Seriously though, you don't want eight do you?' he asked.

I shrugged. 'Not really thought about it.'

'I'd like two.'

'Oh. A boy and a girl I suppose?'

'Don't care as long as they're healthy. The safest time for pregnancy for mums and babies is around mid-twenties so we should plan on having our first when you're twenty-five or so.'

Bloody hell he couldn't be serious! 'Oh right, that's, um, in eight years time then? I better put it in my diary.'

He seemed not to have heard or noticed my sarcastic diary comment because he went on enthusiastically, 'Yeah and hopefully I'll have made registrar by then so I should be earning enough money for you not to work and stay at home if you want to. I hope you will because it's best for young children to be cared for by their mums if possible . . .' He stopped. Finally noticed my sour expression. 'What's wrong?'

'You're talking years in the future. Ages away. I don't know what I want to do next week yet.'

Chris smiled. 'One of us has to be organized. Plan for the future. But if you don't want kids at twen—'

'Well maybe I want *my* future to be a surprise. Why do you have to be so sensible all the time?'

'I'm not sensible all the time.' He smiled wryly. 'You've

obviously forgotten my eighteenth birthday for instance. Wish some more people had.'

I laughed. 'God, yeah. You were a total idiot.'

'I just know what I want, that's all, and go after it.' He paused, gazed at me intently. 'That's how I got you.'

I gazed back at Chris. My gorgeous boyfriend. So, OK, he could be a bit too serious occasionally. Determined. Pushy even. But sometimes that's kind of sexy. He reached for me and pulled me into his arms, pressed his lips to mine. It would have been a very tender, romantic moment if I hadn't just spotted out the side of my eye Danny trying to eat a worm.

Hmm. Perhaps it was time to take Danny home to his mum after all.

SUNDAY MARCH 31ST

Went to Chris's parents' house for dinner. His mum spent most of the time complaining she didn't see enough of him since he moved out. And the rest of it fussing over him and asking endless nosy questions. Was he remembering to separate his dark and light laundry? His woollen jumper looked a bit bobbly – had he forgotten to use the fabric conditioner she'd bought him? Was he eating his greens and fresh fruit every day?

'And always use bran bread not the white stuff,' she

continued. 'Your body needs roughage. There's nothing worse than constipation for making you feel sluggish. Remember that time when you were thirteen and—'

'Right, son,' Chris's dad interrupted. 'Let's go to the pub. Now you're eighteen you can buy your old dad a pint.'

Chris leaped up gratefully. 'Course, Dad.' He threw me an apologetic look. 'You don't mind do you, Kelly Ann?'

Hmm.

As soon as they'd gone Chris's mum started to pump me for information. Were the boys keeping the flat reasonably clean?

'Hmm, yeah reasonably,' I lied. If you can call *Just short of condemned as unfit for human habitation* reasonably clean. But I knew a maternal visit/inspection wouldn't be welcome.

Were there any problems with noisy neighbours?

'No, none at all.' This was true. *They* were the noisy neighbours.

And were they keeping the cupboards and fridge well-stocked? Boys can be forgetful when it came to shopping.

'Yeah. They've usually got plenty in.' Plenty of alcohol anyway. Usually beer was the only item in the fridge.

In an effort to stop her interrogating me any more I turned the subject to my trouble finding a part-time job. She was really nice and gave me a good idea. 'Why don't you try baby-sitting, Kelly Ann? You're good with kids. Chris told me you practically had to look after Danny for nearly all of his first year when your sister had post-natal depression.'

It was true. I really did have experience of looking after kids. Or babies anyway. This was a job made for me.

Chris's mum told me she'd recommend me to a woman she knew who was desperate to find a reliable baby-sitter.

Great. Maybe finally I'd find a job which really suited me.

After that discussion however, she was back on about Chris. She was worried about him having a job at the hospital as well as studying for a demanding medical degree. Wasn't he finding it too much?

'Not really,' I said. 'He doesn't have much free time any more but it's what he wants to do. Definitely. He's planned it for ages.'

'Oh yes, you're right. My Chris has always known exactly what he wants and plans ahead.' She laughed. 'In fact, let me show you something.'

She disappeared off upstairs and came back holding a white envelope which she handed to me.

On the front was written *Mr Santa Claus* in very neat child's writing which I recognized as Chris's even though the letters were larger and not joined up. I looked at Chris's mum curiously.

'It's a letter he wrote for Santa when he was seven,' she said. 'I doubt if Chris actually believed in him then. I think he was just going along with things to keep his parents happy. Have a look.'

I opened the envelope. Spread out the sheet and read:

Dear Mr Claus,

Please could I have the following items?

Item	Qantity	Make/Model
Bike	*1*	*BMX 20 inches*
Football	*1*	*Nike T90*
Meccano set	*1*	*MC 5510*
Selection box	*1*	*Galaxy*
Cream Eggs	*3*	*Cadbury*
Glitter pens	*6*	*Bostik (Red, silver, green, blue, purple, gold)*

Bloody hell. Not even eight yet and only one spelling mistake.

I smiled. 'Yeah, typical Chris. Every item detailed exactly including make and code number. What's with the glitter pens though? Bet he didn't let on to Gary or Ian he was into girly stuff like that.'

'Those were for you. Don't you remember?'

I shook my head guiltily. 'Not really.'

'And the cream eggs.'

'Oh God, yeah. Now I remember. They were delicious.'

She nodded. Stared at me. 'Yes, like I said, Chris has always known exactly what he wanted.'

Felt a lump in my throat. Chris must have loved me even then. At seven years old. And (I now remembered) he'd even let me exchange the glitter pens for his football.

'You won't ever hurt him will you?' Chris's mum asked.

'Course not,' I said, surprised.

She nodded and didn't say anything else about it. Just started chatting about how I was getting on at school and what I was intending to do next year. Usual adult talk. But later I couldn't stop thinking about what she'd asked me. It was a really odd question and she'd sounded genuinely concerned.

I mean, why would I ever want to hurt Chris? I love him. I'd never do anything to hurt him. Never.

MONDAY APRIL 1 ST

Total panic this morning at school when Mr Smith announced over the Tannoy at the end of break that there was to be an inspection of the sixth-year common room by senior members of staff at twelve p.m. exactly.

This was so unfair. There has always been a sort of unspoken agreement that staff stay out of our common room provided we don't cause any problems like playing music so loud it shatters the glass in the head teacher's room in the next block (last year's sixth year) or setting up an illegal gambling club (also last year's sixth year).

It gave us just twenty minutes to get rid of all the alcohol, roulette table (with chips etc) and rude cartoons of teachers stuck to the dartboard. With such a short time there was nothing for it but to pour all the wine and vodka down the toilet and bin the empty bottles along with the gambling stuff and cartoons.

At twelve o'clock exactly there was another Tannoy announcement from Mr Smith saying there wouldn't be any inspection and to remember the date. 'April fools!'

And we could hear other teachers all laughing in the background. *So childish*.

In the afternoon Mrs Kennedy said she'd exciting news about our play. Instead of being performed in school it's going to be staged in a proper theatre in town. Community leaders have heard about what we're doing and say it's a great way to get across the important message about the futility of violence and the evils of gang culture.

'Does this mean we'll get paid for it?' Gerry asked.

Mrs Kennedy frowned. 'It's not about financial gain. It's about art's contribution to the community.'

We took that as a no. Still, it would be cool to perform in a real theatre instead of our assembly-hall stage and we were all pretty excited until Mrs Kennedy gobsmacked us by saying that our audience would be mainly local gang members from the east end of the city.

This news was just a bit too exciting and a murmur of protest got up.

'Of course they are *reformed* gang members,' she assured us, 'who have renounced violence and want to become responsible productive citizens.'

'Yeah right,' several people muttered.

Mrs Kennedy frowned. 'But they will, of course, be frisked for weapons before entry and there will be police in attendance at all times in the unlikely event of any trouble.'

Unlikely my arse. No one was buying this and we almost staged a revolt until she said. 'There will also be several talent scouts from TV and theatre attending the play on the look out for the new young stars of tomorrow.'

Hmm, risk of serious assault from the audience versus the chance of fame and fortune. We'd do it.

At the end of the lesson she asked me to stay behind. 'Kelly Ann,' she said, when everyone had gone. 'I've spoken on the phone with one of the theatre scouts from London. Gave him your name as a person I believe has real talent. Especially for dance. I can't promise anything of course but . . .'

'Oh my God, thanks, Mrs Kennedy,' I said.

I practically floated out of the room. Just imagine. Me, a star. It could happen. *Would* happen if I had anything to do with it. I'd rehearse until I was perfect. And if I got noticed by a talent scout then signed by a top agent, surely even Mum and Dad would believe in me.

Then I had a sudden thought. Ran back to drama where Mrs Kennedy was taking her next class.

I glared at her. 'Yeah very funny but you so didn't fool me. And I'm glad I didn't stop people forging that love letter to Mr Smith from you asking him to meet you behind the bike shed and be sure to bring a condom.'

'I beg your pardon, Kelly Ann. You think I would stoop to such a thing? Make a joke about something so important? Besides, it's after twelve o'clock. And . . . what was that you said about Mr Smith?'

Oh God, why couldn't I just have kept my big mouth shut?

I scuttled out and since I'd a free period made my way home. Saw Mr Smith pacing behind the bike shed looking at his watch.

You'd think he'd have checked her timetable.

TUESDAY APRIL 2ND

It will be the Easter holidays next week but Chris has told me he'll be working full-time in his porter's job and also studying for his exams in May so he won't be able to see me any more than usual. Maybe less. Anyway, I would probably have to start studying for my exams too. He promised summer holidays would be different. He couldn't wait.

Asked Matt what he was doing at Easter and suggested we get together with the rest of the cast to rehearse but he was vague.

'Maybe. We'll see, Kelly Ann. I don't like to plan too far ahead – just go with the flow then see what turns up. I'll call you sometime.'

WEDNESDAY APRIL 3RD

Chris's mum got me an 'interview' for a baby-sitting job with a nursing colleague of hers who lives quite near by so I went along to see the woman tonight.

There were just two kids. An eight-year-old blonde girl called Emma who seemed very polite and well-behaved, and a really cute toddler, Mickey.

Their mum seemed quite impressed with me, I think, and said I'd to come over on Friday at eight p.m. Mickey would already be in bed. Emma's bedtime is nine o'clock. I could help myself to drinks (not alcohol ha ha) and snacks, plus they have Sky TV. She and her husband would be back at midnight and drive me home. They'd pay me £20.

Bloody hell. £20 and I get to pig out and watch Sky all night. Can't believe my luck.

THURSDAY APRIL 4TH

Asked Liz if she wanted to come baby-sit with me as the mum said it was OK to bring a friend (but no boys).

She was tempted by the snacks but had to turn it down as her granny is visiting. She did give me some advice on dealing with kids.

'It's really important to set boundaries, Kelly Ann. Children need to have rules and routine. You should make it clear who is in control and that no means no.'

'Boss them about, you mean? They won't like me if I do that.'

'Maybe at first but they'll realize eventually it was for their own good. Boundaries are essential for children's psychosocial development you know. With proper boundaries children grow into happy, independent, responsible adults. Without them at best they will become sad, insecure, pathetic neurotics. At worst, total drug addicts, yobs or murderers.'

FRIDAY APRIL 5TH

Can't believe my luck. Bloody Liz.

Everything was fine until nine o'clock when I told Emma it was bedtime but she asked to stay up to finish watching her Disney film. It was nearly at the end so I was going to say 'Yeah, fine,' but then I remembered Liz's advice about boundaries. 'Sorry, rules are rules. Off to bed now.'

'But it's only another ten minutes,' she whined.

'No way.'

'You're mean.'

'It's for your own good. You don't want to grow up to be a yob or a murderer do you? Your whole psychosocial—'

'I am not a psycho. That's a bad word. I'm telling my mummy on you.'

I switched off the TV. 'Bed now.'

She scowled at me and stamped her feet. 'I don't wanna go!'

I folded my arms. 'Too bad.'

Tears squeezed from the side of her eyes, her face flushed tomato red and her mouth opened to bawl. Oh God, wish I hadn't listened to Liz. Maybe I should just back down.

But suddenly she gave in. 'OK.'

'OK?'

'I'm tired anyway,' she yawned. 'But can I just go into the garden and get my Barbie? I think I left her on the patio when I was out playing.'

Hmm. Probably a delaying tactic. 'It's dark, you go off and brush your teeth and I'll get it.'

I went out through the kitchen, leaving the door open to light my way, and scanned the patio. Couldn't see the doll so checked the path as far as the gate. Still no doll. Got darker all of a sudden. Turned round. Just like I thought, the door had blown closed. I hurried back up the path.

The door had not blown closed. The door was locked. I yelled at Emma to let me in but . . . no answer. Bollocks.

Made my way round to the front. Front door was locked too of course. Could see Emma through the open curtains curled up on the sofa watching Disney.

I banged on the windows. Shouted. Apart from sticking her tongue out at me – no response.

Oh God, I'd have to call her parents. Tell them I was locked out. How humiliating.

How impossible. I didn't have my mobile with me which had their number in it. Even if I managed to borrow a phone from someone I didn't remember their number.

Shit. I'd have to try and break in somehow.

Checked the downstairs windows front and back. Locked. Looked up. Thought I saw an upstairs bedroom window open just a crack, and there was a drainpipe leading up to the side of it. Yeah, I could make it.

Shimmied up the drainpipe and managed to open the window just enough to squirm through. Sorted.

Except that a cruising police car had spotted me and stupidly assumed I was a burglar or something. I mean honestly, did I look like a house breaker? Didn't help that Emma told them she'd never seen me in her life before and had no idea who I was. But eventually they accepted my explanation and left.

Emma made herself scarce. Just as well or I'd

have beaten her to a pulp, Childline or no Childline.

Decided I deserved a treat after all the carry on so I helped myself to a packet of chocolate digestives and a bottle of Irn Bru from the kitchen, slumped down on the settee and flicked through the channels on Sky to see if there was anything decent to watch. Found a good chick flick even though I'd seen it before when Emma appeared at the living-room door.

'Bed!' I growled.

'OK,' she said. 'But I just thought you should know Mickey's not in his room.'

She turned away and went up the stairs again.

She was probably lying, of course, just to annoy me but I'd have to check.

Mickey wasn't in his room. Or Emma's. He wasn't in his parents' bedroom or the spare one either.

Checked both bathrooms. The kitchen, dining room, cupboard under the stairs. Everywhere.

Oh my God.

Checked the garden, including garden shed, all the time calling, 'Mickey! Mickey!'

Checked every room again.

Nothing.

Oh my God. I'd have to call his parents. Tell them I'd lost him.

Oh. My. God.

Hands shaking, I called his mum's mobile but she

didn't pick up. Probably on silent if she was still at the cinema. Texted instead. SON MISSING. COME HOME. WILL CALL POLICE.

Was just about to press send when Emma said, 'Do you want to know where Mickey is?'

Did I want to know where Mickey was? Oh yes I did. Very, very much. Had to agree to let her watch whatever she liked, and stay up as long as she wanted, before she told me. Would have agreed to anything including taking her clubbing.

Mickey was exactly where she said he'd be. Sleeping contentedly thumb in mouth in the airing cupboard. Apparently ever since he learned to climb out of his cot he quite often wandered into the airing cupboard to sleep. A favourite spot of his.

Even though there were vents in the doors and it was nice and warm, I didn't feel I could leave him there so I prised him gently out, trying not to wake him up. Succeeded but then my bloody phone rang and he started to bawl.

Ignored my phone and tried to calm Mickey down. Took him into the living room to see if the TV might distract him but Emma was watching some horror fantasy movie while munching her way through my biscuits. Thought about asking her to put on a cartoon or something but decided against it. Setting boundaries for Emma was bloody impossible.

Suddenly Mickey stopped wailing and pointed. 'Bicky!' he said.

I gave him a digestive and flopped down on the settee. Mickey munched contentedly. Peace.

'Mickey's not supposed to eat biscuits,' Emma said.

'Just this one,' I said.

'Bicky!' Mickey asked again.

Gave him another biscuit so he'd one for each hand. When he'd finished gave him two more. Also poured some Irn Bru into his bottle when he asked for some of my 'dink'. The hell with Liz and her boundaries. Let the parents do the healthy-diet stuff. One night of pigging out wouldn't do him any harm.

Film was rubbish but otherwise everything was fine until Mickey vomited orange sick over both of us and started to bawl again.

'Told you he's not supposed to eat biscuits,' Emma said smugly, then turned up the TV volume so she could hear it over Mickey's wailing while I frantically tried to wipe the sick off us with paper tissues.

Didn't hear the parents come back because of all the racket. Oh God. I gawped at them. 'Oh, you're, um, early.'

She glared at me. 'I got a missed call from you. I was worried something might be wrong.'

'Everything's fine,' I said brightly.

She looked at her sick-covered toddler then glanced at the TV which Emma was still watching, totally absorbed in the film. 'Do you think that programme is really appropriate for an eight year old?' she asked.

'Well, um, she's very mature for her age.'

But her mum didn't agree. Can't say I blame her. *Lesbian Vampire Killers*. Well, it's not exactly Disney is it?

SATURDAY APRIL 6TH

Thought I'd blown the baby-sitting job, but apparently not. She paid me for the night and she's going to give me another chance. Said that, unlike her last five baby-sitters, at least I hadn't managed to lock myself out of the house.

Hmm. Agreed to do it but obviously Emma and I would have to come to an understanding about who was, and who was definitely not, boss.

My gorgeous nephew Danny is up for Easter but they are all staying with Angela's snobby in-laws so I only got to see him for an hour on a quick visit.

Chris came over but he didn't stay long either as he's spending most of the weekend at his mum's because his uncle and cousins are over. He's promised to spend Easter Monday with me though and maybe go to Loch Lomond if the weather is nice.

He brought up the subject of getting a flat together

again saying he could pay all of the deposit and more than half the rent if need be but I stalled him. Said I probably wouldn't be able to afford even half when I'd have food and fuel bills.

Anyway, to be honest, all the talk about leases and fuel bills sounded too serious and responsible for me. Something for adults to worry about. Not me. Not now. Not yet.

SUNDAY APRIL 7TH

Easter Sunday, and my parents didn't get me an egg! Said I was too old now. I mean, really. Who is ever too old for a chocolate egg?

At least Chris got me one. Well, not an egg exactly – a really cute chocolate rabbit with a basket of tiny eggs wrapped in blue and pink foil.

I didn't eat it right away but kept it until the evening when Liz and Stephanie came over with their eggs for a chocolate fest. (Well, OK I did nibble one ear off but I'm only human.) My parents were over at Angela's in-laws for dinner so we had the place to ourselves.

Liz admired the bunny but then waffled on about how psychologically meaningful it was. 'This is very significant symbolically you know, Kelly Ann. The rabbit represents how Chris views you.'

'Small and cute?' I suggested.

'Or bucktoothed and brainless,' Stephanie said.

Liz shook her head. 'Think what the rabbit symbolizes in our culture.'

'Lots of shagging,' said Stephanie. 'So Chris thinks you're a sl—'

'Fertility,' Liz interrupted. 'Chris views you as highly fertile. A good breeder. The future mother of his children. It's a very positive sign that he's committed to the relationship. Serious.'

I frowned. 'Yeah, too serious.'

Liz and Stephanie stared at me, surprised. No more surprised than me. Where had that come from?

Liz, as usual, was the first to break the silence. 'Chris has always been serious, Kelly Ann. Ambitious. Intense. You know that.'

'Yeah, well, sometimes it's, I don't know, a bit much. And he's changed since leaving school. Got even more sensible. Totally focussed on career stuff and the future. Seems much older somehow.'

'But he's a good laugh too. A nice guy.' Liz sighed. 'Totally well-balanced. No real psychological problems for me to analyse unfortunately.'

Stephanie laughed. 'Yeah, it's too bad, Liz. At least one of us should have dated a psycho you could analyse. Anyway, I still say you're wrong about rabbits. They're definitely best known for shagging. That and eating their own poo.' She looked at me and laughed again. 'Not that Chris was thinking of poo when he bought you the rabbit.'

Hmm, thanks, Stephanie. I eyed my Easter bunny. Could I possibly eat it after all this disgusting talk?

Snapped off its head and bit its face. Definitely. It was chocolate after all.

Stephanie had brought a bottle of red wine – a French *Grand Cru* from some chateau or other – purloined from her mum's kitchen. Liz and I mixed it with the cheap, sweet sparkling white 'champagne' we'd bought to celebrate Easter.

Stephanie talked about her wedding which she's recently put off until next summer – that was the earliest she could get a booking for the exclusive Skibo castle venue she wants. Now she's made up her mind about all the major important arrangements she's going to discuss them with her dad on Wednesday as he'll be paying for it all.

It still seems odd to have a friend who's getting married. Too grown-up somehow. Especially Stephanie, of all people, who always seemed totally irresponsible and boy-mad. She's the last person you'd expect to do something as respectable and mature as getting married. She's had more boyfriends than I've had packed lunches but maybe that's the point – she's kind of done it all already so she's ready to settle.

Unlike me. I've hardly had any proper boyfriends except for Chris. Just a couple of guys I snogged. I suppose if I stay with Chris for ever that's all I'll ever know. Somehow, even though I love Chris to bits and can't imagine ever losing him, the thought depressed me.

Although Liz was travelling to New York in just two days to see Julian she was strangely quiet about it. When Stephanie went off to the toilet I asked Liz why she wasn't more excited.

'I don't know,' she said. 'I think Julian has changed somehow. He doesn't call me any more. And hardly emails. Says he's too busy.'

'Julian won't ever change that much, Liz. And he's mad about you. Maybe he *is* just really busy. And that won't last long. He's going to retire soon so he can laze about all day and night like he used to. That was always his ambition.'

'Hmm, I'm not so sure any more. Maybe he likes working now. Making money. Being responsible.'

I laughed. 'Julian? Never. Julian wouldn't be Julian if he changed that much.'

'That's what worries me,' she said.

Stephanie came back and we didn't talk about it any more but towards the end of the evening I got a horrible twisty feeling in my stomach. Somehow I couldn't help thinking that things were about to change for all three of us. And not in a good way.

MONDAY APRIL 8TH

But maybe the twisty feeling in my stomach last night wasn't due to a premonition but caused by all the wine and chocolate, or the prawn sandwich I had for lunch which I thought tasted a bit dodgy at the time.

Anyway, I've been sick all day and have the runs, so a trip to Loch Lomond was out the question. In fact, wandering more than two metres from a toilet wasn't a good idea.

Chris wanted to come over even though I let him know I was ill but I told him no. Although we've been going out for ages now, I still think keeping me company while I sit on the loo being sick into a basin might spoil the romance. A girl has to maintain a bit of mystery. Even if her boyfriend is a medical student. That's what Stephanie says anyway and she knows everything there is to know about guys.

Chris came over. He was really nice and didn't seem to go off me at all. Maybe Stephanie doesn't know everything about guys. Or not about Chris anyway.

TUESDAY APRIL 9TH

Feeling much better today so have accepted another baby-sitting job. As soon as her mum went out Emma and I had a talk.

It's been decided. Emma gets to stay up until half past ten, watch what she likes on telly, plus eat and drink what she wants. She also gets twenty per cent of my earnings for helping to look after Mickey and telling me where all his favourite hiding places are.

Like Liz said, it's important to set boundaries and I've agreed to mine. Emma has even hinted she might even be flexible about boyfriends visiting. Depends on my behaviour.

WEDNESDAY APRIL 10TH

Got a text from Stephanie. CATASTROPHE. COME NOW.

Oh my God, what had happened? Texted back. HAS SOMEONE DIED?

NO.

GOT CANCER?

NO.

UR FAVE TED BAKER JMPR SHRUNK IN THE WASH?

My phone rang. 'You are totally crap in an emergency, Kelly Ann. Now get ****ing over here.'

Charming.

Ran to Stephanie's. Her mum answered the door. Normally elegant and perfectly co-ordinated, I noticed that her red nail varnish didn't match her pink cashmere top and a couple of strands of hair had worked loose from her complicated chignon. Things must be really bad. 'I'm so glad you're here, Kelly Ann,' she said, ushering me in. 'Stephanie's upstairs.' She rolled her eyes. 'As you can hear.'

Bloody hell she was right. Stephanie was making some racket. Banging and crashing things about, while swearing at the top of her voice.

I hurried up the stairs but paused outside her bedroom door and knocked. 'Stephanie, it's me. Can you stop throwing things so I can get in?'

Don't think she heard me as the banging and crashing continued. Couldn't stand out there for ever so in the end I put my left elbow in front of my face to protect it, shoved her door open, and darted in.

A picture frame crashed on the wall to the left of me, cracking the glass. When it hit the floor I could see it was a photo of her and her dad smiling happily on a beach on holiday together. Stephanie marched over and stamped on it then jumped up and down repeatedly, her high-heeled boots quickly smashing the thing to pieces and mutilating the photo beyond recognition. I guessed the problem must have something to do with her dad.

It was really weird to see Stephanie in this state. Usually nothing bothers her. Her dad must have done something awful to upset her this much.

Took her a while to calm down enough to talk – or talk in a way I could understand at least – but eventually she managed to explain, while pacing up and down the room like an enraged tigress, that her dad was objecting to her wedding plans.

'He says there's a recession on,' Stephanie fumed. 'And we all need to tighten our belts.'

I tried to reason with her. 'Well, I've heard things are pretty bad right now. It's always in the news about loads of businesses going bust because people aren't buying as much any more.'

'Rubbish. Dad owns a portaloo business. People still need toilets don't they?' Stephanie said. 'They don't stop going to the loo just because there's a recession on do they?'

'Hmm, suppose not.'

'He says he can't afford Skibo Castle for the venue, that Lamborghini hire is too expensive and that I could use a local florist instead of having my bridal bouquets flown in from Japan.'

'Well maybe Skibo is quite dear. I mean, Madonna got married there and she's—'

'So what does he expect me to do?' Stephanie interrupted furiously. 'Grab a bunch of daffodils and get a bus to some tacky registry office?'

'No, I'm sure he doesn't mean—'

'And,' she continued, 'he says there's no need for a Michelin-star chef to prepare the buffet. Or a top celebrity band at fifty thousand pounds a night to provide the music.'

'Maybe you *could* find something a bit cheaper?'

'Yeah right. I suppose we could always get a Chinese takeaway then go to a karaoke bar. I don't think so.'

'Um, no, right well, I see that won't work but—'

'But the worst. The absolute lowest point was when he said . . . he said . . .'

Stephanie broke off, too choked up with anger to continue.

God what next? I wondered. A honeymoon in Butlins? Wedding night in a youth hostel? But no, Dave's family were paying for all that.

I offered to go get her a glass of water but she said, 'Screw that' and swilled down some wine straight from a half-empty bottle by her bed.

It seemed to help, as she continued, 'He said, why pay ten thousand pounds for an individually designed, hand-sewn couture wedding dress when I could probably find something *nice*. NICE, mind you' – she paused again before going on – 'In the . . . in the . . . shops.'

She spat this last like it was a dirty word.

'Well, um, I thought you liked shops. I'm sure you could find something you'd look fabulous in.'

She shot me a murderous glance and I decided not to try and argue her round again. Not if I wanted to leave this room alive.

'Like I could just go to the high street and grab some cheap nylon thing from a rack,' she seethed. 'Next he'll be saying I should have my wedding gift list from the Pound Shop.'

'And he's given me a . . . a . . . *budget*! I've not to exceed thirty-thousand pounds. I ask you, a budget of thirty-thousand pounds. For my *wedding*. And my *very first* wedding at that.'

'Your first wedding?'

'Yeah. My *very first* wedding and he's being a cheapskate. I told him *No way*, but he wouldn't budge. So I said "Fine then, the wedding's cancelled".'

'What did he say?'

'He said fine by him, I'd just saved him thirty grand.'

'Oh.'

Stephanie flopped on the bed exhausted and passed me the wine bottle. I shook my head. 'Have you talked to Dave about it?'

She nodded.

'What did he say?'

'He said the wedding-ceremony stuff isn't important to him. He said he couldn't believe I was letting this come between us but, if I was that shallow, he was glad I was calling things off.'

'Oh God, Stephanie.'

'I know,' Stephanie sighed. 'That's the problem with bridegrooms. They're all bloody guys. Don't understand weddings at all.'

FRIDAY APRIL 12TH

Stayed over at Chris's last night but he had to leave just before two in the afternoon and wouldn't be back until nearly eleven as he was working at the hospital. It's a horrible, annoying shift but he told me he didn't have a choice.

I decided just to stay at the flat rather than go home and come back again so I was pleased when Stephanie rang and suggested she come over for a while this evening to keep me company especially as no one would be around then except for Gary.

Having said that I hoped she wasn't still as furious with her dad. I'd spent practically all of yesterday listening to her rant on about him, and how she's going to make him suffer for his meanness but it's kind of hard to sympathize when she talks about the 'miserly thirty thousand pounds' he offered.

Did feel sorry about how gutted she must be about Dave, even though she won't admit to it. When I asked if she was missing him she just said, 'God yeah. I haven't had sex for three days now. Better do something about that soon.'

But I know she didn't mean it. Or I think so anyway.

When Stephanie arrived, Gary greeted her enthusiastically. 'How's my favourite pole dancer then?'

Stephanie scanned the living room. 'Looks like a crypt in here.' And she sat beside one of the three skeletons which were draped over the sofa and armchairs.

Gary broke open a bottle of wine for us. He isn't keen on wine and much prefers beer but always keeps a bottle hidden in his room in case of emergencies i.e. a girl he hopes to sleep with comes round.

'This is very generous of you, Gary,' Stephanie said, taking the large glass of wine he offered. 'Especially as we're not going to sleep with you.'

Gary grinned. 'You girls have always underestimated my pure, charitable nature and assigned base motivations to my desire to please girls.'

I laughed. 'Yeah right. How come you're not seeing Samantha tonight? Have you got fed up waiting for her to sleep with you and dumped her?'

'Of course not. As if I would do something like that. She's been at her mum's since Easter. Got relatives over from America. But she'll be back tomorrow night, although not till pretty late, and she's invited me over.'

'That sounds promising,' Stephanie said. 'Maybe you should have kept the bottle for her.'

'I wish. I'm getting nowhere with Samantha. Won't even give me a proper snog. Says she would feel that was cheating.'

'Cheating? Is she going out with someone else then?' I asked.

'Yeah, the sodding undead.'

'What?'

'She's into vampires. Totally obsessed with super-natural creatures that drink people's blood. I mean, give me a break. The guy's dead and wants to kill her. And that's supposed to be attractive? I'll never understand girls.'

'Maybe she'll grow out of it,' I said.

'No chance,' Gary grumbled. 'I picked her up from her mum's once. She wasn't ready so invited me in and I met her parents. Mum's obsessed with Mr Darcy. You know, the *Pride and Prejudice* guy?'

'Yeah, of course I know who Mr Darcy is. Loads of females fancy him. It's normal.'

'Yeah, well, bet loads of females don't have every square centimetre of wall covered in pictures of him.'

'Well I don't know, some—'

'Or dress in Edwardian clothes with their hair up in ringlets. And all this from a woman who lives in a two-bedroomed tenement in Partick. Nuts.'

'Hmm, no you're right that *is* a bit much. What's her dad like?'

Gary shrugged. 'Seemed normal. An electrician. Didn't say much – he was watching sport on Sky – but Samantha says her mum sometimes makes him dress up as Mr Darcy. Sticks false sideburns on him as well. Poor sod.'

Stephanie laughed. 'Probably the only time he gets a shag.'

'Christ, Stephanie, that's gross. Now I'll have that image in my head all n—' Gary broke off, his expression thoughtful, excited. 'Wait a minute. I've just had an idea.'

'Don't tell me you're going to dump Samantha and date girls who prefer their boyfriends actually living instead of undead?' Stephanie asked.

'Very funny, Steph,' Gary said sourly.

'And who have parents that don't wear ringlets and sideburns,' I giggled. 'Or not at the same time anyway.'

Gary grabbed the half-finished wine bottle from the table. Waved it at us. 'You girls have had too much to drink already. Now, do you want to hear my idea or not?'

I nodded meekly and Gary put the wine bottle back on the table. 'OK,' he said, 'What if I dressed up as a vampire?'

'Might work,' Stephanie said.

'Don't be stupid. Stephanie was only joking. Weren't you?' I said.

Stephanie shrugged. 'Worth a try.'

Gary grinned. 'I might just have something from a fancy-dress party last year. Wait a minute.'

He went off to his room and returned with inch-long, very fake-looking plastic fangs sticking out of his mouth at an unlikely angle. He'd also smudged tomato sauce over his lips and let it drip down his chin.

'Irresistible,' Stephanie laughed.

Gary grimaced which made him look even more stupid. 'Well, I'll have a black cloak of course, and maybe gel my hair. It was just to give you the idea.'

Stephanie shook her head. 'No way. Not even close. You need proper make-up and some black- or red-tinted contacts. And no cloak. Modern vampires are sexier. Haven't you ever heard of *Twilight*?'

Gary's shoulders slumped. 'Yeah, I suppose it was a stupid idea. I don't know anything about make-up or tinted contacts.' But then he brightened, picked up the bottle and refilled Stephanie's glass. 'Not like you, Steph. Bet you're ace at that kind of thing. Of course, turning someone like me into a convincing vampire is probably too difficult. Too much of a challenge. Even for someone as talented as you.'

Stephanie looked at him appraisingly. 'But not impossible.'

Oh God. I tried to argue them both out of this stupid idea but it was too late. They'd decided. Before Stephanie called her taxi home she'd agreed to come over tomorrow and 'work on' Gary's vampire look.

Had a horrible feeling it would all end in disaster.

SATURDAY APRIL 13TH

Woke at nine to find Chris already dressed and ready to leave. I sat up and rubbed my eyes. 'Where are you going?'

'I've got football practice this morning, remember. I told you about it last week. We're trying to get a few extra sessions in before the match next Saturday.' He kissed me. 'I'll text you when I'm finished but I'll probably go straight to work from there. Don't think I'll have time to come back to the flat first.'

'You're working again today!'

'Yeah I told you.'

'No you didn't.'

'I'm sure I did.'

I glared at him. 'And *I'm* sure you didn't.'

He frowned, reached for his mobile and checked his saved sent messages. Trust Chris to keep a record.

I peered at the text he showed me, remembering now. 'Never received that one,' I lied.

He grinned. 'Fibber.'

Then he put his palm to my cheek, gave me another quick kiss and left.

'Away and boil your head,' I muttered under my breath to his retreating back.

Oh my God, what was I doing? I wasn't turning into someone like Mum was I? No, I'd never be like her would I? Never treat Chris the way she treated Dad. I was just annoyed that I'd hardly get to see Chris at all this weekend. That's all.

Thought about going home but decided against it. Mum would probably just make me clean the house. I'd be better off hanging round the flat today.

Hmm, or maybe not. Had to scrub out the bathroom before I showered as it was disgusting. And when I went to make a mug of tea I noticed my feet were practically sticking to the kitchen floor as it hadn't been mopped since, well, probably the last time I mopped it. There wasn't a clean cup or teaspoon either. As for the living room, well, Jamie had come back late with a crowd of medic pals, so don't ask, but the place smelled as though it had been simmered in smelly socks and soaked in beer.

Jamie and Gary made half-hearted attempts at helping with cleaning up but were so useless I eventually shooed them away and did it myself. Strange how supposedly intelligent people can be so stupid at straightforward stuff like housework. Or maybe it's not so strange after all.

Stephanie came round in the evening as promised and started work on Gary. By the time she was finished, he looked amazing. Skin corpse pale, but with no hint of powder, contrasted with deep red-stained lips and gums – but it was the eyes that really grabbed your attention. The irises were black as night so it looked like he'd no pupils at all. Scary as hell.

'You're not really going to go through with this, Gary, are you? Turn up at her flat looking like a vampire without telling her. You'll freak her out.'

Gary grinned. 'She likes being freaked out. Must do if she fancies the undead.'

I shook my head. 'I think you should talk it over with her first.'

'No, that'll spoil the surprise. Make it less exciting for her.'

'What do Chris and Ian think about all this?' I asked.

'Christ, I'm not telling them about it. They'll think I'm nuts. Take the piss out of me for months. You won't tell them anything will you?'

Hmm.

SUNDAY APRIL 14TH

Gary didn't get up until 11.30, but I managed to squeeze ten minutes alone with him in the kitchen before Chris drove me home. Asked him how things had gone with Samantha.

'Not entirely successful.'

'Told you so.'

'Might have been better if I hadn't spotted the open balcony door and decided to climb up and sneak in.'

'You idiot, Gary. Bet Samantha freaked out.'

'Actually, no, she didn't. But the girl whose flat I broke into did. Those balconies all look the same you know.'

'Oh my God.'

'Yeah she made quite a fuss. Wouldn't let me explain – just ran out screaming and called the police. Thank God Samantha was next door and heard her. She managed to convince the girl I wasn't a vampire or pervert prowler but an upright citizen who'd made an honest mistake.'

'Idiot, you mean.'

Gary grinned. 'She may have used that term.'

I shook my head. What a disaster. But then maybe not entirely. 'So,' I said. 'Afterwards how did things go with Samantha? I mean, em, did she like your vampire look?'

Gary shrugged. 'Not really. Told me she's not into vampires any more.'

'I thought she'd grow out of it.'

'She's into werewolves now.'

Chris stopped the car outside my door but didn't cut the engine. He gave me a quick peck. 'Love you. See you next weekend.'

'Yeah, suppose.'

'What's wrong?'

I unbuckled my seat belt. 'Nothing.'

Chris cut the car engine. 'Wait. Have I done something to upset you?'

'No.'

'Said something?'

'No.'

'Please just tell me what's wrong, Kelly Ann. I don't have time to play twenty questions.'

'That's the point. You never have time. I saw more of Gary this weekend than you.'

'I told you I had to work this weekend. You knew that.'

I opened the car door. 'Yeah well you're always working. Or studying.'

'Wait. Don't go. We need to talk about this.'

I closed the door again. Folded my arms. 'So talk.'

'Look, I admit I've been working a lot lately but I need the money right now. As for studying, well, medicine's a challenging course.'

'Jamie's a medic. He doesn't study anything like as much as you. He still passes his exams.'

'Jamie's content with fifty per cent. I'm not. I want to be the best doctor I can be. Rise to the top of my profession. And earn enough to secure my future. Our future.'

'Yeah, well, leave my future out of it.'

'What's that supposed to mean?' he said, bewildered.

I didn't answer. Wasn't sure I knew the answer.

'Listen to me, Kelly Ann,' Chris said earnestly. 'I love you. You're the most important thing in my life. The future means nothing to me without you in it. Do you believe me?'

I sighed. 'Yes.'

'Do you love me?'

'You know I do.'

'Then just try to be patient. It won't be long until summer. We'll go away some place. Just the two of us. That's part of the reason I've been doing so many shifts. Saving up for our holiday. I wanted to surprise you.'

'I can't let you pay for me. It's not right.'

'Of course you can. I love you. I want to make you happy. What could possibly be wrong with that?'

'I . . . I don't know. It's not like you're rich or anything.'

'No, but I've got some money coming to me soon. A trust fund which I should have got after my eighteenth but it's been tied up. It'll mean I won't have to work so many shifts next term. We'll have more time together. Everything is going to be OK. I promise.'

Oh God I hoped so.

MONDAY APRIL 15TH

Back at school. Liz wasn't there as she is still in New York with Julian. She's due back Wednesday. Haven't heard anything from her since she went away, not even a single email which is weird. Hoped it meant she was having such a fantastic time she was too busy to bother. Still, it wasn't like her.

Matt wasn't at school either. I was more disappointed than I should have been.

Got a text from Matt. HI, C U TMRW. MATT X

He'd put an X on it. Was more excited than I should have been.

TUESDAY APRIL 16TH

When I walked into the common room I noticed Matt right away. He was in his usual seat by the window but he wasn't looking outside. Instead, he had his eyes focussed on the doorway. Waiting for me.

I stopped. Gazed at him. He stared back. Smiled.

With my eyes still fixed on his I made my way towards

him, oblivious to everything and everyone like I was hypnotized. Which is probably why I tripped over Ayesha's bag and did a kind of somersault thing over a side table before finally landing on my face on the floor in front of Matt.

'Nice knickers,' Gerry called out.

I flushed as scarlet as my underwear, pulled down my skirt and scrambled to my feet.

Matt took my hand. 'Hey, you OK?' He patted the chair beside him with his other hand. 'Sit down.'

I nodded. Sat beside him.

Matt looked over at a grinning Gerry. 'Don't pay any attention to him. Tosser. Or any of those other idiots laughing at you.'

'I don't. I'm not bothered really,' I lied.

But as Matt started chatting to me, asking me what I'd been doing, telling me the gigs he'd done over the holidays and the places he'd travelled to, I began really not to bother. Matt seemed so much older and more sophisticated than everyone else. He made them all seem childish and stupid. Why should I care what people like that thought of me?

And anyway at least I hadn't been wearing a thong or anything. Found myself wondering if Matt would find red underwear attractive. Also wondered what colour of underwear *he* wore. Probably black. Mmm he'd look good in black boxers.

'What are you thinking about, Kelly Ann?' Matt asked.

Oh my God what was I doing! Speculating about the colour of guys' underwear like some mad nymphomaniac pervert.

I flushed. 'Nothing. I . . . I've got to go.'

I jumped up.

Matt caught my hand. 'What's the rush?'

'Got to, um, go to the toilet. Left my make-up bag there. Hope it's not stolen.'

I hurried out, turned right, dashed along the corridor. Heard Matt's voice behind me call, 'Girls' toilets are the other way!'

So they were.

Oh God, this is getting so bad. Like I'm obsessed or something. I really should avoid him as much as possible. It's a pity then I've agreed to go for another bike ride with him after school today, but I'm determined this will be my last. And nothing will happen. Not even a clunk of helmets.

WEDNESDAY APRIL 17TH

I've spoken to Dad this morning about learning to drive. Mum's against it. She says she wouldn't trust me to drive a Zimmer, even if I was supervised all the time and it was fitted with brakes. But Dad says he'll teach me. And he's even promised me a car – second-hand, of course, but he'll make sure it's in great condition – for my eighteenth birthday in October. It's fantastic of Dad to do this and I'm really grateful but I *so* want a motorbike.

Asked Dad about getting one now, even a cheap one, but he said no. He hasn't seen dead bodies on slabs like Chris but just says Glasgow is too wet for bikes. They're not practical. But they are the most exciting, fantastic way to travel ever. And if I had my own maybe I wouldn't have agreed to ride with Matt again.

At least I didn't clunk helmets yesterday or do anything I couldn't tell Chris about (except for going on a motorbike). But I know I'll have to kiss Matt some day soon. At least twice.

We were going over the script in drama today. Mrs Kennedy discussed the final scene where Matt is knifed to death by a rival gang member and I'm weeping over his corpse, clutching him and kissing him but it's all too late. We're going to act it out properly next week.

At least it's not the earlier kissing scene where he's alive. That one has just got the two of us in it and Mrs Kennedy wants to get the bigger group scenes done first so she's delayed it until later. But I'm still nervous about kissing Matt, even when he's playing a corpse.

It's so annoying. In last year's school play when I had snogging scenes with Gerry, I knew I couldn't trust him and I always had to watch out in case he tried to stick his tongue in my mouth or put his hands up my skirt. This time it's *me* I don't trust. Not that I'd do anything gross like Gerry, of course. But I'm scared of how I'll feel. What if I really like kissing Matt? What if it makes me want to do it for real? And what would that mean for Chris and me?

Never thought I'd say this but I wish Gerry had got the part. Wish all I had to worry about were his wandering hands and probing tongue. Unwanted advances in other words. Not, maybe, wanted ones.

THURSDAY APRIL 18TH

Got a text from Liz. DISASTER. COME QUICK.

Oh my God what could have happened? Texted back: HAS YOUR PLANE CRASHED?

NO.

HAS SOMEONE DIED?

SORT OF.

WHAT DOES 'SORT OF' MEAN?

My mobile rang. Liz. 'You're crap in an emergency, Kelly Ann. Come on over now.'

I ran to Liz's. Her mum answered. 'I'm so glad you're here, Kelly Ann. Liz is in an awful state. She's upstairs in her room. Hasn't come out of it all day.'

I loped up the stairs but stopped outside her room and

listened cautiously. Couldn't hear anything except for Liz's low sobbing so felt it was safe to go in.

Tripped over a huge pile of dirty clothes, shoes and toiletries – the contents of Liz's luggage which she'd tipped onto the floor – and hit my head on the edge of the opened door of her wardrobe which was empty and unused as usual.

Liz was sitting in the middle of her bed clutching a picture of Julian. Her eyes were red and the picture soggy with tear stains. I guessed the crisis probably had something to do with Julian.

'You OK?' Liz asked.

I rubbed my forehead. 'Well, I think I hit my head quite hard. It's really sore.'

'But everyone knows that physical pain is nothing to the pain of emotional and mental anguish,' Liz said.

'Hmm, I don't know. Depends how much you hurt yourself. I mean, if you were put on a rack and stretched until all your bones broke. Or tortured with hot tongs by the Spanish Inquisition or something. Well, that would be pretty bad.'

Liz scowled. 'Mental pain is much, much worse.'

'Oh yeah, you're right of course. Much worse. Of course it is.' I sat on the bed beside her and put an arm round her shoulders. 'So tell me what's wrong, Liz.'

Liz stared at Julian's picture again. 'Oh Julian, Julian,' she sobbed. 'How could this have happened to us?'

'It's Julian isn't it?' I said, gently. 'Something's happened.'

Liz stopped sobbing. 'Of course it's Julian, you idiot.'

Charming.

But her annoyance didn't last long and soon she was gazing at Julian's photo again and sighing. 'It's over, Kelly Ann. Julian and I. We're finished.'

'Oh God, I'm so sorry, Liz. Did he dump you?'

'No, I finished with him.'

'Well, that's not so bad then. At least you've not been chucked.'

'Yeah I suppose my ego won't be damaged by rejection but . . . but . . . I'm gutted, Kelly Ann.'

'Oh God, Liz, why did you dump him then?'

'He's changed. Completely. He's just not my Julian any more. He . . . he's got an American accent.'

'Well that's not surprising. He's been living there for a while. Anyway, American accents are nice. Quite sexy sometimes.'

'And he gets up at five every morning and jogs to work.'

'No, that doesn't sound like Julian but, OK, maybe he just wanted to finish work early so he could spend the afternoon with you.'

'He never finished earlier than seven o'clock. Then he always had a fifteen-minute power nap before eating dinner with clients. After that it was off to the gym for a session, then bed at eight thirty.'

'Oh my God, Liz.'

She shook her head. 'A *power nap*. He actually called it that. Seriously. And he . . . he . . . wears a suit.'

'Julian wears a suit! I don't believe it.'

Liz nodded. 'All the time. Except at the gym.'

Bloody hell he *had* changed. Julian always wore scruffy jeans and jumpers with holes in the elbows, except for a while when he dressed in girls' clothes to annoy his dad. I just couldn't imagine Julian in a suit.

'He's obsessed with work now,' Liz went on glumly. 'Ambitious. Go-getting. It's awful. And he said that successful people were all skinny and that I, that I . . . should think about . . . losing weight.'

'Oh my God that's awful, Liz. No wonder you dumped him.' I hugged her. 'What does Stephanie think about all this?'

'I haven't contacted her, but I expect she knows or will find out soon enough. He's her brother after all.'

'Let's call her. Maybe she can help.'

'No,' Liz said. 'There's no point. Julian is family and Stephanie will have to side with him.' Her eyes teared up again. 'So not only have I lost Julian. I've lost my best friend too.'

'I thought *I* was your best friend?'

She patted my hand kindly. 'Well, you are now.'

Hmm.

SATURDAY APRIL 20TH

Spent the whole day with Liz who is 'grieving' over the loss of Julian and hasn't left her room. I didn't think the bloody awful tragic love songs she insisted on playing all the time helped but she said it was psychologically necessary for the grieving process to wallow in misery for a while bawling your eyes out, or 'catharsis' as she called it. Don't know about Liz, but after five hours of this I was about ready to top myself.

I offered to take her over to Chris's with me tonight, as I didn't want to leave her on her own but she said no, it would be too painful to be with a happy couple. It would just remind her of her loss.

Poor Liz. And Stephanie come to that. Both of them were single now while I was the one with a boyfriend. It felt weird. For years I'd always been the odd one out; the one who couldn't get a date never mind a proper boyfriend. Now it was totally opposite. Although I didn't imagine Stephanie would be without a guy for long – or several come to that.

Talk of the devil. Heard Liz's front doorbell ring and her mum answer, then the determined clacking of high heels stepping rapidly upstairs. The door flew open and Stephanie burst into the room wearing thigh-high boots, a crotch-skimming skirt and sequined pink boob tube. Anyone else would have looked tacky and tarty in an outfit like that. Not Stephanie. Maybe it was the fact that her boots were made of soft expensive leather, her skirt a fine linen from Karen Millen and the boob tube a designer label with hand-sewn sequins. Or maybe it was just that Stephanie couldn't care less what other people thought. Anyway she always looked more classy slut than cheap slapper. Guys loved her. She put her hands on her hips and glared at Liz. 'Right, what's all this about? You've been back two days now and haven't replied to any of my texts or calls, never mind come to see me.'

Liz stared at her sadly. 'I'm sorry, Stephanie, but I thought it best not to answer. You'll probably know by now that Julian and I are finished.'

'Yeah, so?'

'Well, I wanted to spare you any awkwardness. You see, you've no need to explain anything. I understand. Julian is family. Your loyalties lie with him.'

'Bollocks.'

'But he's your brother.'

'And a guy. A total idiot guy as well. I've told him he's made an arse of all this. Now c'mon, it's Saturday night, let's go clubbing. Check out the talent.'

'Oh God, Stephanie, I'm really glad we're still friends and thanks for asking but I couldn't go clubbing so early in the grieving process.'

'Bollocks. You can grieve at the club. Now change that

bloody awful music and let's have a look at your pulling clothes.'

Stephanie marched purposefully into the room but stumbled on one of the piles of self-help books, underwear and empty Diet Irn Bru bottles which always littered Liz's floor. After kicking the pile into a corner she sat on Liz's bed and produced a bottle of vodka from her bag. 'This will get us in the mood.'

I volunteered to run off to the kitchen to ask Liz's mum for glasses and Coke. On my way back heard loud sexy music blasting upstairs. Thank God. Opened the door to see Liz wriggling her way into a tight, low-cut black dress while Stephanie danced around her nodding approval at Liz's choice of outfit.

I poured the three of us large vodka and Cokes, then danced over to join them, singing along to 'Survivor' and slopping the drinks a bit as I did so, but who cared?

Played 'Survivor' again then 'Independent Woman', and loads more stuff like that. Old songs but bloody brilliant. And they were all about how we girls were smart, strong, independent females, so can take care of ourselves and didn't need any stupid guys. Yay!

'I better go ask Dad for some money for tonight,' Liz said. She sashayed out. 'Be back soon.'

'You coming tonight, Kelly Ann?' Stephanie shouted, writhing her hips to the beat.

'No. I'm, um, supposed to be going to Chris's.' I

checked the time. 'In fact, I've gotta go now. Late already.'
I drained the last of my drink, picked up my bag and
shrugged into my jacket.

Liz came back waving two £20 notes. 'Sorted. Oh, is
that you off now, Kelly Ann?'

'Yeah have a good time.'

'You too.'

I left them dancing, giggling, all excited about the night.
Because anything might happen. You never knew. And I
hurried off to meet Chris. My gorgeous, dependable,
loving boyfriend. I knew I was lucky. Knew it. So there
was no reason to feel jealous of Liz and Stephanie tonight.
None.

SUNDAY APRIL 21ST

Liz and I went over to Stephanie's for a girlie night. Face
packs and makeover (all done by Stephanie), chick flick
and chocolates. It had been ages since we'd done this and
I'd been really looking forward to it but Liz and Stephanie
spent quite a lot of the time talking about their night
on Saturday so sometimes I felt kind of left out of
things.

'Do you remember when that really hot-looking guy
asked you to dance, Liz?' Stephanie said. 'But then, when

the music started, he started to jump about like a baboon with its bum on fire?'

'Oh God, yeah. So embarrassing,' Liz giggled. 'I tried to pretend he wasn't with me but every now and then he'd grab my arms and try to swing me under his legs.'

They both collapsed laughing and I joined in but it probably sounded false.

'Oh you should have been there, Kelly Ann,' Stephanie said. 'You'd have wet yourself.'

'Yeah, wish I had,' I said stretching my mouth into a smile.

'And then,' Liz said, looking at Stephanie, 'when you strolled over to the guy with the condom peeking out of his shirt pocket and you said . . . you said . . .'

Liz had another fit of the giggles and couldn't continue so Stephanie took up the story. 'You mean the short skinny guy who was totally up himself? Thought he was some sort of sex god? Yeah I remember. I said, all husky and sexy, *That condom isn't out of date is it?* And he goes, "No, gorgeous, why do you ask?"'

Liz had recovered a bit by this time and finished for her. 'And you said *Because it will be by the time* you *ever need it.*'

Both of them broke into helpless gales of laughter again.

'Oh God, you had to be there,' Liz said.

Really wish I had.

MONDAY APRIL 22ND

Liz was back at school today. I hadn't told anyone about the break-up, so everyone wanted to know how she'd got on in New York, even people who'd been really jealous of her trip. When Liz told them about Julian most of the girls were sympathetic. The boys lost interest and drifted away, except for Mark who'd fancied Liz for a while and asked her out.

But Liz turned him down. 'I'm sorry, Mark, but I'm still in the grieving period.'

'Oh God, sorry, Liz. Didn't realize the guy had copped it. If I'd known I'd have left it till next week to ask you. Is next week OK?'

'And,' Liz continued, 'you're way too stupid for me to ever think about dating you.'

'I suppose the week after next is still a no then?' he asked.

Liz shook her head and walked away. God, Mark was thick. Quite nice looking though. If only he was a bit more muscular he'd have been perfect for Stephanie.

WEDNESDAY APRIL 24TH

Drama class, and the scene I'd dreaded. Matt was sprawled out on the floor having just been stabbed to death. It wasn't a dress rehearsal so there was no fake blood or anything but he still made a fairly convincing corpse. Not that acting a dead person is that difficult, of course.

Kept reminding myself this was a dreadful, poignant scene. A young man is tragically murdered in front of the girl he loves. She kisses him goodbye for ever. It was all terribly sad. And not at all sexy. Or arousing.

At Mrs Kennedy's cue I broke free of people trying to hold me back, ran over to Matt, knelt on the ground beside him and leaned over his body. I cried and wailed for a bit then prepared to kiss him, keeping my mouth tightly closed.

But just then he opened his eyes and winked at me before closing them again. I stopped, drew back a bit and tried not to laugh. Fortunately no one else could see him at this angle so hopefully we could get this last part of the scene finished. I moved closer again aiming to kiss his chin rather than his lips – no one would be the wiser except for Matt – when his arms reached for me and he pulled me on top of him. Then he kissed me hard on the mouth.

I pushed him away and scrambled up. He got to his feet too and took a bow.

Everyone laughed, except for Mrs Kennedy who was furious. Even threatened to drop Matt from the role. But he apologized profusely, said he was just joking around and that it wouldn't happen again, so eventually he managed to charm her.

I wish she had dropped him. I should have been annoyed with Matt for spoiling the scene and probably fuelling rumours that there was something going on between us and I suppose I was a bit. But the truth is I found Matt kissing me like that very sexy. And arousing. Don't ever want to kiss Matt again. Because, well ... I want to kiss Matt so much again.

Oh God.

THURSDAY APRIL 25TH

Ever since the kissing scene I can't seem to stop thinking about Matt all the time. Have confessed to Liz and she's come up with a solution called Aversion Therapy which she says will cure me of my 'obsession'.

Wasn't keen at first, as she said it involves really unpleasant stuff like giving myself pain – maybe with an electric shock – or something to make me feel sick every time I thought about him. However, when she said perhaps just snapping an elastic band on my wrist might be sore enough I decided to give it a try.

Have snapped my elastic band over fifty times today and my wrist is red, but if it works it will be worth it.

FRIDAY APRIL 26TH

Nearly our last period of maths before the exams and Mr Simmons was trying to cover as much as possible but I just found it so boring that I couldn't concentrate. Instead found my mind wandering to Matt all the time.

'Kelly Ann!' Mr Simmons shouted. 'Is it you making that snapping noise?'

'No, sir.' He looked at me suspiciously but was soon droning on again.

But the next time I did it he caught me and gave me a punishment exercise. Refused to do it. A punishment exercise at my age. I'd soon be leaving school for good. I was practically an adult, for God's sake.

Of course, Mr Simmons reported me to Mr Smith for defiance but Mr Smith couldn't be arsed dealing with it, although that's not exactly what he said, and sent me to the guidance teacher Mrs Parker.

She's well-named, as Mrs Parker is the nosiest teacher in the whole school and she questioned me for a whole hour about why I was 'self harming'. Didn't tell her anything, of course, and eventually she gave up so I could go back to my classes.

Hoped that would be the end of the whole stupid thing but no. Last period I was summoned to her guidance room again. Got the shock of my life when I saw both my parents sitting there. Oh God.

'What's this all about?' Dad asked. 'Mrs Parker said she'd something urgent to talk to us about but wanted you present first. You're not, er, you know. Young Chris hasn't got you—'

'No, Dad, it's nothing. Honestly.'

Mum didn't say anything, just glared at me suspiciously, which I knew meant she thought I was somehow responsible for her being called away from her work.

'Now, Kelly Ann,' Mrs Parker said, looking at me kindly. 'You know that's not true. It's a very serious matter. But don't worry, no one is going to blame or condemn you. We just want to help.'

I scowled at her. I mean, really, how petty and stupid could she be? Calling my parents to the school for something as totally trivial as snapping an elastic band – hadn't teachers anything better to do with their time? I was sure my parents would see how stupid she was but I wasn't going to be the one to explain it.

'You tell them,' I said.

Mrs Parker sighed. 'Well, I think it would be better coming from you but if this is what you want.' She turned to my parents. 'I'm sorry to be the one to tell you but I've just discovered Kelly Ann has a problem. She's been abusing her own body at school. Even in classes. Sometimes more than fifty times a day.'

Dad stood up, his face red. 'I don't believe it,' he spluttered.

'I know you're shocked but please try to be calm,' Mrs Parker said in her low soothing voice which infuriates people. 'It's not that uncommon for teenagers—'

'Aye well, maybe some oversexed dirty lad caught with his hands in his pockets too often. But not my Kelly Ann for God's sake—'

'Oh, no, no, no,' Mrs Parker interrupted, 'You misunderstand. I didn't mean . . . well, what I meant was, Kelly Ann has been self harming. You know, inflicting pain on her body. Not, em, anything else.'

Dad sat down. Calmer but puzzled. He glanced at me, then turned his attention to Mrs Parker again. 'Why would she want to do that? Why would anyone want to do that?'

'There are numerous theories but no one is quite sure what drives so many troubled teenagers to burn or cut themselves. A cry for help, perhaps, or just a way of—'

'Burn or cut themselves?' Dad said, aghast. He looked at me. 'Kelly Ann, love, you haven't, you wouldn't—'

'Of course not, Dad. I've just been pinging myself with this elastic band that's all.' I stretched out my arm for Mum and Dad to see my wrist.

Mrs Parker shook her head sadly. 'Don't try to dismiss your pain, Kelly Ann. You may not burn or cut yourself but it's still self harm.'

Mum stood up, reached over and pinged my band so hard it snapped completely. 'Right, that's put an end to

that then. And don't let me hear of you self bloody harming again. Any harming needs done, I'll bloody do it.'

SATURDAY APRIL 27TH

Have decided to abandon Liz's Aversion Therapy idea.
Doesn't work anyway. In fact, it's just made things worse.
Every time I look at an elastic band now, I think of Matt.
    Liz told me this is called Association.
    I told Liz to shut her face.
    For once she did.

TUESDAY APRIL 30TH

*Got a text from Stephanie inviting me over to her house
to talk about plans for her hen night.* Was so excited! She
and Dave were obviously back together and the wedding
on again. I was going to text her with loads of questions
but decided to just run over and get all the details face to
face this time.
    'Oh God, this is fabulous news,' I said as Stephanie
hustled me into the kitchen and opened a bottle of
Chablis. 'So where's Liz? What did she say about you and
Dave getting back together?'
    Stephanie shrugged. 'She'll be over later. Who said

me and Dave were back together? Wedding's still off.'

'But I don't understand. You texted me about your, um, hen night. Didn't you?'

'Yeah, you'll never believe it. My dad is trying to squirm out of paying for that as well,' Stephanie fumed. 'Well, I'm not going to let him get away with it. No chance.'

'But—'

'So he said to me, "I thought you cancelled the wedding." So I said to him, "*Yes, I cancelled the wedding. Not my hen night*". So then he says to me, "Why do you need a hen night if you're not getting married?" I mean, really, can you believe it?'

'Um, well, hen nights are usually before a wedding aren't they?'

Stephanie shrugged. 'I'll probably get married one day. To someone. There's no law says a hen night has to be *right before* a wedding is there?'

'Hmm. Suppose.'

'And even if I don't, why should I not have a hen night just because I never get married?'

'Well, um, put that way—'

'Anyway it'll be fun, and I'm determined my dad is going to pay for it. He's not going to wriggle out of this one.'

To be honest, I think her dad had a point but didn't feel it was a good idea to say so. Instead spent a nice time discussing what we'd like to do on a hen night. And some time discussing what I wouldn't like to do on her hen night, e.g. lap dance etc.

'Do you think there's any chance of you and Dave getting back together, Stephanie?'

'Don't think so. He says he won't go back with me until I've sorted out this wedding thing.' She made a pouty face. 'Won't even have sex with me. Even occasionally. He's being so bloody unreasonable about the whole thing. Just like my dad.'

I nodded sympathetically. It seemed safest.

'So,' Stephanie said. 'Liz tells me you're still gaga over dark-and-dangerous Matt. Practically drooling over him.'

Hmm, so much for Liz's professional confidentiality. When would I ever learn she can no more keep a secret than stick to a 500-calorie-a-day diet. 'I am *not* drooling over him. But yeah, well, I do find him attractive. It . . . it . . . worries me, Stephanie. Feels like cheating.'

Stephanie laughed. 'Don't be stupid. Of course it's not cheating. You don't stop fancying other guys just because you've got a steady boyfriend.'

'Suppose. But it's never happened to me before.'

Stephanie sighed. 'Matt's a good-looking guy. Too thin and complicated for me but, yeah, I can see why most girls think he's hot. Why shouldn't you fancy him?'

'It just feels wrong.'

Stephanie laughed. 'Christ, Sister Kelly Ann, I think

you've forgotten your wimple tonight. Take three Hail Mary's and another glass of Chablis for your penance.'

She refilled my glass. I added some lemonade to it and took a slug. Began to feel better. 'Yeah, maybe I am taking all this too seriously. It's not as though I've done anything.'

'Exactly. You know, when Dave and I were together even though he worked out every day, had a toned, muscular body to die for and was great at shagging, I still fancied other people occasionally.'

This didn't surprise me much to be honest, Stephanie being Stephanie, but I nodded politely. 'You did?'

'Yeah. Like Kenny the cage fighter from Bridgeton. *Mmm*. Or Sam the wrestler from Ruchazie.'

'Oh yeah, I think I remember you mentioning them.'

'Or Wienczyslaw the Polish plumber and Abu the limbo dancer. And then there was—'

'Yeah, I, um, get the idea. But these were guys you just fancied. Nothing happened.'

'Well except for Abu. Mmm he was so strong but, you know, supple and very, very flexible with it. I remember one time when we—'

'Right, so, what you're saying is, there's no harm in fancying other people.'

'Of course not. It's healthy. Normal. Anyway, like I was saying, Abu . . .'

Oh God, there is no stopping Stephanie talking about

sex when she wants to talk about sex. Which is a lot. Unless she is actually having sex. Or shopping. Still, at least it put her in a good mood and stopped her ranting about her dad.

And she'd also made me feel better too. Maybe she was right and my crush on Matt was totally normal. Harmless.

Yeah, in a couple of months school will be over for ever, Matt will disappear and I'll probably never see him again. He'll just be a memory. So there is nothing to worry about. Nothing at all.

WEDNESDAY MAY 1 ST

Why, oh why, is it always sunny when you have to revise for exams? First day of study leave and it's gorgeous. Cloudless blue sky, warm gentle breeze, birds twittering in the trees. Well, I imagine birds are twittering as I've got my iPod in. But still.

I'm with Liz in the library and we're both reading war poetry. All about disease, deformity, death and the futility of existence. It's depressing, especially on such a nice day.

We decided we might as well read this stuff outside so we set off for the park. Everybody else seemed to have the same idea and most of our sixth year were sprawled on the grass by the pond. Some with books and folders out, others not even bothering to pretend.

Couldn't face any more war poetry so tried a love story instead. Hmm, heroine tops herself when the hero marries someone else. Maybe not.

Got out maths. Who was I kidding? Anyway my first exam was a week away. Plenty of time.

Chris called before I went to bed to ask about my day and tell me he loved me. He'd studied all day and evening, of course. Wish I was like Chris so I could go to sleep with a clear conscience knowing I'd had a productive day and got loads of work done. On the other hand, I think I've got the beginnings of a nice tan on my legs so today hadn't been a complete waste of time.

And there was always tomorrow.

THURSDAY MAY 2ND

Slept in till 11 o'clock, so there was no point in starting any revision until the afternoon.

Had cereal, watched some TV, then made lunch – tuna sandwiches and chocolate (not together of course). They say fish is good for the brain and chocolate aids concentration so I reckoned this would help me study.

It was another gorgeous day and still only one o'clock so I thought I'd go for a walk in the park before starting my revision. I've heard exercise increases brain power too.

Was just about to cross the road at the park gates when I spotted Matt on his bike. He saw me too and stopped.

Flipped up his visor. 'Hey, Kelly Ann, I was just thinking about coming over for you. Fancy a ride?'

'Sorry, Matt, I have to study today.'

'Just for an hour? Go on, you know you want to.'

I hesitated. I really did need to study. And it would probably be a good idea not to be alone with Matt. But it would only be for an hour. And I wouldn't be alone with Matt. We'd be on an open road. You couldn't get more public than that. I looked at the motorbike. How would it feel to be speeding along the motorway on a beautiful day like this?

I put on the helmet, mounted the bike and we roared off.

Ended up at Lunderston Bay, a place Dad used to take Angela and me to a lot when we were kids as it's just a forty-minute drive away. Or twenty minutes if you've got a motorbike and ride like Matt.

We walked along the sandy beach until we came to a rocky outcrop then we scrambled up to the top and gazed out at the sparkling sea. If Chris had been here I'd have said it was romantic. But anyway it was still very nice.

Remembered there used to be crabs here and sure enough saw a tiny one hiding in a crevice and managed to catch it. Put it in a small pool of water in a hollow in the rocks. Then I caught another. And another. By the time I'd finished I'd caught eleven. Pretty good going as they are not easy to spot. Matt didn't join in. Just watched me.

'You're like a kid, Kelly Ann.'

I frowned at him. 'You think I'm immature?'

He smiled. 'No. Just, well, just natural, I suppose. It's kind of nice. I like it.' He paused. Stared intently at my face. 'I like you.'

I stood up. 'We should get back now. I've got loads of studying to do.'

'OK, no worries.' He got up. 'I'm just glad you came. Wasn't sure you'd be around any more. Thought you might be spending most of your time at your boyfriend's since we're on study leave. He stays in Byres Road doesn't he?'

'No, um, Chris has to study too. But I'll be seeing him Saturday night. How did you know he stayed in Byres Road? I don't remember telling you.'

He shrugged. 'Just a guess. A lot of students stay there. In fact, I'm going to a student party in Byres Road, Saturday night. Why don't you come? Meet some of the people I hang out with. Musicians. Artists. Interesting types. Bring your boyfriend too, of course.'

'Well . . . I don't know. Maybe.'

'And sometimes dancers. Last party I went to there I met some girls who'd done a pop video. Backing dancers for a rock group. You never know. You might make some contacts.'

'OK then, I'll see if Chris wants to come. But

about today it, um, might be best if you don't mention—'

'Sure, no worries. I won't say we've been here.'

I blushed. 'Not that we've done anything wrong, of course.'

He laughed. 'Not yet.'

SUNDAY MAY 5TH

The party on Saturday didn't go as well as I'd hoped but it wasn't as bad as Chris is making out either and I wish he'd stop going on about it. I mean, nothing really awful happened. In fact it was actually a bit of a laugh – sort of.

Chris, Jamie and I turned up around 11 o'clock. The place was very dimly lit and hoaching so it took me a while to spot Matt who was with a guy I recognized as his drummer Paul.

Was nervous Paul would say something about the night I watched the band play at Ashton Lane but I already had my excuses ready. *Oh, I thought I mentioned that, Chris. Yeah I went to see them one night ages ago. You were working and couldn't make it.*

But after introductions Paul said nothing. Probably didn't even remember me. In any case he was busy rolling a joint while at the same time holding on to a bottle of beer. Not easy. Finally he succeeded. He lit it and inhaled deeply. Noticing me watching him he asked, 'Want some?'

I shook my head. 'No thanks, I don't smoke.'

'Me neither. This is hash – much better for you.'

'No, I'm fine thanks.'

Paul thrust the joint at me. 'Go on it's good stuff. Not cut with any rubbish.'

Felt I ought to take some just to be polite – I wouldn't inhale and just pretend to smoke it – so I reached for the joint.

However Chris pushed Paul's arm back and glared at him. 'She said *No thanks*.'

Paul sneered at Chris then looking at me said, 'Who's this you've brought with you? I thought you said he was your boyfriend? Acts more like your mother. He got some kind of problem?'

I flushed. Chris could seem a bit uptight at times. 'No there's no problem. It's fine. So, um, great party.'

But Paul wouldn't leave it alone. 'He seems to have a problem. He with the fuzz or something?'

I laughed nervously. 'No, Chris is a medical student. His dad's a policeman though. Kind of. A detective anyway. But he's very nice. Broad-minded. He thinks all drugs should be decriminalized and reclassified according to how much harm they do and not—'

Paul turned to Chris. 'Your dad's a pig? That would explain it then.'

Oh my God. He so should not have said that.

Chris grabbed Paul by the throat and smashed him against the wall keeping an elbow at his chest which made him spill his beer and drop his joint on the floor.

Fortunately the carpet had been rolled up for the party so I was able to mop the beer with some paper napkins lying around while Matt picked up the joint and started smoking it.

But Chris still hadn't let go of Paul, and if anything was pressing harder on his throat to stop him struggling.

'Stop it,' I hissed at him. 'Everyone is looking at us. You're embarrassing me.'

'You're also cutting off the blood flow to his left and right carotoid arteries,' Jamie commented mildly. 'Might cause a bit of brain damage after he passes out.'

'I know exactly what I'm doing,' Chris said. He relaxed the pressure on Paul's neck then slowly released him. 'You ever say anything like that again and next time I might not let go.'

The atmosphere kind of soured after that so we moved off.

Later though when I was in the hall queuing for the loo Matt came up to me and I took the opportunity to apologize. 'I'm really sorry about Paul.'

Matt shrugged. 'Paul's mouth is always getting him

in trouble. Your boyfriend's a bit impulsive though.'

'Sorry, yeah, Chris is kind of touchy about some things.'

'I noticed.'

'No really. He used to get a lot of hassle at primary school because of his dad being a policeman. His mum would tell him just to ignore it but Chris couldn't. He was always getting into fights. Went home with a black eye loads of times.'

'He seems to know how to take care of himself OK now.'

'Yeah, he got kind of used to fighting so got quite good at it, then his dad taught him self-defence and martial arts stuff so people stopped bothering him. He's still sensitive about it though. People slagging off his dad because of his job I mean.'

'I can relate to that.'

'Why? Being an accountant's not that bad is it?'

'Where did you get that idea? My dad's not an accountant. He's a minister.'

'A minister? Oh my God. Really?'

'You see, not the coolest job for your dad to have.'

'Oh I'm sorry. I didn't mean. It's just that—'

'I don't look like a minister's son?'

I nodded. 'Not really, no, but then I've never met a minister's son before.'

'No worries. I get that reaction from most people.'

'Must have been difficult for your dad when your mum ran off. Embarrassing.'

He shrugged. 'Yeah but she was never a typical minister's wife. She was always kind of wild. Unconventional. I probably take after her.'

'Is that where you get your musical talent from?'

'Maybe. She could sing but she also used to be a dancer. Like you.' He fixed his deep, dark eyes on mine. 'You could never settle for a conventional, safe life either could you?'

I stared at him mesmerized. 'Well, I'm . . . not sure if . . . um, the toilet's free. Don't want to lose my turn.'

Afterwards I decided it would be best to avoid Matt. Found Chris in the kitchen helping himself to a beer. I wrapped my arms around his waist and rested my head on his chest. 'I love you, Chris.'

Chris smiled down at me. 'You're affectionate all of a sudden. What brought this on? Guilt?'

I flushed guiltily. 'Of course not! Why should I feel guilty?'

'Hey, only kidding. You want another drink?'

Decided I'd better not take any more alcohol. Needed to keep control of myself. 'Just a Coke I think.' I looked around. The table and counter tops groaned with beer cans, wine, whisky and vodka bottles but, except for a single carton of orange juice, no soft drinks. Asked a guy leaning by the sink who I'd thought lived here. 'Do you know where can I find some Coke?'

He looked at me. Frowned. 'Maybe Jack's got some. He usually does but there's a shortage right now. Police confiscated a huge haul a couple of weeks ago.'

'What?' I asked, puzzled.

'She means *Coca Cola*,' Chris said, his voice tense. He turned to me. Put a protective arm round my shoulder. 'Maybe we should think about leaving.'

'We can't go now,' I whispered. 'We only got here an hour ago. People will think we're bad-mannered. Or saddos who don't like parties.'

'I don't actually give a toss what these people think,' Chris said out loud.

'Shh, keep your voice down. We won't stay long. Maybe just another hour or so.' I spotted Paul come into the kitchen with a blonde girl who was holding a large biscuit tin. Decided it might be best to keep him and Chris apart. 'Chris, I saw a twenty-four-hour grocery across the road from here when we came in. Can you get me some Coke from there?'

Chris was reluctant to leave me but I pointed out that Jamie was here – even though he was snogging the face off some girl in tight purple jeans – so eventually he went. I sighed with relief when he'd gone. Hoped he'd come back in a better mood.

I ignored Paul and was going to go back to the living

room when he surprised me by coming over with the girl, who I now recognized as his American girlfriend I'd met in Ashton Lane, and talking all friendly to me. The girl seemed OK too but didn't say much. She didn't seem to remember me so I didn't mention having met her before.

Paul said, 'Isabella's a great cook. Have you tried her chocolate brownies?' He pointed to the box of cakes. 'Go on, try one. You'll love it.'

Mmm. They did look good and I hadn't eaten any-thing since six. 'Thanks.'

I took a bite. It wasn't as delicious as proper chocolate cake from a shop but it was nice and I was starving so I was pleased when Paul put another two on a paper plate and handed them to me. 'I know girls and chocolate cake. One is never enough.'

I smiled my thanks then he and Isabella moved off.

Meant to keep one of the brownies for Chris but he was a while getting back so I'd scoffed the lot by the time he returned, explaining that the so-called twenty-four-hour grocery had closed and he'd to walk to the garage shop.

He wasn't in a better mood like I'd hoped, but some-how I didn't care so much any more. Felt completely relaxed in fact. And it was such a fabulous party. Just seemed to get better and better the longer I stayed.

But there was no one dancing. Probably because the place was heaving and there wasn't any room but I decided to try anyway. Kept tripping over people's feet which made me laugh. Then I started tripping over my own feet like they didn't belong to me, which made me laugh even more.

Chris wanted me to sit down but I refused. I was just having too much fun. The best fun of my life. But when I fell right over in the middle of the floor I laughed so hard, I couldn't get up.

Chris pulled me to my feet and steered me towards an armchair in the corner of the room which Jamie had bagged by putting my jacket and bag on it while he guarded them. It wasn't any distance but took a long time as something weird seemed to have happened to the floor so it felt like I was walking on pillows. I kept losing my balance and it was impossible to walk in a straight line, however Chris didn't seem to be affected at all so finally we got there and he sat me down on the chair.

He frowned. 'Kelly Ann, what's the matter with you?'

'Nothing,' I giggled. 'Oh God, you look so funny when you frown. He he he. You've got a little squiggly line right in the middle of your forehead. Ha ha ha! Right' – I pointed my finger at him – 'there,' I said, poking him in the eye.

Jamie said, 'She's stoned.'

Which made me giggle so much I slid off the chair.

That's the last I remembered until I woke up this morning

feeling awful. By twelve o'clock most of the groggy, tired feeling I'd had all morning had had gone but Chris was still going on about how I'd got stoned last night. 'Are you sure you don't know who gave you the brownies?' he demanded, handing me a mug of tea.

I sipped it gratefully. 'No,' I lied. 'Let's just forget it. It's no big deal.'

'It is to me. Look, I don't know much about this guy Matt but I know I don't like the people he hangs about with.'

'God, you're so uptight. It was just hash not heroin. Lighten up. Everybody takes drugs these days.'

'Not *everyone*. And nobody should be tricked into taking them like you were last night. What if it had been something stronger, or contaminated?'

I shrugged. 'There's no harm done. I'm fine.'

'This time. Next time, who knows. I don't want you to have anything more to do with Matt or his friends.'

'You can't tell me who to see and not to see.'

'I'm not telling you. I'm asking. For your own sake. I think he's trouble. I'm worried you could come to serious harm.'

'I can take care of myself.'

'For my sake then. If anything happened to you I'd have to find the people responsible and kill them. Might be difficult practising medicine with a murder conviction.'

'Oh stop exaggerating.'

'I'm not. I think the BMA might balk at giving a licence to someone with a serious criminal record.'

'Very funny. You know what I meant. Stop making ridiculous threats you'd never carry out.'

'Kelly Ann, you know I've *never* made a threat I wasn't prepared to carry out.'

FRIDAY MAY 1OTH

English exam wasn't too bad but my hand ached with writing.

Afterwards Matt surprised everyone when he invited us all back to his place. Most people accepted, even Gerry; curious I suppose.

Since everyone was going it would have looked odd if I'd refused. Anyway the truth was I wanted to go. I know Chris has asked me not to have anything more to do with Matt but I never promised anything after all. And anyway, like Stephanie said, I didn't need to tell my boyfriend every little detail about my life.

Matt's house was a big high-ceilinged place with old-fashioned furniture, and almost no ornaments or pictures. Just shelves of mostly leather-bound books. Felt more like being in a library than a home.

'Does your dad know you've invited all of us?' I whispered. 'Are you sure it's OK?'

'Why are you whispering?' Matt whispered. 'It isn't a library.' Then in a normal voice he added, 'My Dad's away in Aberdeen for a conference. Going to spend the weekend there.'

He selected some rock music then turned up the volume so it blasted out loud enough to be heard all over the house and probably across the street. 'Drinks in the kitchen, help yourselves,' Matt shouted.

Everyone stampeded to the kitchen. Two kegs of beer, half a dozen boxes of wine, plus bottles of Vodka and whisky dispelled anything left of the library atmosphere.

Not sure whether it was the unexpected supply of alcohol or the relief of finishing the exam but within half an hour everyone was happily drunk and dancing, singing or shouting along to the music.

Probably for the same reason, there was also already a queue for the toilet but Matt told me there was another upstairs so I went there. When I came out I noticed a bedroom door was slightly open and spotted a guitar so I reckoned it was most likely Matt's. There was no one about and yeah, though I knew it was nosy, I couldn't resist a quick look inside.

Like Matt, the room was unusual, dark and different. A black duvet covered the wrought-iron double bed but the sheets and pillow cases were deep red. Black and white posters of rock bands, mainly old ones from the sixties and seventies, completely hid every bit of wall from floor to ceiling.

Except for piles of sheet music, and some old vinyl records there wasn't any clutter or mess. No smelly socks or boxers on the floor. No empty Coke cans or crisp packets under the bed. Not your normal guy's room, but then I guess I hadn't expected that.

There was a photograph in a silver frame on the bedside table of a slim, dark-haired woman in a red dress who looked like she'd been snapped dancing flamenco. I moved closer and peered at it. Yeah. Probably his mum. Apart from that nothing. None of Matt, his dad, friends ... or girl-friends. I picked up the framed picture and inspected it, looking closely for features in common with Matt.

'Found what you're looking for?' Matt asked.

I dropped the photo back on the table and turned round, my face burning with embarrassment. Matt was leaning on the now-closed door watching me.

'Oh God, I'm sorry, Matt. The door was open and I just thought I'd, well—'

'Invade my privacy?'

'No well, um, I thought I heard a noise. Yeah. Over by the window. So I, um, just wanted to make sure no one was—'

'Nosing about in my room?' He smiled. 'Or trying to

burgle me? Yeah, thanks, Kelly Ann. Very thoughtful.'

I hung my head. 'Sorry.'

Matt moved away from the door and came right up to me. Stood in front of me. He put his hand under my chin and tilted my face up to look at him. 'It's OK, you were just curious about me. I understand that.'

'You do?' I said, relieved. 'Thanks, Matt, I'm really sorry about—'

'Yeah, because I'm curious about you too. Interested.'

Suddenly I was very aware that we were in Matt's bedroom. Just the two of us. Standing right by his bed. 'Well, we better get back downstairs. People will wonder where we are.' I laughed nervously, skirted round him and hurried to the door. I grasped the handle and pulled. It didn't budge.

Matt's arms were either side of me keeping it closed and trapping me between him and the door.

I squirmed round to face him. 'We . . . we really should get going. You're supposed to be the, um, host.'

'It's going to happen, you know, Kelly Ann. You and me. It's only a matter of time.'

'Nothing's going to happen. I've got a boyfriend.'

'We don't need to tell him. He never has to know.'

'Yes he will. He'd find out.'

'You're right.' Matt took his hands away from the door and moved back a little. 'He would find out. Especially as we're going to do it in public.'

'What!'

'The kissing scene in the play. The one where I'm not a corpse. We'll be performing in public so he'll find out. What did you think I was talking about?'

'Oh yeah right. Of course that was what I was thinking about. But well, yeah, it's, um, difficult to explain to a boyfriend. But you're right. Chris will have to know. I'll, um, tell him. He'll understand.'

'Great. You know we haven't rehearsed that bit yet. Why don't we—'

I turned round again and opened the door. 'Sorry I've got to go I need—'

'Wait, don't tell me you need the toilet again. You've just been.'

'Vodka,' I said, hurrying downstairs.

Decided not to tell Chris about the party as I know he doesn't approve of Matt. But I'd nothing to feel ashamed or guilty about. Nothing happened between me and Matt. I didn't even dance with him, never mind snog him. But I don't feel relieved. Just somehow . . . dissatisfied. Oh God.

SATURDAY MAY 11TH

Spent all day and evening studying at Chris's flat. Everyone else, even Gary, was doing the same so at least I didn't feel I was missing anything. Chris helped me with my maths. He's very good at maths – very good at most things really – but patient with people who aren't, so he never gets frustrated when, after explaining something for the umpteenth time, I still don't get it. Unlike me.

I got a lot of work done but can't say it was the most fun weekend ever. Didn't get to bed until two o'clock when I curled up in an exhausted heap next to Chris.

Although he'd been working longer and more intensely than me he still wanted to make love but I wasn't in the mood. My head was stuffed full of algebra and irregular French subjunctives. Very unsexy.

So he just spooned me for a while and gently massaged my back and shoulders until I relaxed. Stroked my thighs, the backs of my knees and elbows; kissed that exact spot on my neck. Mmm. And soon I forgot all about formulae and French. There was only Chris and me. Nothing else mattered.

Yeah, Chris is good at most things.

But afterwards, nestling in his arms, tears dripped down my cheeks onto the pillow. Not sure why. Just had a feeling that maybe this was the happiest I'd be in a long, long time.

FRIDAY MAY 17TH

Sat my last exam today. Yay, finally! Liz's last too.

'Just think, Liz,' I said as we walked home. 'No more exams ever again!'

'Well,' Liz said, 'no more exams *in school* ever again. There will be at least another three years of assessments, tests and stuff at uni.'

Hmm.

'No more maths exams ever again!' I yelled, throwing my calculator in the air and watching it nose dive to a watery death as it slid down a drain.

Liz grinned. 'And no more school uniform ever again!' She took off her blazer and tossed it into a skip at the side of the road.

'Erm, Liz. That was Rachel's blazer. You borrowed it because you spilt Irn Bru on yours last week. Remember?'

Liz hesitated. Looked in the filthy skip. Walked past and shrugged. 'She won't need it any more either.' She giggled, then started singing, 'School's Out.'

Even though we'd need to go back a few times, especially me for rehearsals, I joined in. Because *real* school, with lessons, reports and Mr Simmons's punishment exercises was over. Forever.

Although Stephanie still had one written exam left at college she never takes stuff like that seriously and invited us over to her house to celebrate. She'd put a bottle of champagne on ice.

And she had something to celebrate too as it turned out. 'Dave just left. The wedding's back on.'

'Oh my God, Stephanie! That's great. What happened?' I asked.

She shrugged. 'Couldn't go any longer without some decent sex' – she took a swig of champagne and laughed – 'or indecent sex . . . Kelly Ann, are you eating gummy bears with a bottle of Dom Perignon champagne vintage 1995 at one hundred and fifty pounds a bottle? No, don't take them out your mouth, for God's sake.'

I quickly swallowed the last bits. 'Well, Liz is eating chocolate.'

'Liz is eating the Neuhaus Tiramisu Truffles luxury Belgian chocolate which Dave brought me. That's different. Classy and sophisticated. You haven't finished them all have you, Liz?'

Liz flushed. 'Well, um, I think there's one left.' She put the gold-foil gift box down and fished out a half-full pack of chocolate buttons from her pocket. 'I'll move on to these.'

Stephanie sighed theatrically. 'Oh God, I give up.'

'So,' Liz said, 'what's happening about your wedding plans. Did your dad give in?'

'Hmm, no not really. But he *did* say I could buy any wedding dress I liked. Money no object. So what do you think of this?' She handed over an opened newspaper and pointed to the picture at the top of a page.

Liz and I peered at it. A tall slender model was wearing a long dress made entirely from $100 notes.

'Costs two million dollars,' Stephanie said. 'But unfortunately, it's too tacky for a wedding. I've heard Renée Strauss might be designing another diamond-studded bridal creation this year though.'

Not quite sure whether Stephanie was joking or not. But in any case I'm dead certain her dad will have to shell out an awful lot on her dress. From the gleam in Stephanie's eye, it would be probably be nearly as expensive as the rest of her wedding put together.

Apart from the wedding stuff, Stephanie had other news too. 'Oh, by the way, Julian will be in Glasgow for a conference next week,' she said casually.

Liz stiffened. 'Oh.'

Stephanie eyed Liz speculatively. 'Says he'd like to see you.'

'No way.'

She shrugged. 'Quite right. He doesn't deserve it.'

Talk turned to Stephanie's wedding again, how she and Dave made up, and the week in Tenerife they've booked at the end of May to celebrate. Although Liz asked loads of questions she wasn't nearly as nosy as usual, and it was obvious she was thinking about Julian's visit.

Poor Liz. Wish she and Julian were back together again too, but there was no possibility of that. He'd suggested Liz needed to lose weight. There was more chance of a guy rising from the grave than any boyfriend being forgiven after a comment like that.

SATURDAY MAY 18TH

Couldn't see Chris at all this weekend as he's got so much work to do for his exams still.

He texted me this morning: MISS YOU, LOVE YOU. SEE YOU SOON XX

Matt texted me this afternoon. REHEARSAL SOON? X

TUESDAY MAY 21ST

Julian has called, texted and emailed Liz, even though she's blocked him, because he can hack his way in. She's not answered any of his messages except to say that if he comes to her house her dad will hang him from the lamppost outside, and anyway she won't be there.

Stephanie said he's due to go back to New York tomorrow morning so at least she won't be bothered by him any more.

Liz is gutted about Julian going away without seeing her.

I went over to her house to see if I could cheer her up and found her in the living room arguing with her dad, who can't understand why she's upset. 'I thought you said you didn't want to see him?' he asked.

'I didn't.'

'So how come you're disappointed you didn't see him?'

'Oh, you wouldn't understand.'

'Try me.'

'Cognitive dissonance,' Liz snapped.

She was right. He didn't understand. Neither did I, but at least I knew not to argue with Liz when she's upset.

To cheer her up I suggested we call Stephanie and all go for lunch at Pizza Express. Stephanie's mobile was off so I called her house but no one was in. Maybe they were seeing Julian off at the airport. I left a message saying where we'd be if she wanted to meet us.

Although Liz had seemed keen on the idea, when we got there she was kind of quiet and subdued. Well, for Liz anyway. I mean she gossiped about the possibility Mr Simmons had moved in with Ms Conner, that Gerry was cheating on Felicity with blonde twins (Suzanne and Mary-Jo in fifth year) and that Ms McElwee had run off with the janitor. But her heart wasn't really in it. I could tell. Especially when she agreed the rumour about Ms McElwee probably wasn't true without seeming that disappointed.

Had just started on my dessert when I spotted a man in a really expensive suit walk in, and wondered what he was doing in a Pizza Express. Looked more like he belonged in the Rogano. To my surprise he came right up to our table by the window. Stood in front of us. Gazed adoringly at Liz. 'I couldn't leave without seeing you,' he said.

Oh my God. *Julian!*

Liz glared at him. 'What are you doing here?'

'I got Kelly Ann's message on the answering machine. Please, we need to talk.'

'There's nothing more to say,' Liz said. 'It's all been said. Your psychosocial development has deviated so far from mine that the dynamics of our relationship have been altered beyond repair. I'm sorry, but our compatibility quotient is simply no longer capable of sustaining a mutually supportive, positive bond. Any attempt to do so would risk damaging my self-esteem, and have a negative impact on my achieving the psychological pinnacle of self actualization.'

Bloody hell. For someone who'd nothing more to say she certainly said a lot.

Julian looked as puzzled as I felt. 'So,' he said, 'does that mean you're going to talk to me or not?'

Liz sighed. 'It's over, Julian.'

'But I still love you, Liz. And I know you love me.'

Liz hesitated and her gaze softened for a moment, but then she pressed her lips together. 'I formed an attachment, yes.'

Julian smiled triumphantly. 'You love me.'

'I loved *Julian*. You're not the same person any more.'

'But I am, Liz. Just the same.'

Liz pointed to his suit. 'My Julian would never wear that . . . that thing.'

He shrugged. 'It's just a suit.'

Liz shook her head. 'It's not *just a suit*. It's a symbol. A symbol of convention. Of corporate control. Of—'

'OK,' Julian interrupted. 'If that's all that's stopping you from talking to me it's easily sorted.'

He shrugged out of his jacket and tossed it behind him, where it landed on someone's lasagne. He removed his tie, dropped it on our table ruining my chocolate and raspberry double-cream dessert. He started unbuttoning his shirt . . .

'For God's sake, Liz,' I said. 'Just talk to him. Everyone is looking at us.'

But she wouldn't.

The shirt went the same way as the jacket. One of the waitresses asked him to leave and threatened to call the manager but Julian ignored her. He slipped out of his shoes and started unzipping his trousers.

'Liz, stop him,' I begged.

But she did nothing. By this time it wasn't just people in the restaurant staring at us. Passers-by on the street had stopped and were peering through the window at us.

Julian was down to his pants and socks. He put his hands on the waistband of his boxers. 'Last chance, Liz. Are you going to talk to me?'

Liz turned away.

Oh God, I had to stop this. I leaped up and launched myself at his middle. He toppled over and I went with him landing on top of him. Which is how we were when the police stormed in and arrested us both.

Took me ages to convince the police I was trying to *prevent* an act of public indecency, not commit one, by which time they'd already contacted my dad so I had to wait until he came to collect me before they would let me go.

When Dad arrived he looked at me with wary incomprehension and concern. Like an exorcist had just told him I'd been possessed by an evil spirit and he was afraid my head was about to spin around while spewing green vomit.

'I can explain everything, Dad.'

'Sshh, don't say a word till we're out of here!' Dad hissed.

Dad was quite bolshy with the police. What did they

mean arresting a young girl for a completely innocent show of natural affection? They weren't the ruddy Taliban were they? So bolshy, in fact, that they nearly arrested him but eventually they let us both go.

They wanted to release Julian too as they said they'd better things to do with their time than look after some exhibitionist clown like him making an arse of himself over an ex-girlfriend, but Julian is refusing to put his clothes back on until Liz talks to him and Liz is refusing to talk to him, so he's still in jail.

On the way home I tried to explain to Dad what happened but he wouldn't let me. Told me that he really, really didn't want to know, then added, 'At least your mother hasn't heard anything about this. Let's keep it that way. Unless, of course, the story gets in the ruddy papers.'

THURSDAY MAY 23TH

Story didn't get in the papers but someone must have recorded it as the video clip is on YouTube. The sound quality is rubbish so it looks as though I've been driven mad with lust by Julian's strip and jumped on him in a frenzy of desire. It's had 200,000 hits so far. Thank God my parents are computer illiterates.

Unfortunately no one else is and I've been called and

texted about it all day. I've told everyone it wasn't me of course but just someone who looks a bit like me wearing the same kind of clothes. And, yes, it was a coincidence that the girl happened to be wearing a hand-crafted pendant very similar to the one Stephanie made for me in her jewellery class last Christmas. Also the person sitting behind did look a lot like Liz. But the girl in YouTube wasn't me, OK?!

Thank God school is nearly over completely. A lot of people have left already to go on holiday or start jobs. The rest of us will just go in occasionally; mainly to help organize the prom or, like me, finish rehearsing the school charity musical. Matt has promised he'll be there.

FRIDAY MAY 24TH

Liz has decided to forgive Julian after all, so he's out of jail and they've gone shopping for new casual clothes. He's resigned from his job which is just as well as they were going to sack him anyway for bringing the company into disrepute by getting arrested for indecency.

After shopping, Julian is going to take Liz out for dinner to celebrate getting back together and also to make sure Liz is eating enough – he thinks she's lost a few pounds since he last saw her and he doesn't want her wasting away.

They're not going to Pizza Express though.

SATURDAY MAY 25TH

Chris's exams finished yesterday so he went out with Ian, Gary and Jamie to get pissed. They all have to be packed and out of the flat by Sunday morning as the lease is up then. I've promised to go help them clean the flat. Stupid, I know. Have made it clear I am not cleaning the toilet.

Didn't go round until nearly six o'clock hoping that they'd have done the bulk of the cleaning up by then. Should have known better. They were all sitting round drinking beer out of cans, talking about how pissed they'd got last night, and the good times they'd had in the flat. The place was a tip.

Fortunately Gary and Chris's mums came over ten minutes after me.

'I know I shouldn't,' Gary's mum sighed, 'but I couldn't bear the shame of strangers knowing what a disgusting, filthy tip my lazy son was prepared to live in. I'm not cleaning the toilet though. Potty training was enough.'

Gary obviously hadn't been expecting her as he bolted into his room to remove the posters from his wall. Don't ask.

Ian and Jamie's mums came just after that. For the same reason as Gary's mum, I suspect. Even so we weren't finished until nearly midnight.

Although they'd meant to stay until morning everyone went home to their own houses afterwards. Their mums said they didn't want to give anyone the chance to mess things up again. Since Chris had been drinking beer earlier his mum drove us back and dropped me off at my house.

Chris walked me to the door. 'Thanks for helping out, Kelly Ann.'

'Yeah, well, tell Gary I didn't appreciate the stink bomb in the toilet after I'd cleaned it. He needs to grow up.'

Chris shrugged. Grinned at me. 'That's never going to happen.'

'Hmm.'

'Sorry we couldn't spend one last night in the flat, but at least the exams are over and we'll be able to see each other every day if we want. And I've got a surprise for you next week.'

'What is it?' I asked suspiciously.

'Wouldn't be a surprise if I told you. Something I want you to see. I hope you'll like it.'

Oh God, I've always hated surprises. Well, ever since Mum bought me a baby doll for my seventh birthday that cried and wet itself instead of the skateboard I'd asked for. So disappointing. And bloody annoying when it peed over my jeans. No wonder I'd let Gary tear its head off and use it as a football. I mean, it's not as though I could have converted the thing to a skateboard was it? No, surprises are usually things I really, really don't want.

Was interrupted in these musings by the sound of a man screaming in terror behind us. Looked round to see an obviously drunk guy staring in horror at the back seat of Chris's car then he ran off as fast as his staggering legs would take him.

'Your mum was right,' I said. 'You should have put the skeletons in the boot.'

Chris smiled. Gave me a quick kiss. 'See you soon.'

I was really tired and went straight off to bed but annoyingly couldn't get to sleep. Kept thinking about Chris's 'surprise'. From his excited expression I guessed it was something quite big. Had a horrible feeling I was going to like it about as much as the drunk had enjoyed his encounter with Percy and Jenny. Just hope Chris won't be disappointed when I run off screaming.

MONDAY MAY 27TH

Back at school today. Went earlier than I normally would, as it's kind of nice to go there when you don't have to do anything at all you don't want to do. A lot of other people had the same idea and after we'd returned books and stuff we just sat around chatting and seeing off fifth years who were trying to take over our common room.

Most of the girls were talking about the prom at the end of June. Formal invitations had already been sent to everyone including people like Stephanie, Chris and Gary who left school after fifth year. I suppose it's a bit weird going to a prom a year after you've left school for good but I'm glad they organize it this way because it means that everyone who started school together gets the chance to celebrate leaving together as well.

It soon became obvious that absolutely everyone seemed to have bought their dress except for me, which panicked me a bit, but at least I knew I had a date to go with unlike Rebecca, who'd split up with her boyfriend before the exams, and Rachel, who hadn't found anyone yet.

I wondered if Matt would go and if so whether he'd bring a date. He wasn't in the common room this morning but he'd promised to be in by midday as the cast had arranged to see Mrs Kennedy and start rehearsing.

By 11:55 a.m. he hadn't showed so I texted him. WHERE R U?

He sent me a picture of his large wrought-iron bed with its black duvet and scarlet sheets. Then he texted, JOIN ME? X

There was no lol or anything, but obviously this was a joke. Even so, I got a funny fluttery feeling looking at that picture and text. It was hard not to imagine what it would be like to be there with Matt. Very hard.

I closed the message but didn't delete it and hurried off to the drama room.

Matt didn't show. I should have been annoyed – Mrs Kennedy definitely was – but instead I felt disappointed and relieved. Oh God, I was so mixed up about Matt.

Chris texted me at lunch time. WHERE R U? C U 2NIGHT? XX

SCHOOL. Y C U L8R

Went back to drama after lunch. Matt was already there apologizing to Mrs Kennedy. When he can be bothered he can be totally charming, and she was soon smiling her forgiveness and agreeing with him that we should do the first kissing scene.

The fluttery feeling in the pit of my stomach returned and my face flushed red hot. Oh God, I so didn't want to do this. Because I so much wanted to do it. But Mrs Kennedy was beckoning me over and it would look stupid, and maybe suspicious, if I refused.

Matt was looking at me, his expression kind of calm and amused at the same time. Wish I could be that cool and controlled. Forced myself to walk over to them as normally as possible.

Mrs Kennedy frowned at me. 'This isn't an execution

scene, Kelly Ann. You look as though you're walking to the gallows.'

'I'm, um, just concentrating. Trying to remember my lines.'

Mrs Kennedy sighed impatiently. 'There aren't any lines in this scene, Kelly Ann. It's all done with facial expression and body language. Remember? Now stand in front of Matt, just about half a metre apart at first. No, closer. That's right.'

Oh God. I must remember this is a play. *Just a play*. We were acting a role. It didn't mean anything in real life.

Mrs Kennedy turned to the rest of the class. 'Could someone dim the lights please? Good, that's better. Now I want you all to watch this scene. Some people imagine it's easy to kiss on stage but it isn't. Just because you've all snogged someone before doesn't mean you can perform on stage correctly. You don't want to look as though you're hoovering someone's face. I'm going to direct each move here and I want you all to listen and watch closely.

'Right now, Matt. Take Kelly Ann's hands in yours and stare deeply into her eyes. Good. Good, that's excellent. Now glance at her mouth and yes, that's right, stare back into her eyes again. Now, yes, good idea you've put one hand on her cheek and the other round her waist and pulled her gently closer to you. Yes and now you've leaned in for the kiss. Excellent. Gentle kiss at first that's right ... Yes and, um, and becoming more and more passionate. Right. Well done. That's, um, fine so . . . When you're ready.'

Matt and I weren't ready for a while.

Matt was as good at kissing as he was on the guitar and the only guy who's ever really affected me this way except for Chris. Oh God, Chris. Just thinking about him made me feel so guilty. But this was only a play so I hadn't done anything wrong. Not really. Not yet anyway.

TUESDAY MAY 28TH

Just went into school for the rehearsal today which Mrs Kennedy has organized to run over the lunch hour from twelve until two o'clock as that's the only time the drama rooms are free.

Chris had come round to see me in the morning, seemingly determined to make up for all the times he was too busy during term, and before he starts his summer job at the hospital.

We talked for a bit about the prom. He, Ian and Gary are going to hire dinner suits (these things are so much easier for boys) and Gary is hoping to go with Samantha but will come even if he hasn't got a date. Chris told me that as far as he knew most of the people who left early in fifth year are coming as there hadn't been a fifth year prom so this will be their last and only chance to meet up with everyone from school.

The thought made me sad somehow.

Chris must have picked up on my mood. 'What's wrong, Kelly Ann?'

I sighed. 'Don't know. Just feels like everything familiar is going to change for ever and there's nothing anyone can do to stop it.'

'Well, some changes are inevitable.' Chris smiled. 'You can't stay in school all your life repeating your maths Higher.'

'Thank God for that. I definitely won't miss maths,' I laughed.

'But other things won't ever change. Like how I feel about you, for example.' He put his palm on my cheek, tilted my face up to his and kissed me. 'Nothing and no one could ever change that.'

My face burned with guilt. Even though I'd done nothing.

'You OK?' Chris asked.

'Yeah, yeah course I am. Why wouldn't I be?'

'No reason. It's just that you've seemed different recently. Preoccupied. Are you worried about something? Maybe I could help.'

Oh God. Chris has always been my best friend as well as my boyfriend. How I wished I could talk to him about how I feel, but he's the last person I can confide in now.

'No it's nothing,' I said. 'Just, um, my prom dress. I'll need to look for something soon.'

Chris dropped me off at school. 'Want me to pick you up again at two?' he offered.

'No, it's OK. I might hang around for a bit afterwards anyway.'

Actually I'd no intention of staying. Just didn't want to be with Chris too much until I'd sorted out how I felt about Matt and why I was so restless all of a sudden. Already Chris seems to sense there is something wrong so I thought it would be safest to keep a distance for a while in case I give too much away.

Most of the two hours was spent on large group scenes so I hardly talked to Matt at all during rehearsal but when it was over he walked with me out through the car park towards the school gates.

When we got to his motorbike he climbed on and said, 'Hey, it's only two o'clock, why don't we go for a ride somewhere?'

This was the last thing I needed now. 'No thanks, Matt, I've got stuff to do.'

Matt raised a sceptical eyebrow. 'Studying? The exams are over remember.'

'No, just, well, things to do. Important stuff.'

'What could be more important than enjoying yourself?'

'No really I'm too busy—'

Heard a voice behind us. 'She said no.'

Chris. Oh my God. And he didn't sound happy.

Matt seemed to understand this too. He raised his hands, palms out. 'No worries. It's cool. See you, Kelly Ann.' He pulled on his helmet and roared off.

'I thought I told you to steer clear of him,' Chris said.

'You didn't *tell* me anything. You asked. What are you doing here anyway? Checking up on me?'

'No, of course not.'

'So why are you here?'

'Just, well, I wanted to see you and . . . I don't know . . . you've been odd lately. Distant. I wondered if, you know, you were keeping something from me. Something important.'

'So you *were* checking up on me.'

'No. I . . . I trust you. I was just worried that's all.' He paused and his expression hardened. 'But I don't trust Matt. He and his friends can't seem to take no for an answer. And I don't like the way he looks at you.'

'What do you mean how he looks at me?'

'Well, you know, like he finds you attractive. Like he'd want to . . . well, not that I blame him for that.' He gazed at me. 'You're beautiful, Kelly Ann. What guy wouldn't find you attractive? But you're right. I'm being stupid. I shouldn't be jealous. I'm the lucky guy you belong to after all.'

So Chris thinks Matt finds me attractive. And guys could probably tell that kind of thing. Felt elated and guilty. My life was so much simpler before Matt came along.

WEDNESDAY MAY 29TH

Went into school even though there was no rehearsal scheduled today as most of the sixth years who are still around have arranged to meet in the common room for the last time. Next month fifth years will be starting their new timetable and it will probably be impossible to keep them out of our room.

We played pool and Monopoly then just sat around and chatted for a while. Someone had brought fairy cakes they'd baked in the home economics kitchen and then we watched video clips of *Dirty Dancing*, my favourite film ever, which also had the effect of getting rid of any guys.

Afterwards talk turned to girlie stuff like how we were going to wear our hair at the prom, whether luscious mascara really thickens lashes by up to seven times and what uni had the fittest guys, Strathclyde or Glasgow. Strathclyde was eventually voted best after a heated debate and much internet searching of images of freshers' week.

'Sod it,' I said laughing. 'Why don't career teachers warn you? If I'd known that I'd never have put Glasgow as my first choice.'

'Yeah me too,' Rebecca giggled. 'But it doesn't matter that much to you does it, Kelly Ann? I mean, you've got Chris.'

So I had. So I wouldn't be checking out the talent, getting plastered and snogging random guys during freshers' week like I'd just seen on YouTube. I would be having a few drinks then most probably meeting Chris and going to the cinema or something. Maybe even just going home to make a start on studying the course books I'd bought. Fun stuff like that. 'Well I can always look,' I said, sounding like someone's granny.

'You're so lucky,' Rebecca said, meaning it. 'Chris is a fantastic guy and he's perfect for you. Must be nice to have found your ideal match already.'

'Yeah, he's great,' I agreed. But I wasn't so sure about the *already* bit. Sometimes I wish I'd found Chris a bit later. Might have been nice to have gone out with a few more people before meeting my ideal match. Even if they weren't perfect for me. Even if they were maybe a bit dangerous, perhaps.

THURSDAY MAY 30TH

In school for another rehearsal today. Afterwards Matt asked again if I'd like to go for a ride. I told him no thanks.

'What's the matter – don't you trust me, Kelly Ann?' he asked.

'Of course I trust you.'

He stared deeply into my eyes. 'Don't.'

Chris called. 'Remember the surprise I told you about? I'll pick you up tomorrow. One o'clock.'

Oh God, I'd forgotten about that. 'Aren't you going to tell me what it is? What if I don't like it?'

'You will. Trust me.'

Wish people would stop talking in mysterious riddles and just say what they mean.

Stephanie called. 'Dave and I just got back. Amazing holiday. Weather was crap but we never left the hotel anyway. Stayed in our room and shagged all week.' And she went into more detail. Wish Stephanie was a bit more mysterious sometimes.

FRIDAY MAY 31 ST

It took less than two minutes for the letting-agency rep to show us around the small apartment. It had one bedroom, a living-room-cum-kitchen area combined and a bathroom. The furniture was modern and in good condition compared to his last flat.

Chris grinned at me. 'What do you think?'

It was clear from his expression that he was really excited about it, so I tried my best to be enthusiastic. 'Yeah it's nice and, um, clean but I'm not sure. I know Gary and the rest of them can be pains but, well, won't you be a bit lonely living by yourself like this? And it's dearer too.'

'But I won't be living by myself. It's for us of course.'

'*For us?* Chris, I already told you there's no way I can afford to live away from home.'

'You can if I pay the rent. Remember the trust fund for my eighteenth? Well it finally got released and it means I can afford this flat for both of us. So what do you think?' He was looking at me expectantly, his expression proud and animated like he'd just given me the best present ever. Instead of my worst nightmare.

'*No!*' It was almost a scream and took us both by surprise. I flushed. Tried to get a hold on my rising panic. 'I mean, no I . . . I don't want this.'

'You don't like it?' Chris said, obviously deflated. But he forced a smile and went on. 'Well, OK, we can look at others. I'm sure we'll find something—'

'No, you don't understand. I don't want to look at any more flats. I . . . I don't want to live with you.'

'You don't want to live with me?' Chris said, puzzled. 'But why not? This means we can be together all the time. Just the two of us. I thought that's what you wanted.'

I sighed. 'That's what *you* want. Not me.'

Chris was silent for a while, studying my face as though looking for an answer there. 'What *do* you want then?' he said slowly.

I hesitated. Chris wasn't just asking about living together or not. We both knew it was more serious than that. He was talking about us. 'I don't know.'

'You don't know? But you must know. I mean, do you want to break up or something?'

'No. Well, yeah. In a way. Maybe . . . just for a while.'

'For a while!'

'Yeah, you know, a kind of trial separation. See how it feels.'

'Why are you doing this to us, Kelly Ann? Please don't do this. I'm begging you.'

'I'm sorry, Chris. I . . . I just have to. I need to be free. For a while anyway. You're the first proper boyfriend I've ever had and, well, I'm only seventeen.'

'You want to split up so you can date other guys. Is that it?' Chris asked angrily. 'Or is it just one guy? It's Matt isn't it. He's the reason you're doing this.'

'No he isn't. Or not the only reason anyway. I'm just not ready to do the whole *Till death do us part stuff*. I want to be young and single and . . . and not know what the future might hold.' I paused. Looked at his stricken face. 'Oh God, I'm sorry, Chris. I never wanted to hurt you.'

'Hurt me? I feel like you've just ripped out my heart and stomped on it.'

'I'm sorry. If there was any other way—'

'How long?' Chris interrupted.

'What?'

'The trial separation. How long?'

'I, well, I don't know.'

'A week? A month? A year? Make a decision.'

'I . . . I'm not sure.'

'Right. I'll make it then. One month. The night of the prom. But know this. If you sleep with anyone else I won't take you back.'

'That's not fair. I took you back after I found out about Linda. And Amy.'

'That was different. Linda happened before we got together in the first place. And Amy, well, you'd finished with me if you remember.'

'It's not different. Amy, anyway.'

'OK, maybe it's double standards but I just couldn't do it. If you shag anyone I'll never take you back. We'd be finished for good.'

We said nothing after that. Just glared at each other.

'So,' the letting rep said. 'I take it you don't want to look at any other properties today then?'

Oh God. Not sure whether I've done the right thing or not. Maybe this is the start of a new independent and exciting period of my life. On the other hand it might turn out that I've just made a catastrophic mistake which I'll regret until the day I die.

Matt texted: REHEARSAL TOMORROW NIGHT MY PLACE 7PM?

Texted back: Y c u I hesitated then typed x. Pressed send.

SATURDAY JUNE 1 ST

Stephanie and Liz can't believe what I've done.

'I can't believe what you've done, Kelly Ann,' Liz said.

Stephanie closed the catalogue of wedding cakes we'd been scrutinizing in her room, having reluctantly settled on the four tier one with silver-leaf decorations rather than the six-tier model with gold. Stephanie isn't used to economizing.

'Are you really that stupid?' she said. 'I can't believe what you've done.'

'You think I've made a mistake?' I asked.

'Duh,' they both chorused.

Hmm so much for supportive friends. Well, that's not really fair; I know that Liz and Stephanie are super-loyal friends who really care about me. They're just concerned that I might have made a mistake that's all. Or, as Liz put it, a monumentally disastrous error which could ruin my entire future life. At the very least.

Both of them suggested I call Chris and ask him to forget about the month separation thing – put the idea down to PMT or something – but I can't do that. I'd sound weak and stupid. Anyway, I had to find out what I'd been missing by going steady with Chris. Like Matt for instance.

'It's only a month,' I said. 'Maybe by the end of it I'll realize Chris definitely is the one for me and we'll get back together. But I need to know for sure. Need to be free to, um, experiment first.'

'With Matt you mean?' Stephanie said.

'Not just Matt. Lots of things. Like, um, parties and clubbing and stuff.'

Stephanie raised her eyebrows sceptically. 'Bollocks.' Her mobile buzzed. 'It's Dave.' She smiled mischievously. 'I'm going to take this downstairs. We've, er, private stuff to discuss. About the wedding. When I come back I hope Liz will have talked some sense into you.'

Thank God she went out. Overhearing Stephanie's sexy phone calls with Dave could be very embarrassing.

When Stephanie left the room Liz gave me a concerned look. 'What if Chris experiments too?'

'What! Chris wouldn't do that.'

'Why not? He's free as well isn't he?'

'I suppose.'

'And loads of girls fancy Chris.'

'I never noticed anybody trying to pull him.'

'That's because everybody knew he was crazy about you so they'd no chance. But now that he's free . . .'

'You think he'd find someone that quickly?'

Liz shrugged. 'Well, he's intelligent, good at sports, funny, kind, strong, protective, generous and really good-looking. So, nah, you're probably safe. Can't imagine there will be too many girls looking for a boyfriend like that.'

Oh God. But Chris wouldn't be interested would he? I was the one who wanted the break, not him. He'd wait a month for me. I was sure.

Went over to Matt's. Got there at seven p.m. exactly and realized I was too early. For a first date – and I now admitted to myself this was what it was – I should have been at least ten minutes late. Obviously, I wasn't used to dating etiquette any more but hopefully Matt would be too sophisticated to play stupid conventional games like that.

Or maybe not. The door was answered by his dad who told me Matt had gone out but he expected him back shortly and invited me in to wait. I knew it was Matt's dad from the white collar, the fact that he lived in Matt's house and because he told me so. Otherwise I'd never have guessed as he looked nothing like him. He was quite small, maybe just a few inches bigger than me, with grey hair receding at the front and a round pink face.

He was nice though and made me a cup of tea in the kitchen while chatting to me about how I knew his son and the good weather we'd been having. I wanted to call Matt to ask when exactly when he'd be here but thought that might look even more desperately keen than coming on time. After ten minutes though, when I'd finished my tea and Matt's dad had gone off to answer the phone, I was just about to dial him when I heard the door open, and a few seconds later Matt strolled into the kitchen.

He seemed surprised to see me. 'Hey, Kelly Ann, you're early aren't you?'

I was surprised too. He had his arm draped round the shoulders of a girl with long, almost white-blonde hair and a pale pretty face. Like Matt she was dressed all in black: jeans, T-shirt and wrist bands, but a wide silver belt and lots of large silver rings on her fingers broke the monotony. As did the shiny red electric guitar she was carrying.

Maybe he had a sister he'd never told me about. There was a lot, after all, he'd never told me and he hardly ever talked about his family. She didn't look like his sister, of course, but then Matt didn't look like his dad.

Matt noticed me staring at her. 'Oh yeah, this is my girlfriend Marnie. Been on a gap year but got bored and came back early. Marnie, this is Kelly Ann. Friend of mine from school.'

'Well, um, nice to meet you,' I said.

Probably the biggest lie of my entire life.

Matt talked on smoothly as though nothing unusual had happened, and Marnie blabbed away about her travels as she slipped a possessive arm round his waist. I stretched my face into a smile and nodded often, hoping I didn't look how I felt. Totally gutted.

Marnie explained she had been on a gap year and wasn't due back until September but had got 'bored with beaches' and come home early. She hadn't told Matt as she wanted to surprise him. She insisted I stayed and rehearsed the play with Matt. She'd love to watch.

She'd sounded all friendly and warm, even exchanged mobile numbers with me and suggested we meet up sometime, but her cold shark's eyes as she studied me made me feel as welcome as a wart.

My cheeks were getting sore from keeping my fixed grin in place, and anyway I suspected my false smile and the constant nodding was probably making me look slightly retarded. Time to go. I pretended I'd just remembered an incredibly important thing I was supposed to do, that I'd forgotten right up until that very second, and left.

Oh God, I'd risked so much for a chance to go out with Matt and now it was impossible. What had I done?

But I'd other reasons for breaking off with Chris, didn't I? Being free and single would be fun. At least for a while. Wouldn't it?

SUNDAY JUNE 2ND

Liz and Stephanie were really sympathetic when they heard about Marnie and agreed that Matt might have mentioned his rock-chick girlfriend before, but when they tried to persuade me to go back with Chris I refused.

'The trial separation wasn't just about Matt,' I said. 'In fact, it's probably better this way. I can be totally free, single and independent for a while.'

'But who will you shag?' Stephanie asked, all concerned. 'You've never been into casual boyfriends, so what will you do for sex? A month is a long time.'

'And what about the prom?' Liz asked. 'Who's going to be your date?'

'Oh God. I hadn't thought about that.'

'And remember,' Liz warned. 'Chris may find someone else. A month is a long time.'

'Chris will wait for me,' I said confidently. 'I think he will anyway.'

It was a sunny day so Liz suggested a stroll in the park and an ice cream by the pond.

'You're not going to try to eat it with chopsticks are you, Liz?' I warned.

'Of course not. Well, maybe just the chocolate flake bit.'

I'd just bought my ice cream and taken the first lick when an enormous Great Dane broke free from its owner and galloped towards me. I froze and stared at the thing in horror. Should I make a run for it or try to fight it off? Both seemed ludicrously impossible. Before I could decide, Titan bounded up and put his front paws on my shoulder knocking me to the ground and my ice cream into the pond.

If you've never had your entire face licked by a Great Dane's tongue I can tell you it's not a great experience. Also a dog's breath smells disgusting. However, it is, on balance, better than having your face *eaten* by a Great Dane which is what I'd thought was going to happen. Obviously Titan remembered me and must have liked me. Problem was, his enthusiastic greeting was practically crushing the life out of me.

Liz and Stephanie tried to pull Titan off without success, partly because they were still trying to hang on to their ice creams and, in Liz's case, still licking it.

The owner, when she eventually arrived, wasn't much better. Just lightly tugged on the dog's leash, while gently remonstrating with it. 'Oh, Titan, you naughty boy. Yes, I know you're just trying to be affectionate but you don't know your own strength, you silly thing.'

This wasn't the most dignified way to run into your sort of ex-boyfriend (at least temporarily anyway) but honestly I was relieved to see Chris, Gary and Ian heading towards us en route to the five-a-side football pitch. Maybe between the three of them they could drag Titan off me.

Or maybe not. Titan looked up and snarled menacingly before returning to his task of washing my face while keeping a cautious eye on them.

'Oh dear, don't come near. I'm afraid Titan doesn't like boys,' his owner said.

Ian backed away. Some friend! But to be fair I remember his mum saying he's been scared of dogs since a terrier bit him when he was seven.

Gary tried throwing a stick for Titan to fetch but the dog ignored it.

Chris picked up a stick too and I thought he was going to do the same thing as Gary but instead he slid it under Titan's chain collar and quickly twisted the stick until the chain tightened around the dog's throat, choking him. A firm yank on the collar pulled Titan off me and I scrambled to my feet. Chris untwisted the stick a few turns which loosened the collar a bit, then ordered the dog to sit in a kind of stern policeman's voice. Titan obeyed. Chris talked firmly but soothingly to the dog in a low voice for a while until he was sure it was calm. Finally he dropped the stick, and gave Titan a pat. 'Good boy.' He turned to me. 'You OK?'

'Um, yeah. Thanks. That was, well, quite impressive really.'

But Titan's owner wasn't impressed. She was furious. 'You shouldn't have done that,' she spat. 'You could have choked my Titan.'

Chris glared at her. 'And you shouldn't keep an animal you can't control.'

'I beg your pardon!'

'You heard me.'

She looked for a moment as though she was going to argue some more but thought the better of it and hurried off muttering something about young people these days.

We all stared at Chris. It wasn't like him to be so bad-mannered.

He stared back, then without another word jogged off to the pitch.

'He's been like this since you two broke up,' Gary moaned. 'Grumpy as a giraffe with a sore throat. Why *did* you split anyway? Chris won't say.'

'That's because it's none of your business.'

'OK, OK. Don't bite my head off. Bloody hell, you're as bad as he is. I've a good mind not to invite either of you to my party on Friday.'

'What party?' Liz and Stephanie chorused.

'A party at my house to celebrate my parents' wedding anniversary.'

'Oh, um, that's nice,' I said, politely, 'but I don't think—'

'They won't be there of course,' Gary continued. 'They're having dinner at a hotel in Perth and staying overnight. However I thought it my duty to raise a glass or two to them in their absence.'

Liz grinned. 'Sounds good but I'm not sure Julian can make it. He's—'

'Great. Come without him. We're really short of girls. You too, Stephanie. I'm sure you could do without Dave for one night.'

'Bollocks. There are always way too many girls at your dos and never enough fit guys,' Stephanie said. 'But, OK, if you're going, Kelly Ann?' She turned to look at me. 'The three of us might have a laugh.'

'I'm not sure,' I said. 'Could be awkward with Chris there.'

'Bollocks,' Stephanie said.

After a bit of argument I agreed to go along. I suspected that they were all hoping that Chris and I would get together again at the party but I was determined this wasn't going to happen until the month was up. I needed to be sure, or as sure as I could be anyway, that I wasn't missing out on anything by being with Chris who I've known practically all my life. But yeah, it might be nice to see Chris again at Gary's party. Just to chat to him or maybe have a dance or something. I did miss him so much. And I had to admit he'd looked quite fit jogging off in his footballer's gear.

FRIDAY JUNE 7TH

Just as Stephanie had predicted, Gary's party was hoaching with nice-looking girls. There were only a couple of fit, available guys who were, of course, constantly surrounded by girls trying to pull them. The only girls they showed any interest in however were Liz and Stephanie i.e. the only two at the party who were not actually single. Typical.

No one showed any interest in me except for one guy called Bobby who had large, sticky-out ears the size of satellite dishes, cross-eyes which both seemed to be focussed on his tiny-flattened piggy nose, and breath smellier than Titan's. Nor was he one of those ugly guys with a great personality and fantastic sense of humour that you might consider dating if face-transplant technology improves and he can be persuaded to go for one. No, he droned on incessantly about his hobbies – making papier-mâché aeroplanes which don't fly and collecting 'interesting' bus schedules from around Europe, although he's never travelled outside Glasgow. And he wouldn't take a hint. Followed me around for most of the night even though I made it totally obvious I wasn't interested. Thank God the music was so loud I couldn't make out most of the boring stuff he was on about.

Yet I'd heard that this guy was single only because he'd dumped his girlfriend last week. She's gutted and wants him back. It's so depressing. I can't imagine any girl desperate enough to want a guy like that. But I've been told she's quite OK looking and really nice. Normal anyway. Bloody hell, maybe Liz is right and I shouldn't have split with Chris. Judging by tonight there doesn't seem to be a lot of talent out there.

I kept looking for Chris, but by twelve o'clock he still hadn't showed and I was about to give up and go home when I heard his voice in the hall. Felt a little twist of excitement in my stomach the way I used to when we first started dating and my eyes fixed on the door waiting for him.

But the first person I saw was a tall, slim girl with honey-blonde hair and long legs that seemed to go all the way up to her armpits. Just behind her was Chris, only a few inches taller than the blonde, with his hands resting lightly on her hips.

I hoped at first that she was a platonic friend – maybe a study buddy I hadn't heard about – but when she twisted round and kissed him on the mouth I had to admit she was probably a girlfriend. Can't believe he's done this. But maybe it's what I deserved.

Liz had warned me Chris would have no bother getting another girlfriend and she was right. He'd found someone else already, and she was stunning. What if he prefers her to me? Falls in love with her. That couldn't happen, could it? Not in just one month.

I was still staring open-mouthed at the pair of them when Chris noticed me and gave me a nod of recognition.

I looked away quickly. Turned and gave a false, bright smile to Bobby, my constant companion of the night. 'So, tell me more about your bus-schedule collection.' Unfortunately the loud music that had been playing up until this point stopped abruptly and everyone looked over to see who was shouting this naff comment.

Bobbie frowned. 'Look, Kelly Ann,' he shouted loudly back at me. 'It's been nice talking to you but I think I may have given you the wrong idea. So, um, no offence but, you know, the chemistry just isn't there for me.'

He walked off shaking his big-eared head and rolling his cross-eyes (asymmetrically) like I'd been stalking him all night and he'd just managed to wriggle free.

Most people who say they've never been so insulted in their life are lying. Not me. I'd have remembered. Definitely.

Just wanted the floor to open up and swallow me, or alternatively just wanted the floor to open up so I could push that big-eared, cross-eyed arrogant moron into it. And Chris's blonde girlfriend too.

I stayed on at the party just long enough to show that I wasn't leaving because Bobby had totally humiliated me or because Chris had turned up with a gorgeous blonde girlfriend and I was jealous. Which I wasn't, of course. Liz and Stephanie didn't want to go and tried to persuade me to stay but I couldn't take any more.

Gary said I should get a taxi back but there was no way I was paying for that when my home was just ten minutes walk away.

However, Ian offered to walk with me and though I told him he didn't have to, I'd be fine, he insisted so I let him. Thought it was nice of him to bother especially as it meant dragging himself away from Valerie and a party awash with alcohol and told him so when we got to my house. 'Thanks, Ian.'

Ian shrugged his massive shoulders. 'It was no bother, Kelly Ann. Anyway Chris asked me to see you home. Make sure you didn't get mugged or anything.'

This was typical of Chris. Even though we'd split and he'd already found himself another girlfriend he was still trying to control my life. 'He'd no right to that,' I fumed. 'I don't need anyone to look after me.'

Ian shook his head. 'Chris said you do need looking after.' He smiled. 'Said you'd as much sense as a turkey looking forward to Christmas.'

'Chris should mind his own business.'

'C'mon, Kelly Ann, don't get mad at him. He just cares about you that's all. Worries about you.'

And suddenly I wasn't mad any more. It was true. Chris must still care about me. Think about me. Felt tears sting my eyes and I turned my face away so Ian wouldn't see.

'You know Chris,' Ian went on. 'Always had a soft spot for people too weak or daft to look after themselves.'

Was so mad I punched Ian on the nose. Had to jump up to do it because of his height and the punch didn't land as hard as I'd have liked but it did make him wince at least.

Ian rubbed his nose. 'Christ that was sore, Kelly Ann,' he said admiringly.

'Sorry, but you asked for it.'

'Hmm, well, for what it's worth, we were wrong about you. You've no need of protecting.' He shook his head as he turned to go back to Gary's place. 'Bloody hell, why is it always the little ones that are so sodding vicious?'

SATURDAY JUNE 8TH

Liz phoned me this afternoon with gossip about the party and information about Chris's new girlfriend, Jade. None of it was good news. For me anyway. She offered to come round and give me more details, plus counselling if necessary.

But I didn't want any more details, and I'd rather put my head in a mincer than be counselled on my failed love life by Liz, so I just told her maybe later and hung up before she could say *You're in denial again, Kelly Ann*.

But afterwards I couldn't stop thinking about Chris

and Jade. Picturing the two of them together; chatting, holding hands, snogging. Liz had told me Jade's got a flat which she's keeping on over the summer as her parents are loaded. Had he been to her flat yet? Seen her bedroom? Maybe even . . . No, Chris wouldn't do *that* to me, would he? Not yet anyway. He'd wait until the month was up at least.

Hmm. Or then again maybe not. Jade was a really fantastic-looking girl and Chris was just a guy. How long could he resist her? A month might be too risky.

In a panic I reached for my mobile and almost dialled him, but stopped myself in time. How pathetic would it look if I called Chris this soon and asked to go back with him? Would he ever respect me again? And what if he refused? I'd never live down the humiliation. No, I'd keep to our agreed time. Savour being free, single and independent. Enjoy myself. Even if enjoying myself hadn't seemed like much fun lately.

I put my mobile firmly back in my pocket but had to take it out again as it rang almost immediately. Had a mad notion it might have been Chris begging me to drop this stupid separation thing and get back with him but it was Gary who asked me to come over as he'd something urgent and important to discuss with me.

'What about?' I asked, annoyed and intrigued.

'Come over and you'll find out.' Then he hung up.

When I called him back it went straight to answer

phone. Should have stayed put but curiosity got the better of me as Gary knew it would.

'Knew you'd come,' Gary grinned at me as he ushered me inside.

The place was a tip. Worse than Liz's room at its worst, which I'd have thought impossible until I saw it with my own eyes. It looked as though several tribes of hungry, drunken baboons had invaded the place and laid waste to it.

There were dozens of lager cans scattered on the floor, some seeping, ash-polluted sticky liquid. Part-chewed sausage rolls, pizza and tuna sandwiches were every-where – trodden into the carpet, mashed onto chairs, sofa, cushions and even (the extra-cheesy pizza with pepperoni) congealed on the window.

There were a couple of empty plastic tomato-sauce bottles and a can of shaving cream, also empty, which probably explained how pink frothy slogans and draw-ings had appeared on the walls and ceiling. Don't ask, but they'd definitely been done by guys.

And of course the whole place stank of beer, whisky, stale sweat and tobacco smoke with a hint of vomit.

'For God's sake, Gary. Haven't you at least started to clear up yet?'

'The party only ended half an hour ago. It might have ruined the atmosphere if I'd started hoovering while people were still here.'

'When are your parents due back?'

Gary shrugged. 'Not for a couple of hours.'

'*A couple of hours!*' I tore off my jacket and dropped it on the least dirty bit of chair I could find (although it would still need washing when I got home) then ran into the kitchen to grab a bin bag and cleaning stuff. Oh God. Incredible as it sounds it was worse than the living room. Well, Gary could start in there.

When I returned to the living room I ran around frantically grabbing armfuls of rubbish and shoving them into an enormous black bin bag. Then I stopped. Gary had put on Sky Sports and was sitting on a chair watching the football.

'What do you think you're doing?' I screamed.

'It's just the last ten minutes. Unless it goes to extra time. I'll help you out after that. I promise.'

I dropped the bag on his lap and switched off the TV. 'You'll help *me* out?'

Gary got up. 'OK, OK, I'll start now.'

'Wait a minute.' I grabbed my jacket. 'This is why you wanted me over isn't it? To help you clear up. Nothing to do with discussing anything. Well, that's it. I'm off.'

'No wait, Kelly Ann! I really did want to talk to you. It's about Chris.'

I put my jacket back down. 'What about Chris?'

'Well, I think you should ask him back. He's really suffering, you know.'

'Didn't look like he was suffering last night.'

'Oh, Jade, you mean. I'm sure she's just some blonde bimbo he's seeing to help dull the pain temporarily.'

'Liz told me she's an astrophysics student.'

'Is she? Hmm must be pretty bright then. But brainy girls who spend all their time in a library can be pretty boring.'

'Her hobbies are windsurfing, white-water rafting and parkour.'

'Parkour?' Gary said, unable to hide his admiration. 'Never knew any girls who liked extreme urban gymnastics. She really jumps roof to roof and summersaults over bridges and stuff like that?'

'Yeah she parkoured all over the west end of Glasgow in a bikini last summer for charity. Raised £10,000 for the sick-children's hospital.'

'In a bikini? God, I'd like to have seen that.' He paused, no doubt to imagine Jade parkouring half-naked as he was smiling stupidly. However, when he noticed me scowling at him he quickly continued, 'But, anyway, I'm sure there's still lots of assets you have that she doesn't.'

'Like what?'

He thought for a while. Quite a long while. 'Your bum.'

'My what?!'

'Yeah, you've got a much better bum than she has. You might not know this but you were voted rear of the year twice at school. Won by a landslide each time.'

'And that's it?'

'All I can think of for now,' Gary admitted.

I handed him a bin bag. 'I'll do the living room. You start in the kitchen. And remember I am definitely not cleaning the toilet.'

He took the bag. 'Chris still loves you, Kelly Ann. Why don't you make the first move? Ask him back.'

Felt tears well in my eyes and tried to blink them away. 'I just can't, Gary. I can't.'

Gary put his arms round my shoulders and gave me a hug. 'Don't cry, Kelly Ann. I really will clean the toilet. I promise.'

I broke free of him, gave him a gentle slap and smiled. 'Idiot.'

I turned away and got on with picking up the rubbish from the floor. Bent down to get some cans stuck underneath the sofa. When I got up I noticed Gary hadn't gone yet but was standing at the door looking at me.

'What are you waiting for? We'll never get the place done in time for your parents getting back at this rate.'

'I was just thinking,' Gary said, 'that you really underestimate the power of a nice bum.'

Threw the lager cans at him but missed.

I wasn't really annoyed with Gary. It's impossible to be mad at him for long and he always makes me laugh. I didn't really mind cleaning up either as it helped stop me thinking too much about Chris and Jade. Or Matt and Marnie.

Somehow Gary and I managed to get the place reasonably cleared before his parents got back although we had to quickly emulsion one living-room wall and there is still a faint pink drawing of a pair of boobs on the ceiling.

'Thanks, Kelly Ann.' Gary said. 'Oh and by the way don't worry about Bobby knocking you back in public last night.'

I flushed at the memory. 'He didn't knock me back. *Ugh*. You don't really think I fancied him, did you?'

'Course not. It's just his ploy. Home in on the nicest-looking girl at the party then make it look like you're turning her down. Other girls start thinking there must be something special about a guy who knocks back a girl like that so . . . It's worked a few times for him. I'm thinking of trying it myself.'

I smiled. 'Thanks, Gary. You know, that's the first real compliment you've ever given me. I don't count the good bum.'

'You should.'

When I finally got back I called Liz and Stephanie to see if they wanted to do anything tonight but they were both out with their boyfriends. Julian and Liz. Stephanie and Dave. Everybody seemed to be in happy couples except for me. But I'd wanted to be free and single, hadn't

I? I stayed in and watched a repeat of *Friends* on TV. Wish being single was as exciting as that.

MONDAY JUNE 1OTH

Mrs Kennedy had to stage the rehearsal after school this time as she was busy with regular classes all day. Matt turned up but, like last week, we didn't rehearse any bits with both of us in the scene so I hardly spoke to him at all. Afterwards I hurried off ignoring him.

When I got back home he was waiting outside my house on his bike. 'What are you doing here?' I asked.

He smiled. 'Waiting for you.'

I scowled. 'Isn't your girlfriend annoyed about that?'

'Why would she be?' he asked, sounding genuinely puzzled.

Oh God, Matt obviously hasn't ever been interested in me at all. At least not in that way. He just saw me as a friend, so why should his girlfriend be annoyed? And he'd probably no idea I fancied him either. Wanted to make sure he never found out how I'd really felt.

'No reason, I suppose,' I said, trying to sound casual. 'It's just, you know, with her being away a long while and only getting back a week or so ago, I imagined she'd want to spend loads of time with you.'

'Marnie's not like that. She's, you know, kind of a free

spirit. Like me. Neither of us believes in crowding one another. Shit like that. We like to give each other plenty of space.'

'Oh, right, well that's fine. Yeah, I'm like that too.'

'Good. It's just that you've been giving me an awful lot of space since last Saturday. I got the impression that you were maybe pissed off with me.'

'God, no, why would I be?'

He shrugged. 'Don't know but you seemed kind of upset about Marnie. Maybe even j—'

'Of course not,' I interrupted. 'Just surprised that's all. I mean you never mentioned her before.'

'You never asked.'

'And, um, she's blonde. I thought you didn't like blondes.'

'I never said that.'

'Yeah you did.'

He shook his head. 'I said, I prefer brunettes. Not that I didn't like blondes. Besides Marnie has a lot of other things going for her. She's very talented you know.'

'Yeah, must be nice to have a girlfriend who plays the guitar too. Common interests.'

He laughed. 'Oh she's shit on the guitar. That wasn't the kind of talent I was talking about. Anyway, since you're not bothered about Marnie, you know, jealous or any of that bullshit—'

'Course not!' I laughed. Too loudly.

'And she's cool about you, so there's no reason why we can't meet up, say tomorrow night my place, and we can have that rehearsal we missed out on.'

'Yeah cool.'

'Great. Seven OK for you?'

'Yeah seven's fine.'

He gave me one of his dark meaningful stares. 'I really do prefer brunettes you know.'

TUESDAY JUNE 11TH

Went over to Matt's about seven. Well, quarter past seven, actually. Not that it was a date or anything but I didn't want to be forced to wait for Matt again.

I pressed the bell and Matt answered right away. He smiled. 'You're late. I was worried you'd chickened out.'

'Oh am I? Sorry I've been so busy today.'

He ushered me in. 'Doing what?' he asked.

'Oh this and that,' I said vaguely. 'You know how it is. So, is your dad in tonight?'

'No, he'll be away all night so we've got the place to ourselves. No one to interrupt us.'

My throat felt suddenly dry. 'Oh, um, right. Well, it won't take long.'

'No point rushing.' He opened the door to the kitchen. 'I've got nothing else planned so I'm yours for the night.'

He took two bottles of Pilsner from the fridge. 'Want a beer?'

'No thanks.'

He put them both back. 'So where do you want to do this? Living room? Or my bedroom maybe? More comfortable probably.'

'Living room,' I said firmly.

He gave me an amused smile, led the way to the living room and sat on the sofa.

I sat opposite him and pulled the script from my bag. 'Right, where should we start,' I said, briskly.

'What about our first kiss? We've only done that once. I think it needs some work.'

'Mrs Kennedy said it was fine.'

'Mrs Kennedy doesn't know how much better I could do it.' He fixed me with that annoying amused smile again. 'Neither do you.'

I blushed. 'Look, Matt I . . . I think I should go now.'

'Why? You don't think I'm using this as an excuse to jump on you do you? Like I'm some kind of sex pest.'

'Oh God, no, of course not. I wouldn't—'

'OK, so let's rehearse. That's what we're here for, isn't it?'

He stood and crossed over to stand in front of me. Took hold of my hands.

I let go of the script and got up too.

'So,' Matt said in a low, sexy voice. 'First we hold

hands and stare deeply into each others eyes. That's it. Now I look down at your lips. Let my gaze linger there for a while. Now I look into your eyes again. Your eyes say *yes* you want to be kissed. But first I put one hand on your cheek like . . . this. And the other round your waist like . . . that. And now I pull you gently closer to my body. You stand on tiptoe reaching for me and I lean down until my lips gently brush yours. Like that. And then . . .'

We 'rehearsed' for a good five minutes longer than the scene needed. But when Matt manoeuvred me on to the sofa and pressed himself down on top of me I pushed him away. 'Stop!'

He let go of me immediately. 'What's wrong?'

I got off the sofa, picked up my bag and stuffed the unused script into it. 'This is wrong. You've got a girlfriend.'

'So?'

'So it's cheating.'

He laughed. 'Cheating's for kids. Marnie doesn't mind me seeing other people. We're not into this whole exclusive-relationship conventional bullshit.'

'You mean she doesn't care if you cheat?'

'It's not cheating if you're honest about it.' He stood up, reached for my hands again and leaned towards me. 'So, want to rehearse some more?'

Not sure whether or not I would have settled for a part-share of a boyfriend, even if he is the most amazing guy I'd ever met, as before I got time to think about it a rock with a note attached crashed through the large bow windows and landed about six centimetres from our feet.

I gawped at it for a few seconds, too stunned to react, but then looked outside and saw a red-faced Marnie sitting astride her motorbike shaking a fist in the air.

Matt picked up the rock, removed the note which had been attached by a black hair band and read it. He handed it to me. 'I believe this is meant for you.'

Written in red lipstick a single word. *SLUT*.

We managed to dive out of the way before the second rock crashed through. I looked up just in time to see Marnie make a very unfriendly gesture before roaring off on her bike.

Matt was reading the second note. It had, in red lipstick again, *BASTARD*.

Matt said, 'I believe this one is for me.'

FRIDAY JUNE 14TH

Matt has admitted he might have been wrong about Marnie as she obviously has more conventional views on relationships than he'd thought. She's called him and apologized for the broken windows but warned him to keep away from me. However he's dumped her as he says he was getting bored with her anyway.

So at last it's happened. Matt is my boyfriend. Don't know exactly what the future holds for me now but with Matt it's bound to be exciting, surprising and maybe just a bit scary. Can't wait.

SATURDAY JUNE 15TH

My first argument with Matt. He suggested going for a bike ride 'somewhere up north' this afternoon but I told him I needed to shop for a prom dress.

'You're not going to the school prom are you?' he said in an amused, superior voice.

'Well, um, yeah. Of course. I am now anyway. You're going too aren't you? With me I mean?'

'Sorry, Kelly Ann. Not my thing. But you go. Enjoy.'

'I can't go on my own!'

'Of course you can. You can do anything you like.'

'But I don't want to go on my own.'

He shrugged. 'Suit yourself.'

'I'll pay the extra for you,' I offered desperately.

'It's not the money. Just the whole prom thing. Not my scene.'

So annoying. I mean a boyfriend who won't go to a graduation prom with you? It's practically against the law. Or should be anyway.

Eventually after a lot of pleading Matt agreed to go with me but he wasn't dressing up 'in some monkey suit or hiring a naff limo'.

It would have to do.

Liz and Stephanie can't believe I've left it this late to buy a prom dress.

'There will be practically nothing left in the shops by this time,' Stephanie warned.

'You'll be lucky to find something even half decent by now,' Liz said.

The very first dress I tried on was perfect. A red floaty thing which fitted me exactly and looked fabulous. Not only that, but it came with matching long gloves and had been reduced to half price. Now I know Liz and Stephanie are the best, most loyal and caring friends anyone could ever have, but I think they were a bit annoyed that their dire predictions were proved so completely wrong.

'You'll never find heels to match,' Stephanie huffed.

'Have you even thought about what you're doing with your hair yet?' Liz grumbled.

But I didn't care about their grumpy moods because tonight I was meeting Matt for our very first proper date.

We were supposed to go hear one of Matt's favourite live bands playing in Ashton Lane but I stupidly forgot my fake ID and we got knocked back. Matt wasn't really annoyed though. 'We'll just go back to my place, have a few beers and chill,' he said.

Suited me. Except for the beer. I've never understood how guys can enjoy drinking something that smells so awful.

But when we got back I was a bit disappointed that Matt's dad was in. No reason why he shouldn't be. It's his house after all. It's just I got the impression he was out a lot and I kind of hoped he wouldn't be there tonight. But when we went into the kitchen he was sitting there drinking tea and reading the paper.

His dad smiled at me, offered me a cup of tea and tried to start a conversation but Matt just grunted, 'We're going upstairs.' Then he took a beer and Coke from the fridge and ushered me quickly up to his bedroom.

Felt a bit nervous at first to be in a guy's bedroom that wasn't Chris's. Matt put on some nice relaxing music and we just sat on his bed for a while chatting about favourite bands, films, holidays we'd been on. Usual stuff. I liked that he hadn't tried to snog me right away like most guys would the first time they get a girl in their bedroom. In fact, it was me who made the first move. I wrapped my arms around his neck and kissed him long and slow without having to pretend I was playing a part. And with no guilt about cheating.

It was nice, but somehow not as exciting as when I had

to pretend I was playing a part and felt guilty about cheating. Suppose Liz could explain it to me if I was ever stupid enough to ask her. Perish the thought.

We drew apart and Matt smiled at me. Then he took off his T-shirt and started to unzip his trousers.

I sprang up from the bed. 'What do you think you're doing?!'

He seemed puzzled. 'Getting undressed. What's the matter? Oh, I get it. Sorry.' He took his hand from his zip, sat on the edge of the bed and started peeling off his socks. 'Pretty uncool not taking my socks off first.'

'No, stop it! Your dad's downstairs.'

He stopped. Looked up at me with an amused smile. 'Well, I take it you don't expect me to invite him up? Look, don't worry, we'll keep the music on. He won't hear anything.'

'No.'

He frowned. 'What's wrong?'

'It's . . . it's too soon. This is only our first proper date.'

He sighed. 'I was kind of hoping for an *improper* date. But seriously, I don't get it. We've known each other a while now. We fancy each other. What's your problem? It's not as though you've never done this before.'

'Yeah, but I haven't done it with you before.'

'And your point is?'

Wasn't sure what my point was. It just seemed like such a big step. Especially as I knew it would mean giving up any thought of ever getting back with Chris. My first time with Matt would have to be totally romantic. Perfect. So I would know I'd made the right decision. Maybe after the prom when I'm wearing my red dress and he's ... well, OK he's in his usual stuff but it would still be better than this. And no parents around, definitely not. Especially not a minister. Also it's decision date. Yes, the night of the prom would be the right time.

Couldn't explain all this to Matt but he seemed to accept that after the prom and no parents were the important points.

'Hey prom it is. At least it will give me something to look forward to after all the shit.'

SUNDAY JUNE 16TH

Have told mum and Dad about matt. They didn't even realize that Chris and I had split which just goes to show how much attention they pay to me – although usually that's a good thing.

Dad especially is not pleased and he was cool to the point of really rude when Matt came over to see me today.

When Matt left I tackled Dad about it. 'But you're the one who said I was too young for a serious relationship with Chris, Dad. I thought you'd be happy.'

'I just meant for you not to be so serious about Chris. I didn't mean for you to finish with him and take up with this Matt character.'

'He's called Matt. Not This Matt Character.'

'I don't like him.'

'Well I do.'

We argued some more but Dad wouldn't budge. Honestly, just because Matt has a tattoo, rides a bike and plays in a rock band Dad thinks he's some total degenerate into drugs and sex. Which is just so not true. Or not completely true anyway.

MONDAY JUNE 17TH

Was at Matt's house this evening watching a movie in the living room when his dad walked in. He said hello and tried to chat to us for a bit. How had our evening been? What was the movie we were watching?

But Matt cut him dead. 'The movie we're *trying* to watch, you mean?'

I flushed. 'It's OK we can pause it.'

Matt didn't pause it. Just continued to stare at the screen and ignore his dad.

'Matt, pause the—'

'It's OK,' his dad said. 'I was just going upstairs anyway. Hope you enjoy the film.'

When he left I rounded on Matt. 'Why are you so horrible to your dad?'

Matt shrugged. 'He's a loser.'

'How come? Seems OK to me. Really nice actually.'

'Too nice.'

'How do you mean?'

'Guy's got no backbone. Few years after my mother took off she dumped the plumber. Came back to Glasgow. Guess what my dad does?'

'What?'

'Begged her to come back. I heard him on the phone. She turned him down.'

'But that's so sad, Matt. He must have really loved her.'

'*He's* sad you mean. Should have told her to shove it. I've no respect for a guy like that.'

I thought this was really unfair. If he was going to be mad with anyone, it should have been with his mum, but I didn't argue as I'd never seen Matt like this before. Usually he was so laid back he'd make a basking lizard look hyper. Now he seemed about as relaxed as a snarling grizzly.

Instead of trying to defend his dad I asked him about his mum. 'So, have you seen your mum since she got back to Glasgow? Kids usually still see their parents after they get divorced don't they?'

'They're not divorced. I suppose she can't be bothered and he doesn't want to. Like I said. He's a sad loser.'

'But you could still see your mum.'

He shrugged. 'She called me and asked. I told her I wasn't interested.'

'But she's your mum.'

'So what? Look, she decided to disappear without so much as a goodbye. That's cool. Her choice. Doesn't mean she can just drop by again and pick up where she left off. I'm not my dad.'

Hmm, I was wrong about him not being angry with his mum. Wondered why he kept her photo in his room though.

'So why—'

'Kelly Ann, are we going to watch this movie or not?'

'I *am* watching it.'

'Bullshit. We've been talking for the last ten minutes.'

'I can watch and talk. I'm a girl.'

'Yeah right. What's been happening then?'

'The bomb-disposal expert, Lee Rogers, is on his way to the embassy to defuse a bomb which has been planted in the office of the Russian ambassador and is due to explode in fifty-five minutes. But Lee has just found out his wife and kids are being held hostage and the kidnappers want him to reset the timer to go off when the evacuated people go back into the embassy or they'll kill his entire family horribly. Meantime Jennifer, the woman he's having an affair with, has discovered she's pregnant with his baby and has to decide—'

'Jeezus. OK you win. Girls can talk and watch,' Matt said admiringly.

My mobile buzzed. I checked the message while watching the movie.

'Who's that from?' Matt asked.

'Liz, answering the text I just sent her.'

'Christ.' He was silent for a while. Pretty awestruck I think. But then he smiled, pulled me towards him and kissed me. 'So can you concentrate on the movie and do this?'

He kissed me again.

'No,' I lied.

WEDNESDAY JUNE 19TH

There's to be a full dress rehearsal at the theatre tomorrow night so Mrs Kennedy asked us all to come to the drama room after school to try on our costumes. They'd been pretty easy and cheap to make for this play. The guys all wore trackie suits and trainers with caps tilted high on their heads. Most also wore chunky knuckle-duster rings. To make the two gangs recognizably different one wore their trackies tucked into socks while the other didn't.

The girls' costumes consisted of tacky, very skimpy clothes with clanky fake gold chains and huge hooped earrings the size of Wagon Wheel biscuits. The only problem was that I needed a flared skirt to do a lot of my dance numbers and the only skirts available that fitted me were tight lycra. Mrs Kennedy managed to solve the problem by making me a skirt from a length of silky cloth tacked and velcroed together. It looked OK and since the play was only running one night it would do.

The theatre was going to provide us with scenery backdrops so the only other props we needed were fake knives and blood. Also bottles of Bucky and cans of extra-strength lager, which pleased some of the boys, until they discovered Mrs Kennedy had emptied all the alcohol out of them and filled them with water. Typical teacher.

Afterwards we went to the pub and had a laugh about how nedish or tarty we'd looked in our costumes. The truth is though Matt, even wearing a naff black tracksuit, cap and tacky gold rings, had looked sexy. Hmm, maybe I shouldn't wait until after the prom. From what I hear Chris is still going out with Jade anyway. And no wonder. She's super-smart and brilliant at everything. Just like Chris. Jade is much better suited to him than I am. Probably he already knows that and prefers her. I couldn't go back to Chris even if I wanted to. So why should I make Matt wait?

But Matt left early. Said he was meeting Paul about a possible gig in London. I took this as a sign. I'd wait until prom night. The perfect time.

THURSDAY JUNE 20TH

Dress rehearsal at the theatre today was amazing. It was exciting to practise in a real theatre like we were professionals and everyone acted, danced and sang their heart out. Even Matt seemed a bit less laid-back and took his role more seriously than usual. We made it to the end with hardly a mistake, except for Matt's death scene where his fake-blood bag spurted yellow paint instead of oozing red liquid. Don't think this was really a mistake either as Gerry is in charge of props and he's still mad at not getting Matt's role. He's been relegated instead to chorus and – the final insult – understudy for Matt.

Mrs Kennedy has told Gerry this had better not happen Saturday night or he'd be in trouble. I've told Gerry this better not happen Saturday night or he's dead.

Apart from Gerry, the only problem tonight was the news that Matt's band has been offered a gig in London tomorrow night. They've been asked to fill in for a supporting group who had to pull out at the last minute due to them all being arrested for drug possession and suspected dealing.

I know Matt is excited, as the audience is the biggest they've ever had but I was worried. When we got back to his house after the rehearsal I tried to be enthusiastic for him but I couldn't help letting him know how anxious I was. 'Wish you didn't have to go to London the day before our play,' I said.

Matt shrugged. 'Don't worry, I don't need to rehearse any more.' He pointed to his forehead. 'Got it all up here.' He smiled and draped an arm round my shoulder. 'We'll knock 'em dead.'

'But suppose something goes wrong and you don't get back in time.'

He frowned impatiently. 'I told you already. We're gonna leave first thing Saturday morning. I'm going to do most of the driving on the way back and I'll keep my foot on the accelerator the whole way. I'll make it with time to spare. Chill.'

I didn't say anything after that as I've learned he just gets in a bad mood and ignores me. I was rewarded by seeing him smile again then he picked up his guitar and played a medley of my favourite pieces. God, he's just so sexy when he's strumming on his guitar. Could forgive him almost anything then.

SATURDAY JUNE 22ND

It's the morning of the play. My stomach is all twisted in nervous knots. Wish Matt was here to calm me down. He never gets stressed about anything and maybe some of his couldn't-care-less attitude would have rubbed off on me.

As it is I'm stressing about Matt too. I know he said he'd make it back to Glasgow with time to spare but I've texted him four times and called twice but got no answer.

Maybe he's switched off his mobile because he's driving the van but he doesn't usually do that. In fact, even though you're not supposed to, I've seen him take calls while he's on his bike going really fast.

1 2.OO P.M.

Finally got a call from Matt. He said the gig went really well and went on about it for ages. I tried to sound enthusiastic but all I could think about was tonight.

'So where are you now?' I interrupted.

'Oh, still in London. We're just about to hit the road.'

'*Still in London!*' I screeched.

'Yeah. Late night last night. After the gig we got invited to a club by one of the organizers. Free tickets and drinks so a great time but we are all pretty rough this morning.'

'But—'

'Chill. I'll make it OK. Gotta go now. Battery's running low.'

4 P.M.

Text from *Matt*: TRAFFIC BAD. BUT OK C U 8 ISH.

6 P.M.

Text from *Matt*: GOT A FLAT. RUNNING L8. TRY TO STALL.

8:45 P.M.

Mrs Kennedy said we couldn't wait any more. The audience were getting restless and starting to graffiti the theatre. Gerry would have to play Matt's lead role. He was the understudy.

Oh God. Knew Gerry hadn't bothered to learn the lines or anything because he'd been pissed off about not getting a proper role, but Mrs Kennedy wouldn't listen to anyone's objections and said the show had to go on. She'd prompt him from the wings if and when he got a bit stuck.

A bit stuck? He hadn't learned a word so just made it all up and only hummed the songs. It was awful. But the worst was the dancing. He knew none of the moves so just kind of shuffled about the stage waving his arms and bumping into people like a wooden puppet whose strings were being pulled by a drunk.

I'd been dreading the scene where it would be just the two of us dancing and sure enough it was a total disaster.

'Just stand still and let me dance round you,' I hissed. 'If you move anything I swear I'll cut it off.'

Have to say he did exactly as I asked and everything was OK until the end when I launched myself at him and he was supposed to catch me but didn't. Of course I landed flat on my face.

'Sorry but you told me not to move,' Gerry said.

He tried to help me up then but stood on my flared skirt which ripped at the back when he hauled me to my feet exposing my knickers. For the whole of the rest of the play I had to act and dance facing the audience with one hand holding my skirt closed at the back.

It was the longest, most humiliating hour of my life. Needless to add the talent scout didn't sign me.

Mrs Kennedy tried to comfort me afterwards backstage even though she looked mortified too. 'It's not your fault, Kelly Ann. You did your best.'

'No, it's all Gerry's fault. I'll kill him for this,' I fumed. 'Where is he anyway?'

She gave me a tight smile. 'I sent him home in a taxi for his own safety. You're not the only one he annoyed.'

'Won't save him. I know where he lives.'

She frowned. 'Yes, Gerry should have taken his role as understudy more seriously. He let us down. But what about Matt?'

Hmm yeah. What about Matt? He'd rubbished my worries about timing and promised me that he'd make it. But he hadn't. His gig had been a huge success but my big chance had gone for ever. Still, he wasn't responsible for the traffic was he? Or the flat tyre?

'Matt couldn't help it. He . . . well, it was the traffic's fault.'

Even as I said this I couldn't help feeling that Matt should have got everyone to leave London earlier. Or checked the tyres to make sure they were OK before the journey. It was the sort of thing Chris would have done.

Mrs Kennedy raised her eyebrows sceptically as though thinking the same thing but didn't say anything more about Matt. Just told me my parents were waiting outside to take me home.

Liz and Stephanie were there too.

'Don't even think about offering me counselling, Liz,' I warned, as Dad put a comforting arm round my shoulders and guided me along the corridor towards the rear exit.

'Not even a bit of anger management therapy?' Liz asked hopefully.

'Especially not anger management therapy,' I said firmly.

'It wasn't that bad,' Dad said. 'I thought you were really good, love.'

'Your costume was great,' Stephanie offered. 'Well, erm, until it ripped right up the back.'

Mum rolled her eyes impatiently. 'Whole thing was a bloody disaster but for once it's not your fault. Sodding school couldn't organize a piss up in a pub. And if I ever I get my hands on—'

She was interrupted by loud banging and shouting noises coming from the front of the theatre, plus what sounded like dozens of police sirens outside.

Hmm. Don't think the message of the futility of violence has worked somehow. Another failure, like this whole awful night.

SUNDAY JUNE 23RD

According to the local press a brawl broke out in the audience after the play, between people who thought it was total crap and those who thought it was so crap it was sometimes quite funny in parts. The good news is that the fight didn't run along gang lines as people from rival groups fought alongside each other depending on their view of the play. Local community leaders hailed it as progress of a sort.

Even though there were dozens of arrests the only picture in the local papers was one of me showing my knickers. Typical of the standards of the gutter press these days.

Gerry telephoned. Spent half an hour grovelling

and ran out of credit. He's so not off the hook though.

Matt didn't answer my calls but eventually came round about eight to see me. He was very apologetic at first but when I didn't accept his excuses right away, and made it plain I was still mad, he got annoyed. He wasn't responsible for the traffic and the flat tyre for Christ's sake.

I suppose not. But then somehow I didn't think Chris would ever have let me down like that. No matter what. But Chris had always been completely reliable, responsible, and dependable. That was his nature. Matt was the opposite. Unpredictable, impulsive, sometimes reckless. Someone different and dangerous. Exciting. And that's what I'd wanted. Wasn't it?

MONDAY JUNE 24TH

Liz isn't having an eighteenth birthday party because it's too near the prom. Instead she's having a family celebration at home and a piss up with Julian and all her pals at the pub. Stephanie, Dave and I went round to her house at nine. Julian was already there. After opening her presents, Liz ceremoniously burned her false I.D. card before setting off with a wad of money to get legally plastered for the first time.

Except that she hadn't organized a proper I.D. card and no one would serve her or even let us buy drinks for her. And 'no' they would not take her word for it and her 18 today badge was not a legally recognized ID.

It was a pretty subdued eighteenth birthday celebration. For Liz anyway. For me too actually. Matt couldn't come as he was busy with stuff at Paul's. Or so he said. Sometimes I think he can't be bothered with my friends. Gary, Ian and Chris were there. So was Jade looking casually stunning as only really beautiful people can.

She seemed a very nice person too. Talked to everyone and took a real interest in what they had to say. In fact, Jade was so nice I couldn't even dislike her which is very annoying.

Chris and I hardly spoke. It's difficult to believe we only split up less than a month ago. And impossible to think we'd once been so close. Everyone, including me, had thought our relationship was rock solid. Unbreakable. Instead it's been proved more rocky than solid and now it was destroyed beyond repair. We were almost like complete strangers.

The prom night was supposed to be decision time but I realized now it was over really as soon as we split. Maybe earlier. Probably from the day I first set eyes on Matt. Or heard him play guitar. I've betrayed Chris and there's no going back. Chris's future is with Jade or someone just like her. My future is with Matt. I hope.

But why did I feel so miserable?

TUESDAY JUNE 25TH

Only four days now until the prom. And also the first night Matt and I will make love which means I've had to buy nice underwear as well as my prom outfit. Just as well I'll be getting more babysitting work during the summer school holidays.

Have never done it with anyone except for Chris and feel a bit nervous. What if I'm not any good at it but Chris has been too kind to say because he loved me and didn't want to hurt my feelings?

Or maybe Matt will go off me as soon as I sleep with him because he just enjoyed the challenge of trying to get me into bed with him. Like King Henry the Eighth with Anne Boleyn. He was so keen on her that he fell out with the pope and had his best friend executed just so he could divorce his wife and get Anne to have sex with him. But afterwards he slept with other people and sent her to the tower to have her head cut off. Not that Matt would kill me or anything. But he might just dump me afterwards because he was bored. He seems to get bored with people quite easily.

WEDNESDAY JUNE 26TH

Matt says Henry the Eighth dumped Anne Boleyn and had her beheaded because he wanted a son and because he was a murderous megalomaniacal psychopath. I was safe because Matt didn't want any kids, male or female, and beheadings were rare in the UK.

And 'no' he wasn't just interested in me because I hadn't had sex with him. Millions of girls hadn't had sex with him. He'd go so far as to say the majority of females he'd met hadn't had sex with him. That didn't make them interesting. I was random sometimes.

Anyway Matt has told me that his dad, who was supposed to be away this weekend, has cancelled and will be at home the night of the prom. Also Paul is having an all night party on Saturday and Matt wants us to go there after the prom is over. So I suppose it will be a while before Matt and I make love for the first time. Don't know whether I'm bitterly disappointed or relieved. Maybe both. Life is so much more complicated now I'm with Matt.

FRIDAY JUNE 28TH

Last assembly ever. Have always hated assemblies. Boring, pointless waste of time. But this one was different. The very last assembly of my very last day at school.

Even before Mr Smith addressed us I was feeling all sad and emotional but when he started to talk about us leaving school for ever I could feel the tears well in my eyes.

'So,' Mr Smith said, to a hushed hall. 'After today you leave the carefree world of childhood behind for ever and venture out into the real world as young, conscientious adults.'

Loud farting noises from the back of the hall interrupted Mr Smith here. He frowned. Sighed. Waited for the noises and laughing to stop.

'A world of self-discipline, duty and responsibility—'

A helium filled condom balloon with a face drawn on the end, which looked a lot like Mr Smith's bald head, floated gently along the aisle, up onto the stage and rose above Mr Smith's head before he could catch it. It was inscribed with the message 'Goodbye Johnny'. So that's what the J stood for in Mr J Smith. I'd always wondered.

'Right that's it,' Mr Smith said. 'Get lost the lot of you. Go on, get out. And good riddance.'

Charming.

Still, as I made my way to the school gates with Liz for the very last time must admit I was all choked up. Heard someone calling my name and looked back. Mr Simmons.

'Kelly Ann, wait!' he shouted.

I stopped and watched him hurry towards me. My eyes filled with tears.

'Kelly Ann I just wanted to say—'

'I know what you're going to say Mr Simmons and I feel it too.'

'You do?'

'Yes. You're going to say that though we've had our differences over the years, everything you did was for my own good, and that you're really going to miss me,' I sobbed. 'And, you know, I'll . . . I'll miss you too.'

I threw my arms round his shoulders and gave him a hug. It was like hugging a statue.

Mr Simmons unwrapped my arms and moved back. 'Actually I was going to say you still haven't returned the calculator you borrowed.'

Oh God.

SATURDAY JUNE 29TH

Couldn't believe how grown up and sophisticated I looked in the floaty red dress and long gloves with my hair all swept up.

Mum looked at me, her eyes a bit shiny. 'You'll do, I suppose.' She hugged me. Glanced over at Dad. 'Our Kelly Ann scrubs up not too bad doesn't she? Who'd have believed just a few years ago all she'd wear were jeans with holes in the knees and arse.'

'You look really nice, love,' Dad said gruffly. 'Right then, when is this Matt character due?'

'Oh he's out there now. Waiting for me in the taxi.'

Mum scowled. 'He's not hired a limo then? Cheapskate.'

Mum and Dad have still not taken to Matt. They'd have been even less impressed if they knew he was waiting for me on his motorbike. To be honest I wasn't keen either espcially as it was drizzling rain.

I hurried out teetering on my high-heels and closed the door quickly behind me so Mum and Dad wouldn't see him.

I was a bit disappointed when Matt didn't comment on how I looked but just handed me my yellow and black helmet which so didn't go with my dress and didn't fit well over my complicated swept up hairdo either. Also it wasn't easy to get on the bike and balance properly wearing high heels and yards of chiffon. Had to kind of hitch up my skirt then fold the material round my legs and trap it there. I suppose I could have felt daring, different and unconventional. In fact, I just felt uncomfortable, damp and, well, a bit stupid really.

When we drew up at the hotel I spotted Stephanie and Liz getting out of a silver stretch limo with Dave and Julian. They both looked amazing. Liz wore a very low-cut deep-blue dress which showed off her curves and pale creamy skin perfectly. Stephanie had on (sort of) a skin-tight black dress slashed to the thigh, with diamond-shaped bits cut out at waist and midriff. They saw me too and waved over enthusiastically.

Excited, I scrambled off the motorbike, got my heel caught in the hem of my skirt, and landed in a puddle on the pavement.

Liz and Stephanie rushed over while Matt helped me up. 'You OK?'

'Oh never mind that. Is your dress OK?' Stephanie asked. She examined the skirt. 'It's not torn. Just damp. We'll dry it off in the toilets. Is the back all right?'

Noticed that other people arriving were gawping at us. 'Stop making a fuss. I'm fine. Let's get in out of the rain.'

I hurried off.

'Wait, Kelly Ann!' Stephanie shouted. But I ignored her. The sooner I got inside away from the gawpers and got my dress dried off the better.

The hotel reception was lovely. All marble and glass and deep, dark mahogany wood. I followed the signs to our party room and went in. It was gorgeous. Crystal chandeliers sparkled above long tables covered in snow-white linen with fresh flowers and pink candles.

A lot of people were already there including Gary, Ian and Chris, who looked all sophisticated in their dinner suits and bow ties – like something from a *James Bond* movie. Valerie wore a shocking-pink satin dress which looked amazing with her long red hair. Samantha had on a white spaghetti-strap dress and Gary was gazing adoringly at her cleavage. Chris's new girlfriend wasn't there. I expected she'd be along soon and probably out-shine everyone.

My feet sank into the thick, soft carpets as I made my way in, gathering my skirt to hide the, thankfully small, wet patch as a respectful waiter in a smart black and white uniform approached me. 'May I take your, em, motorcycle helmet, Miss?'

We all sat at the same table as Chris which was a bit awk-ward but not too bad as my place was as far away from him as possible.

Matt was difficult though. All through the five-course meal he hardly said anything except for repeatedly point-ing out to anyone who would listen (not many) that this type of thing wasn't his scene. As if his black T-shirt and jeans weren't enough to have made this obvious anyway!

I was surprised that Jade never made an appearance. Maybe she and Chris had split up already. Or maybe she just couldn't make the prom. I certainly wasn't going to ask. Anyway, Liz would no doubt find out for me later.

As soon as the meal was over Matt disappeared out-side for a smoke. He took ages, so when the dancing started he still hadn't got back and I was left sitting by myself when everyone got up on the floor. Well actually not quite everyone.

'Would you like to dance, Kelly Ann?' Chris said.

Hmm. Dance with my ex who still tugged dangerously at my emotions or look like a sad wall flower?

I took his outstretched hand and he led me on to the floor. I thought it might be a bit odd now *not* to ask where Jade was. I tried to be as neutral as possible. 'So how come Jade couldn't make it tonight?'

'We split up a few days ago.'

'Oh.'

I said nothing more, but Chris continued without being prompted, 'Yeah, Jade's a beautiful girl. Talented too. But she wasn't right for me.'

Curious now, I couldn't help myself asking even though I knew I shouldn't, 'Why not?'

'She wasn't you.'

'Oh.'

I was right. I shouldn't have asked. We danced, careful not to get too close, but even so the touch of Chris's hand on mine, the nearness of his body, even his familiar scent after so long apart, was almost overwhelming and so many memories flooded back. It was hard not to rest my head on his chest the way I used to, or gently press my lips to his.

By the time the dance ended I was close to tears and

feeling strangely shaky. I broke away abruptly and hurried off to the toilet to get myself together.

I splashed cold water on my face and immediately realized I should have gone for waterproof mascara and liner like Stephanie suggested. Had to fix my make-up which somehow helped calm me down. You need to concentrate to apply eyeliner in a thin accurate line very close to your lashes after all. By the time I'd finished coating my lashes twice with the mascara (never sure why I open my mouth like a fish to do this but can't help it) and reapplied blusher to the apples of my cheeks by grinning like a mental person at myself in the mirror, I was much more composed.

Yeah, just because I got upset when I danced with Chris didn't mean I'd made a mistake and wanted to go back with him. It was normal to feel a bit nostalgic about an ex-boyfriend. Especially one as important as Chris had been.

No. Matt was the most exciting, different, amazing guy I'd ever met. If I didn't take this chance now I'd never know what I'd missed. I was doing the right thing. Definitely.

I returned to the party and scanned the room for Matt but couldn't see him. Began to feel anxious again. The sooner Matt got back the better.

He did reappear eventually. 'You want to go now?' he asked.

'Of course not. The party's just starting.'

'Christ, you're kidding me? Feels like we've been here for ever.' He put his arms round my waist. Kissed me. 'Anyway, haven't we got better things to do? I think you promised me a hot date tonight.'

'A hot date? But your dad's at home. We're going to a party at Paul's. Remember?'

'So? Paul's going to lend us his room. For a couple of hours anyway.' He kissed me again. 'Can't wait.'

'Oh my God, you asked him?!' I squealed.

He frowned. 'Yeah why not? It's cool. He's fine with it.'

'But, it's not, you know, very romantic. For our first time.'

He leaned away from me. 'Look, if you're not interested I'll head off.'

'No wait! It's not that it's just—'

'What?'

I'd never seen Matt like this before. Impatient and pissed off. Maybe I *was* being stupid. After all it wasn't as though this was my first time ever. And he had waited a whole month. Loads of girls would have given anything to get off with Matt. Would jump at the chance if he dumped me. 'Nothing. It's OK. But, well, let's wait till the end of the prom. No one's leaving until the last dance at midnight.'

Matt reluctantly agreed. But for the rest of the party he was even more antisocial than before, and spent most of the time sitting in a corner with his feet up on the table, until Mr Simmons and a waiter told him off. Afterwards he kept wandering off outside to smoke. It was so annoying. He'd never smoked this much before.

At least after the first dance most people didn't stick with their prom date. Everyone danced and chatted with everyone else – even teachers – so it was just like a big fancy expensive party.

I decided to ignore Matt's moodiness and try to enjoy myself. This was my first prom and probably the last time me and all my friends from school would be together like this in our lives. I was going to have a good time if it killed me.

And I did. For a few hours I put all my worries out of my mind then danced and laughed the night away. Couldn't believe it and was disappointed when, at nearly midnight, they announced the last dance of the evening.

Matt wasn't. 'Thank God that's over. I'm going to go for a smoke. Meet me in the car park at the side entrance.'

'But it's the last d—'

Too late, he'd gone. Thought about just joining Matt outside but I wanted to say goodbye to everyone first.

Chris came over and asked me to dance.

'Thanks, Chris, but I'll just sit this one out. I'm tired.'

'C'mon, Kelly Ann. One more dance won't hurt.'

It did seem stupid for the two of us just to sit there so, steeling myself, I got up.

'Did you enjoy the prom?' I asked, trying to sound casually relaxed and probably failing.

'No.'

'Oh.' That kind of put an end to my attempt at neutral social chitchat, so I said nothing more and we danced in silence for a minute, avoiding each other's eyes, until suddenly Chris stopped, took my hands in his and looked down at me.

'So, technically this was decision day,' he said. 'But I guess since you're here with Matt and not me there's no need for me to ask.'

'I'm sorry, Chris.'

'I'll ask anyway. I still love you. Still want you back. Last chance, Kelly Ann. Are you sure this is what you want?'

'Chris, don't.'

'Look, I know I got things wrong sometimes. I was too serious. Too, I don't know, overwhelming. But I can change. Be more laid-back. Give you more—'

Oh God, I couldn't bear for Chris to beg like this. I had to find some way to stop him. 'Stop it, Chris! Don't. I've made up my mind. It's, well, it's too late.'

'It's never too late. Please, Kelly Ann. You know we belong together.'

Oh God, I was going to have to say it. He wasn't going to give up otherwise. 'But it *is* too late. You see, Matt and I are already sleeping together. And you said if I ever shagged anyone you could never—'

I stopped. The expression on Chris's face looked like he'd just been punched in the stomach by a ramrod. He let my hands go and I turned away quickly so I couldn't see the pain I'd caused him.

The dance ended shortly after anyway, the lights came on full and after a loud cheer everyone started to drift towards the entrance chattering and hugging goodbye.

I felt strangely out of it somehow. Still thinking about Chris and how much I'd hurt him with my lie, while also wondering how the rest of the night would go with Matt. The night which would make my lie true. I hated the idea of using Paul's room, especially at a party, but at least everyone would probably be too drunk or stoned to know or care what Matt and I were doing.

I said goodbye to Liz and Stephanie who, like most people, were going to the front entrance. After collecting my helmet from the cloakroom I made my way to the side entrance which leads to the car park. Matt wasn't there and I couldn't see his motorbike either. Knew he wouldn't just have left me here. Or hoped not anyway. He had been in a strange mood all evening. But no, he wouldn't do that. Probably he'd got bored and gone for a ride while waiting for the prom to end.

I was right. Heard the now-familiar sound of Matt's bike roar into the car park so I walked out and waved.

'Kelly Ann, what are you doing here?' Chris called from behind me.

I spun round. 'Waiting for Matt. That's him now. What are *you* doing here?'

Matt roared to a stop just in front of us. I turned and made to run towards him but Chris grasped me by my elbow holding me back.

'Let go of me!' I hissed.

Chris ignored me. Spoke to Matt. 'You're not fit to drive that tonight. Leave it here. Get a taxi.'

'Oh for God's sake, he only had one beer,' I said. 'Anyway it's none of your business.'

Matt put up his visor. 'Like she said. None of your ****ing business. Now why don't you just **** off?'

'Kelly Ann, he's stoned,' Chris pleaded. 'You're not seriously thinking of riding back with him.'

I hesitated. Maybe Chris was right and Matt had been nipping out for more than a cigarette. But then again Matt wouldn't get stoned when he knew he'd be driving would he? He'd never done that before. No. Chris was mistaken. Or exaggerating. Anyway, this had nothing do with him.

'This is none of your business any more,' I said.

But he wouldn't let me go and I couldn't shake him.

Matt got off the bike and made to move towards us. Chris eyeballed him. 'She gets on that bike with you over my dead body or yours. And we both know it will be yours. Even if you weren't stoned out of your head.'

Matt hesitated. Stared at Chris but then seemed to lose focus and swayed a bit. Finally he shrugged. Got back on his bike. 'You want her that much, you have her. I was getting bored anyway.'

When Matt took off Chris let go of me. Probably not a wise thing to do. Didn't know who I was more furious with. Matt, because he obviously didn't care about me at all, or Chris, for setting up a situation which proved that Matt didn't care about me at all. But I only had Chris here at the moment to vent my fury.

I slapped and punched him while screaming that his interference had ruined my life. Chris just stood and let me hit him while saying over and over he was sorry. So annoying. Violence isn't nearly as satisfying when someone lets you do it and keeps apologizing all the time.

Mr Simmons, who'd come to see what all the noise and commotion was about, eventually dragged me off him. 'I don't bloody believe this,' Mr Simmons said to me. 'After six years you've left the school and I'm finally rid of you but you're still causing me ******* grief.'

'Mr Simmons,' I said, shocked. 'You're not supposed to swear. You're my teacher.'

'Not any ******* more.'

But at least he couldn't give me a punishment exercise.

MONDAY JULY 1 ST

It's annoying to basically owe your life to someone you're really, really furious with, but as usual I have to admit that Chris was right. Matt shouldn't have been driving on Saturday night. Not that he was off his face like Chris made out but yeah, his reactions probably weren't as good as they should be to drive a motorbike.

After Mr Simmons found out what Chris and I were arguing about he phoned the police and gave them Matt's licence number to try and intercept him, but they were too late.

Matt jumped a red light, which to be honest he's done before with no problems, but this time a car coming the other way clipped his back wheel and sent him spinning headfirst into a wall. He managed to turn away at the last second, but the back of the bike hit the wall and knocked him off. He's in hospital with a broken leg and some cracked ribs. I would have been dead for sure if I'd been on the bike too.

I got all this from Matt's dad who used his son's mobile to call me. He told me only family were allowed to see Matt today but I could visit tomorrow if I liked. Matt had asked to see me.

Not sure I'll go. I don't like hospitals and it's over with Matt and me. Not even sure for Matt there was ever anything much there in the first place.

TUESDAY JULY 2ND

News has spread about the accident, and everyone has been calling and texting me about Matt all day. Everyone except Chris, that is, who hasn't even called to say *I told you so* like any normal person would. This is typical of Chris. And very annoying. Which he probably knows.

WEDNESDAY JULY 3RD

Chris texted. U OK?
I texted back. Y
But I wasn't OK. Not OK at all. And the only person who could fix it was the last person I could ask.

THURSDAY JULY 4TH

Finally went to see Matt after he'd texted me. Said no one else could make it this afternoon and I wouldn't want him to have no visitors, would I?

But as I waited in the corridor for visiting time to start I noticed a tall, elegant, dark-haired woman who I was sure was Matt's mum. However, when the nurse finally opened the ward doors and everyone piled in, she stopped her, 'I'm sorry, Mrs Davies. Matt says he doesn't want to see you today.'

The woman didn't argue or get mad. Instead her shoulders slumped and she just turned back resignedly.

I went on in. Matt was sitting up in bed, his face a bit bruised and swollen and his plastered foot raised in a pulley thing. Somehow he still managed to look really attractive.

He gave me a rueful smile. 'Hi, Kelly Ann.'

I sat down on the chair beside his bed. 'Hi.'

Wasn't really sure what to say after that so just blurted out, 'So, I've always wondered, what do you do if your leg gets itchy under the plaster?'

Matt smiled. 'Hasn't happened yet. I'll let you know.' He shook his head. 'God you're random sometimes, Kelly Ann. I thought you might have wanted to talk about Saturday night. About us.'

'Not really. Nothing much to say is there?'

'I think there is. I'm sorry, Kelly Ann. I didn't mean what I said to your ex. I was a bit stoned. Not as stoned as he made out but yeah, not totally in control either.'

'It's OK.'

'It's not. I'm never gonna get like that again. Cost me my bike, and I'll be banned for at least a year. And there's nothing more important than my bike to me. Except my guitar that is.'

Noticed that I wasn't anywhere in there. 'That's good.'

'So you forgive me?'

'Yeah.'

'But it's still over between us?' Matt guessed.

'Yeah, well, I think I need someone a bit more reliable. And, there's, um, your bike and guitar. Too much competition for me. For any girl probably.'

Matt looked disappointed, but he didn't argue. We spent the next while chatting about nothing much while I ate the Quality Streets and seedless grapes his dad had brought him yesterday as Matt said he wasn't that keen on them.

A nice-looking nurse interrupted us saying she needed to take a blood test but I could come back in five minutes. I was secretly quite pleased as I've always found it awkward talking to patients during hospital visiting hour.

I wandered to the ward exit. Was surprised to see

Matt's mum still sitting there. She looked at me. 'The nurses say you know Matt.'

'Well, yeah. A bit.'

'I'm his mother. Could you do me a favour? Could you please ask him if he'll see me? Please. Just for five minutes.'

I flushed, embarrassed for her. 'Yeah, um, course.'

As I passed the reception area to go back into the ward a plump middle-aged staff nurse stopped me. 'Excuse me. Can I have a quick word?' she said in a soft Irish accent.'

I nodded.

'I saw you talking to Matt's mum. You know, she comes every visiting time. Afternoon and evening. Stays the whole hour, hoping he'll change his mind and see her. He never does. Now, I don't know what the problem is. Not my business. But I just think it's a crying shame, so it is.'

'Yeah. It's kinda sad.'

'So, you're his girlfriend then?'

'Just a friend. Sort of.'

She nodded. 'Well, I just wondered if you could have a word with him? Try and persuaded him to let her visit.'

'I'll try,' I promised.

When I went back Matt was flirting with the pretty nurse and she was loving it, but scuttled off when she saw me.

'Matt, your mum's out there,' I said. 'It's rude to keep her waiting like this.'

He shrugged and his face hardened. 'She kept me waiting for five years.'

'But—'

'No, Kelly Ann. Sometimes a person can let you down so badly, hurt you so much, you can never forgive them. Never go back.'

I argued some more, but eventually gave up as I could see it was useless. Matt was absolutely determined not to see his mum and there was nothing I could say to change his mind.

The nurse who he'd been flirting with earlier passed by again on her way to fix some flowers for a patient. Maybe she thought we'd been fighting as she stopped by his bed. 'Everything OK?'

'Fine,' Matt said without looking at her.

'So, nothing I can do for you?' she asked, giving him a bright smile.

'No thanks.'

She kept the smile on her face but it couldn't hide the disappointment in her eyes as she moved away.

'Matt,' I said. 'Why me?'

'What?'

'Why did you pick me? To go out with I mean.'

He shrugged, which made him wince. 'Why not you?'

'Well, loads of girls fancy you. You could have gone

out with practically anyone. So why pick me? A girl who already had a boyfriend.'

He didn't bother to deny what I'd said about girls fancying him. 'I don't know. Never really thought about it.'

'But you must have had a reason. Was it the challenge of getting me from another guy?'

'Christ, no. Don't think so anyway. Like I said, I'm not used to analysing stuff like this. But, hey, tell you what. You coming back to visit me again?'

'Maybe.'

'Right. I'll have a think about it over the next day or two and let you know.'

I left shortly after that as there was only five minutes of visiting time left and I'd run out of stuff to chat about. His mum was still sitting in the corridor. She looked up at me hopefully but I shook my head. 'I'm sorry, Mrs Davies.'

She looked sad but not surprised. 'Thank you for trying anyway.'

I started to make my way along the corridor but then turned back. 'He keeps your photo in his bedroom,' I said.

Before she could ask any more I hurried out.

Later, after I got back home, I couldn't stop thinking about Matt's mum and what he'd said about her. It saddened and depressed me. But not only because of his mum.

FRIDAY JULY 5TH

Liz and I went over to Stephanie's to discuss wedding stuff, including the hen night and bridesmaid dresses, but my heart wasn't really in it.

'What's the matter, Kelly Ann?' Liz asked gently. 'Still too upset about Matt to be bothered with this just now?'

'No, it's not Matt. I'm over him.'

'You are? But you've not had time to grieve and—'

'Can't miss what you never had. Or not much anyway. Matt wasn't all mysterious and sophisticated like I'd thought. He's just a boy who's been hurt by his mum so much he can't trust any girl enough to really get close.'

Liz was staring at me like I'd grown another head. 'That's really quite deep, Kelly Ann,' she said in a voice that made it plain she never expected an intelligent thought to enter my head.

'I'm not totally stupid, you know. Not all the time. Just sometimes. Like with Chris for example. I had a fantastic boyfriend and threw it all away to go chasing after Matt. I made a total mess of that, didn't I?'

'Yeah,' Liz and Stephanie chorused immediately.

'Complete arse,' Stephanie added.

'Monumental, catastrophic error of judgement,' Liz said. 'Honestly you've been so incredibly stu—'

'Thanks. I think I get the picture,' I interrupted.

Stephanie shrugged. 'So you screwed up. Just call Chris and tell him you've changed your mind.'

I shook my head. 'I can't do that.'

'She's right,' Liz said. 'These type of discussions are far better done in person.'

Stephanie nodded. 'Yeah, good point. You need to be looking your sexiest. Heels, stockings, shortest pulling skirt and—'

'That won't work with Chris,' I said.

Stephanie disagreed. 'Works with every guy.'

I shook my head miserably. 'Not with Chris. I've hurt him too much. You didn't see his face that night I told him it was over. He'll never take me back now. Never.'

'Rubbish. And you'll have to wear your Wonderbra, of course, with maybe that red silky spaghetti-strap top or perhaps the black lacy one . . .'

Stephanie continued to talk about various options for my get-up while Liz suggested couple's counselling but I wasn't listening because I knew it was hopeless. Like Matt said, sometimes you can hurt someone so much they can never forgive you. Never take you back.

SATURDAY JULY 6TH

But I did want to tell Chris I hadn't slept with Matt, even though I knew it wouldn't make any difference. The fact that I'd said it to hurt him so he knew I'd decided for Matt and against him was unforgivable anyway. But I felt he'd a right to know.

I texted Chris and asked him to meet me in the park by the pond tomorrow afternoon as I'd something I wanted to tell him.

He didn't answer until nearly midnight and I thought he was going to ignore me. But eventually he texted back.
MET OFF FORECAST RAIN. MY PLC 4 P.M.

Trust Chris to check the weather forecast.

SUNDAY JULY 7TH

Wasn't keen to meet Chris at his mum's house, especially as I was sure she'd be mad at me for being horrible to her son, but didn't want to complain in case he refused to see me at all.

Was glad when I went over and Chris answered the door. There was no sign of his parents inside either.

'They're away on holiday for a fortnight,' Chris said. 'Went two days ago.' He pointed to an armchair by the fireplace. 'You want to sit down?'

'No, I'll, um, just stand thanks. This won't take long.'

'OK, so you'd something you wanted to tell me?'

'Yeah. Well, it's about Matt.'

'I already heard it's over. Can't say I'm sorry.'

'That's not what I wanted to tell you. It's about, you know, what I said about Matt and me sleeping tog—'

'I don't want to hear it.'

'But I need—'

'I said I don't want to hear it.'

'But—'

'Not a word, Kelly Ann. Not a single word. I don't want to know.'

His voice was harsh, cold. Final. There was no point in continuing. 'Oh. Right. Well, I . . . I suppose I'd better go then.'

'Wait. I've got something I need to tell you now,' Chris said.

'Don't bother. I know what you're going to say.'

'You do?'

'Yeah. You're going to say there's no way you'd ever take me back. It's too late.'

'Actually—'

'And I don't blame you. I've hurt you way too much for you ever to forgive me.'

'Kelly Ann—'

'Don't, Chris. I . . . I understand. I've been so stupid. If I thought it would work I'd get down on my knees and beg you to take me back, but it's hopeless I know. I don't deserve you. But I want you to know that I'm really sorry. That I'll regret what I've done until the day I die. And that, well, I'll miss you. Every day of my life.'

Chris put his hand on my cheek, brushed a tear away from my lashes with his thumb. 'Kelly Ann,' he said softly, 'that isn't what I was going to tell you.'

'It isn't?'

'No. I was going to tell you that I never want to know about you and Matt. What happened between you—'

'Yeah, you said.'

'But despite everything . . . well, fact is, I still love you. Still want you back.'

'Oh.'

'So, what do you say?'

What do I say? A huge wave of relief and happiness surged through me. I wasn't too late. Chris loved me! Wanted me back. That's what he'd wanted to tell me. What he was going to let me know before I opened my mouth. And said all those things.

'Oh my God.' I blushed furiously. 'Why didn't you stop me!'

'I tried to but you kept interrupt—'

'I didn't mean it about the begging thing. Not, um, literally anyway.'

'That's a pity. I might have enjoyed that.'

'And obviously I wasn't the only one at fault. I mean you *are* a bit too serious at times. And we're way too young to move in together.'

'Agreed.'

'And, well, you can be a bit controlling sometimes. Bossy.'

'Maybe.'

'And stubborn.'

'I've been told that.'

'And argumentative.'

'I'm not argumentative.'

'Yeah you are.' Saw Chris grinning at me. 'Oh yeah, very funny.'

'Kelly Ann, do you still love me?' Chris asked.

'God, yes.'

'Do you want me back?'

'More than anything.'

He took me in his arms. Kissed me gently then whispered in my ear. 'Are you wearing stockings?'

MONDAY JULY 8TH

Visited Matt again today for the last time as I'd heard he would probably get out tomorrow. Chris wasn't pleased even though he now knows I've never slept with Matt. Despite his protests I insisted on telling him the truth yesterday. Have never seen a guy look so happy to have his instructions ignored. He wasn't so happy when I ignored his annoyance at my plan to visit Matt but I told him I'd promised to go and that was that.

In the end he agreed reluctantly and even drove me to the hospital but waited outside in the car park while I went in to see Matt.

I'd deliberately gone a bit late to avoid having to spend a whole hour thinking of things to chat about, so the ward doors were open and visitors already inside by the time I turned up.

Was gobsmacked to see Matt's mum there sitting by his bed. Oh my God, he must have finally agreed to see her.

I smiled as I approached them. 'Hi.'

Can't say they were all easy and happy. Matt was a bit stilted and tense. His mum anxious and hesitant. But they were talking. And when she tactfully left five minutes before the end of visiting hour so Matt and I could have a bit of time by ourselves, he let her squeeze his hand and agreed to meet her in a few days.

After she'd gone we chatted for a bit about nothing too important carefully keeping off the subject of his mum, which I could tell was a bit too touchy for Matt to want to talk about.

I was just getting ready to leave when Matt looked at me solemnly. 'So, Kelly Ann, last time you were here you asked me a question and I think you deserve an honest answer.'

I nodded. 'Yeah. I'd really like to know.'

'Knitting needle.'

'What?'

He smiled. 'For the itch. If you slide one inside the plaster you can scratch it.'

'Very funny. Now be serious. You promised.'

'OK, so you wanted to know why I picked you. Right?'

'Yeah.'

'Well you're warm, funny, gutsy and the most genuine person I've ever met. That's very attractive.'

I blushed. 'Thanks, Matt.'

'You're welcome.'

'I, well, I better go now. See you.'

'Bye, Kelly Ann.'

I was almost at the ward door when I heard Matt shout. 'Kelly Ann!'

I turned round.

'I just thought of another reason I picked you,' he shouted. 'Great bum!'

Hmm.

I was surprised to see Matt's mum waiting for me in the corridor. 'I just want to thank you,' she said. 'I was on the verge of giving up when you told me about the photograph. It gave me hope.'

'Oh, em, right, you're welcome,' I mumbled, hoping she wouldn't ask how I knew it was in his bedroom.

I was going to hurry away but she stopped me. 'Kelly Ann, I don't know whether Matt told you I used to be a professional dancer?' She smiled. 'Quite a successful one too before I married Matt's father and gave it up.'

'Yeah, he mentioned something about it.'

'I run a dance class now.' She handed me a card. 'Matt tells me you're good. Why not come along. Free lessons are the least I can do.'

'Oh, well, I don't know.'

'I've helped quite a number of young people get their first start in the dance world. It would be a pleasure to help you. Please say you'll give it a try.'

I grinned. 'OK then, yeah, thanks. Thanks very much.'

I skipped out to the car park where Chris was waiting for me. Hadn't felt as happy as this in years. When he saw my face though he looked worried. Tense. Oh God, probably he thinks I'm this happy just about seeing Matt. It would take a while for him to trust me completely again. I'd have to be patient.

I ran over, threw myself into his arms and kissed him full on the mouth. 'I love you, Chris.'

This helped. A lot.

Chris drove past school on the way back. I looked at it sadly, knowing I'd never be back again.

My old life was over and a new one about to begin. I don't know what the future holds for me. Maybe I'll be a famous dancer or actress one day. Maybe not. Perhaps I'll have two kids, or ten. I could settle in Glasgow or end up in Australia. The future is a mystery. But of one thing I am totally sure. Wherever I am. Whatever I do. I want Chris to be with me.

Although, OK, probably not for the bikini wax which Stephanie has finally persuaded me to have. She was waiting for me now at the beauty salon and was going to have hers first. This would prove to me bikini waxing was a routine treatment and not the extreme torture I imagined.

Decided to call her and tell her I was on my way. Switched on my mobile which I'd turned off for the hospital visit.

It bleeped. Three new text messages.

School: PLEASE RETURN CALCULATOR TO MR SIMMONS.

Mum: ANN SUMMERS PARTY AT GREAT-AUNT WINNIE'S TONIGHT. SHE'S FAMILY. BE THERE.

Stephanie: DISASTER. COME QUICK.

Oh God.